Bound to the Alpha Trio

Stephanie Swann

Book Cover by getcovers.com

Formatting by Stephanie Swann

Editing by Beth A. Freely

First edition 2023

Contents

Dedication

To the only three people I'd live for.

Author Note

This book is many things, but one thing it is not is suitable for anyone under 18. If this is you, please put this down. It'll be here when you're of age.

Rating: R

Warnings: children, pregnancy, multiple mates, loss, grief, lots of hot, sweaty sex, adventure, twists, turns, darkness. Generally just an adult book. It does not have infant loss or animal loss. This book has less sex than book one and is mainly focused on adventure and coming into oneself.

1: Amrin

T he last thing I remembered is that split-second decision. As Roman was running towards the portal, I watched Avery's face crumble, and I knew that nothing in this world would divert her love for them... and nothing that would change mine for her. Pushing Roman aside as I crashed through that dark entrance, my body splintered, and then everything went black.

I lost track of time, wandering with sightless eyes. There was no smell, taste, or feel but the abyss I was thrown into until a brilliant light illuminated a treacherous path. My choice was simple: undertake the task of climbing through the void or stay and dwell. I chose to climb.

As I scaled the tunnel walls, energy coursed through my body. Every step was an effort, but the more I climbed, the stronger I became. My movements were smoother and more precise as the crystals beneath my feet glistened in pink, purple, blue, and green hues.

My arms and legs tingled with excitement as I ascended the winding passageway. Soft voices sang from the shadows. They echoed faintly throughout the tunnel like a beautiful symphony of souls.

A warmth filled my heart, and their harmonious melodies brought me peace. My strength seemed to multiply with every note, and as the crescendo echoed, I felt invincible. Then suddenly, just when their song had reached its climax— the tunnel opened into a vast sky with stars twinkling brightly.

I gazed in wonder at this beautiful sight, and for a moment, I had no other thought than that of sheer awe and admiration for this world beyond worlds before me now. one which seemed to welcome me home with open arms.

"Welcome home, my firstborn wolf." Her voice was light and airy as I twisted and turned to look for her. "You will not find me here. Climb higher."

My chest heaved with exhaustion. My legs trembled beneath the weight of my body as my hands grasped the crystals jutting out of the walls. I wasn't sure how much higher I could climb, but she was my Goddess, and I couldn't fail her now, not after everything I'd done. Moving forward, my senses were on alert as I searched for any sign of her.

The stars seemed to glow brighter, and the world around me became more vibrant. An unfamiliar sense of excitement and anticipation overwhelmed me as I moved forward. Suddenly, at the edge of my vision, a warm light hovered in the sky. My heart raced: my Goddess, Creator, and the divine Selene.

I carefully stepped out onto the plain and found myself standing overtop a starscape so magnificent it was almost overwhelming. My soul surged with power as I looked down at the moonlight gleaming. It was pure. Whole.

Then, suddenly, she was there - standing before me in all her glory. Her eyes sparkled with love and compassion as she extended her graceful hands towards me. I ran into her embrace without hesitation, feeling her warmth and unconditional love course through me.

At that moment, I realized why she had brought me here - to experience pure beauty beyond anything I had ever known. To know that wholeness could come from within instead of seeking it from without, understanding that through this connection with herself, we can create our unique destiny filled with joy and abundance beyond measure.

She smiled down at me as she whispered in my ear, "Welcome home."

"My Goddess," I wept as my knees gave out, "I have failed you. I have failed everyone."

"Amrin..." her hand wrapped around my chin, "look at me, my child."

Shaking my head, I knew I could not. I was not deserving of the forgiveness she was extending.

"You are deserving. I understand that decades of being trapped inside men who did not value their mates drove you to the brink. Amrin... please..."

Looking up at her, compassion reflected on me. "I forgive you, not because you may or may not deserve it, but because of your heart. I want to give you a second chance."

Her words took me aback. A second chance? After everything I had done. But then again, this was the divine Selene, and if she thought I deserved a second chance, who was I to argue?

"What do I need to do?" I asked, looking up at her.

"You must learn to control your inner wolf," she said, "You were not born to be a killer, Amrin. You were born out of love and compassion."

Tears streamed down my face as I realized the truth in her words. My inner desires had consumed me, and I had become a weapon of destruction.

"I will do anything you need, Selene."

She smiled at me again, but it was warm and proud. "I know you will, my child."

As we stood there, I felt a sense of purpose wash over me that I hadn't felt since the decline of my human counterparts. I would do anything to make things right, to make up for the lives I had taken and the pain I had caused. And with Selene's guidance, I knew I could make it happen.

"I have a mate for you," she started, guiding me to walk with her.

"Already? But I only just died!"

"Yes, but this is rather... urgent."

"Who is she?" I was curious as to who she thought would complete my soul.

"She has been used and abused by a mighty warlock. Beta Lucas, you know him, claims he is her mate, but she wants nothing to do with him. Seeing my children suffer is the greatest point of pain for me. She needs a kind soul. A gentle yet protective mate, who will help her overcome her trauma and grow into the person she was always meant to be." She sighed, "I do not usually meddle in my children's affairs, but I cannot seem to let her go, or you, for that matter. This is your chance to accept someone for who they are, in this moment, and put in the work to help her trust again."

My heart skipped a beat as Selene spoke of this mystery woman. As an Alpha, I had always assumed I would mate with someone of equal stature, but Selene's words stirred something profound within me. I wanted nothing more than to help this woman and perhaps open her to falling in love with me.

"Tell me what I need to do," I said.

Selene placed a hand on my shoulder. "First, you must earn her trust. She has been through unspeakable horrors, and it will take time for her to open up to you. Beta Lucas has been a constant presence in her life, and he will not give up easily. He has been stalking her since she arrived at the Alpha Trio's pack. You will also need to know... she is human."

I felt a twinge of anxiety at that last revelation. A human? I had never considered mating with someone who wasn't a werewolf before. But if Selene trusted this woman enough to make her my mate, I trusted her too. And with everything Selene told me, I was determined to protect and care for this woman who had suffered so much.

"Thank you, Selene. I will do everything in my power to protect and care for her," I said, feeling a wave of determination wash over me.

"Good. Her name is Emma, and she's currently in the pack-house. It has been rebuilt, though our Alphas do not know yet."

"Can I go to her now?" I asked, eager to meet this Emma.

Selene laughed, "No child. There is something I need you to do for me first.

"What is it? Anything!" My heart pounded. I just wanted to meet her and love her. I'd been waiting for so long to accept a mate and have them accept me.

"You need a body to go back into. You cannot show up as you are, as beautiful as that is."

"Great, put me in someone!"

"Woah, Amrin, not so fast. It takes a lot of work.

"So... what now?" I felt deflated.

"Well, you have two options. Your previous host is here; he is a bit... mangled and will bear the scars, but we can wipe his memory. You may choose him and rename him. Or, if that is too personal for you, we will have to wait until a werewolf host dies."

I considered my options. I didn't want to wait for someone to die, and wiping someone's memory felt wrong. My earlier host may have been damaged, but I could work with that.

"I'll take Braden," I said. "I don't mind the scars, and I can make amends for any harm I caused him. But I want him to bear a new name. Mine."

Selene nodded, "Very well. Let's go."

2: Avery

Alara came waltzing into the cave like there were no cares in the world as if walking in on Nik eating me out was just another everyday occurrence.

"Uh... do you mind?" He growled.

"I do. You two have spent the last two days frolicking and copulating, and now it's time to awaken Osric." She said, her eyes glinted.

"Can I finish what I am doing here?" He said, desperation crossing his features.

I giggled. Nik with blue balls would not be good. For anyone. Least of all me.

"Fine," she huffed. "I will be back in one hour; if you are not out here, dressed and waiting by then, I will drag you out by that thing you call 'big.'"

She disappeared through the cave entrance, leaving us alone. Despite the awkward interruption, a twinge of excitement ran through me at finishing what we had started. Nik's arm tightened around my waist, pulling me close to him.

"Sorry about that. I didn't want to stop," he muttered, his lips brushing against my earlobe.

"It's fine," I whispered. "I don't want to stop either."

The deep rumble of his laughter set my body alight. "Good. Now, where were we?"

He leaned down and captured my lips in a searing kiss, his tongue exploring mine with passion and fervor. Moaning into his mouth, my body ignited with need as his hands traced the curves of my body. He pulled away, his dark eyes smoldering with desire.

"Perhaps we should move... you know, in case more 'co-incidences' show up," he said, a mischievous glint in his eye.

A wicked grin spread over my face as I reached for his hand and led him deeper into the cave, away from potentially prying eyes. We found a secluded spot amongst the rocks, and Nik didn't waste time. He pushed me up against the wall, his hands roaming my body as he kissed me fiercely. The stone was cold against my bare skin, but the heat of his body pressed against me warmed me. Our bodies melded together, moving in unison as we sought to satisfy our mutual carnal desires.

His hands slid down to the hem of my dress, lifting it up and over my head in one fluid motion. I'd been testing making clothing while in the dream realm, petty, but watching his face as he found me dressed up with that feral gleam in my eyes made me giddy. Naked except for my boots, I was vulnerable yet empowered by his intense gaze. He stepped back slightly, admiring the view before him with hungry eyes. He was still fully clothed, his muscular arms bulging against the tight fabric of his shirt. More importantly, a tent was pitched in his pants; my mouth watered at the sight.

Without a word, he lunged forward and grabbed my face with his hands, his teeth pulling on my bottom lip. He roamed over my curves, teasing and caressing me in all the right places. I moaned against his mouth, lost in the sensations that were coursing through my body. As he trailed kisses down my neck and across my collarbone, I reached for the buttons of his shirt, eager to explore the rippling muscles beneath.

With trembling fingers, I undid the last button, pulling his shirt off and tossing it aside. his body was a work of art, all bronzed skin and sculpted muscle. A rock bit into my back as he pressed me up against the wall, flicking my nipples before he pinched, and a bolt of pleasure pooled between my legs. My legs almost gave out as a low, guttural moan escaped me; he took one into his mouth, sucking and nipping gently. My hands tangled in his hair, pulling him closer as my back arched in ecstasy.

Nik's fingers trailed lower, teasing my inner thighs before delving into my pussy. I gasped as he found my clit, circling it with deft strokes that had me trembling. He added another finger, pumping in and out as I rode the waves of pleasure that crashed over me.

There wasn't much time before Alara would come looking for us, but I wanted more. Needed more. I pushed at him, compelling him to move back and allowing me the access I needed to undo his trousers. My hands reached in, freeing his throbbing cock. He cupped my breasts as I caught the first drop of precum before it fell.

My tongue swirled around the head, taking my time to enjoy him before pushing him down my throat, savoring the salty taste of his skin. He triggered my gag reflex as I pushed him deeper, cutting off my air supply. Adding in my hands, I sucked him eagerly with every stroke as he grew harder and thicker. He gripped my hair as he pushed closer to the edge of ecstasy, my rhythm encouraging him to the precipice.

Pulling away with a gasp, I trailed kisses over his hard stomach before looking into his eyes with a coy smile. He growled softly, bending down to sweep me into his arms and set me down. My hands steadied as they settled on the hard wall. His lips caressed my neck and shoulders, stealing my breath as he positioned himself at my entrance. A loud smack and a sting caused my pussy to clench and release.

"Ready?" He smacked my ass again before running a soothing hand over his mark.

"Please," I wiggled my ass, trying to force him to enter me.

He filled me with one thrust, stretching me to the limit as he claimed me for his own.

I wrapped my calves around him, digging my heels into his ass and pulling him deeper. His palms were warm as they tightened around my chest, holding me as we rocked together. Just before I lost control, my feet hit the ground, and I bent over. His pace quickened, and I met his thrusts with the rock of my hips.

He let out a low growl, pounding into me as I held onto the wall. His passion was loud, and he moaned dirty words of encouragement as he drove us closer to the edge. His hands explored my body, his fingers strumming my aching clit until I could take no more.

"I'm close, so close," I gasped, clinging to the wall as I climbed up to the wave of my peak.

"Cum for me," he urged, fucking me even harder.

I did as commanded, tilting my head back and allowing a moan to escape from between my lips as I tumbled into bliss. His hips stuttered as I squeezed him tight, pulling him into me until nothing remained. His seed spilled into me, filling me with all the pleasure he could give. Collapsing against him, I savored the feeling.

He opened his arms as I turned to lean into him, strong arms holding me as my legs regained their strength. Grinning, I reached up to cup his cheek as his hand found mine, kissing my fingertips before pulling me tight against his chest.

My hair had stuck to my forehead, and he tucked it behind my ear as he simply held me. Tilting my chin up with his finger, he bent down and kissed me slowly. His tongue fluttered against mine in a dance of sensual delight, igniting new desire deep in my belly. Damn you, Alara.

When he finally pulled away, he smiled down at me.

"Thank you," he said.

"For what?" I asked, utterly confused. "I should be thanking you."

"I didn't hurt you, did I?"

"No, it was amazing, as always," I yelped as he smacked me on the ass, my hands hiding my burning cheeks.

"You are," he chuckled. "That was hotter than my hottest dreams. Something about the whole cave thing made it so sexy."

"Hell, it was hotter than mine, and we're in one," I ran my fingertip along his jaw. "We better get dressed."

"Uh, about that," he chuckled, motioning to our tattered clothes.

I sighed, "right. New ones." In a few seconds, I had us clothed in new attire, and we marched towards the entrance where Alara stood, tapping her foot impatiently.

"That was longer than an hour."

"My bad," I said.

"You didn't sound like you were doing bad. Anyway. It's time. You ready?" She walked away without waiting for an answer.

"I guess it's now or never, baby girl," Nik grabbed my hand as we followed.

The trees became thicker, their branches forming a canopy above us. The moon's light filtered through, here and there, illuminating our path. With each step, I felt my courage grow.

Suddenly, Alara stopped and motioned for us to stay put. She then pointed to a clearing a few yards away where something shimmered in the moonlight. We crept closer until we could see what it was: Osric, his bottom half frozen in stone, his eyes betraying his boredom at being stuck that way for an eternity.

"Well. Look who finally decided to show up." He said, his eyes boring into mine. "Come back to free me, pet?"

"Yes. Unfortunately, it has come to my attention that you placed an infection inside me that won't disappear until you're freed. So, long story short, here we are." I said dryly.

"Wonderful. I'm glad you came to your senses. Now, who will be my blood sacrifice." He was toying with us. He knew it would be Nik.

Alara spoke quickly, interrupting Nik as he stepped forward, "Here's what's going to happen. Nik will submit to your energy, you will drain him, and I will heal him and restore his life force with my own. Understood?"

He gasped, "Wait, you are giving up your life for mine?"

She smiled, but it didn't quite reach her eyes, "I have no other purpose than keeping my girl safe. I cannot leave the dream realm, but you can. You bring her life, Nik. You will carry a piece of my soul in yours, and it will help you guide Avery as she walks this path."

Osric nodded, "Very well then. No time for long goodbyes; we have stuff to do. Let us begin." He raised his arms and closed his eyes, beckoning for my mate to go closer. He stepped forward and knelt before Osric, the force of his aura causing Nik to bare his neck.

My heart stopped at I watched my strong man on his knees before this monster. His skin turned ashen as he raised his eyes in defiance before he grunted, his lips twisting into a grimace. *Goddess, please.*

The ritual began, unease settled in my gut as Osric's hands glowed brightly and the air around them swirled with energy. His chants filled the air as his hands moved closer to Nik's chest. Nik began to contort, his features seizing in pain, but he refused to utter a sound. Osric's mouth curled in a grin as he reveled in his power, using Nik's energy to replace his own.

Slowly, the rock began to melt, and Osric stepped out just as Nik collapsed. Running to him, I held him as he gasped for breath, his bones straining against his skin—a mere skeleton of the man I loved.

"Step aside, child," Alara knelt beside me. "I don't have much time."

Looking at her, tears welled in my eyes, "I love you, Alara, please don't go."

"You must decide, child, me or your mate."

"Don't make me choose," I wailed.

"Then I will choose for you." She said, cupping my face in hers.

She spat out a quick sentence and disappeared without pomp and circumstance. Gone. Just like that.

3: Nikolai

As Avery held me, rocking back and forth, the life flowed back through my veins, but this time, it was different. I felt... whole. Alara had given me her soul; with it, there was a different feel to my body. A sense of peace and understanding replaced the darkness that once ripped against my flesh. Neutrality. River lurked in the shadows, but even he felt at ease. It was strange.

"Hey, Nik... Nik... are you okay?" Avery asked, looking down at me.

"Yeah, baby girl, I am just fine. In fact, I feel better than I have in... well, ever." I sat up, turning to look at Osric.

"Ah, the happy couple lives on. How unfortunate. I hoped to be the last Lycan again, but Alara had other plans. Never mind. Now, what task would you have me do so that I might do it and continue on my merry way." Osric smiled maliciously.

Avery sighed, "We need your help to destroy Belial and put him back in his realm, along with any demons or portals he has left here. Though you already know that. Otherwise, why would we be here? Besides this infection. Which I wouldn't mind you removing now. My body is wasting away."

"Hmmm... I shall think about your request, but first, I am starving. Time to hunt." Osric stood up, stretching his limbs. His face twisted, a grin forming. "You know how it is," he said. "A guy's got to eat."

Without waiting for a response, he darted into the darkness, his form disappearing into the shadows. Avery and I exchanged a glance, wondering what the hell was wrong with him.

"We should go after him," Avery stood, brushing dirt off her knees. "We need to ensure he doesn't do anything stupid and stays on task."

"I'll go. You stay here. Rest a while." I offered, giving her hand a quick squeeze before darting after Osric. I didn't want her near him. He was a bad, bad guy.

"Ah, so the little Lycan prince has decided to join me. Come, let's take this bear."

My eyes widened. This guy was well and truly insane. I watched Osric taunt the bear, his body flowing seamlessly from one movement to the next. It was like watching a dance of death, and I was drawn to it. Osric drew himself up to his full height as the bear charged us and released a ferocious snarl. The bear faltered for just a moment, giving Osric the opportunity he needed to strike. He lunged toward the bear with lightning-fast movements, his fangs bared and his claws extended.

I held my breath as Osric and the bear collided, their bodies slamming into each other with a resounding thud. His fangs sank deep into the bear's neck, and I watched the life drain out of the animal's eyes. As the bear fell to the ground, Osric stood over it triumphantly, blood dripping from his jaws before he tore into its flesh.

"That was impressive," I said, trying not to show my awe.

Osric turned to me, his eyes gleaming with ferocious hunger. "Impressive? Just wait until we take down Belial. That will be truly impressive. This was nothing. You could take one too if you weren't so pathetic."

My teeth grit—the nerve. Working with Osric would be dangerous, but a small part of me was excited that I finally wasn't alone. I had someone who might be able to teach and guide me on what it meant to be a Lycan. As much darkness as he radiated from every pore, Avery was every part light, which meant that I was free to be the middleman, learning from both of them how to control my own balance.

"Osric," I said hesitantly, "can you teach me what it means to be a Lycan? What does it mean to have this power? What power do we even have?"

Osric smiled at my naivete. "Ah, the power of a Lycan--a powerful gift bestowed on us by the great Selene." He gazed at the night sky as if searching for her in the stars. "To be a Lycan is to embrace both our light and dark sides. To use both in balance, without allowing one side to dominate. It is an art form that requires dedication, practice, and connection to the other Lycans around you. Your power comes from us; we are this Earth's most ancient and pure lineage. When the time comes for us to rule again, you and I shall oversee it together."

I started at his proclamation, suddenly fearful of his impending power. What was I getting myself into?

"If we are balanced, then why are you just all darkness? It doesn't make sense. Selene made you first; you're basically a God amongst us, so why wouldn't you try to help her maintain the balance?"

"I grew weary watching our kind be decimated by hunters, other supernaturals, and random herbs that witches thought to throw together. As the last of us were wiped out, I flew into a rage. I killed an entire village of humans sleeping peacefully nearby." He said matter-of-factly.

"And... Selene, just let you get away with that?" I asked, shocked at his confession and how he was nonchalantly picking the bear out of his teeth.

"No, you stupid kid. She put me in that stone and called for a truce long enough to throw my soul in Belial's pit. I've been down there for Centuries." He started walking away.

I was rooted to the spot. Is that why he is so willing to help us defeat Belial?

"Your legs broken? Get walking." He snarled, "As for your question, yes, I want to rid the world of him. There is only room for one dark entity, and that isn't going to be him. Despite what you may think of me, I have your best interests at heart. Those align somewhere with destroying those who oppose and hate us and teaching you how to wield your mate as a weapon... to destroy those who oppose and hate us."

"Right, that's not going to be a thing. Avery is mine to protect, and I won't have her light extinguished by your darkness." I finally caught up to him, "anyway, she would never agree."

"Didn't you ever stop wondering why Belial became an issue?"

"Because Amrin released him?" I said, puzzled.

"Yes, but it's because the world sits very precariously. The balance must always be maintained. When your girlfriend decided to absorb the Spirit Stone, the Gods had no choice but to continue allowing Belial free reign... or to release me." We had finally walked back to the clearing where Avery sat waiting. She listened intently to the tail end of his spiel.

"Are you saying you're worse than a literal demon?"

"You can decide for yourself, but I know there will only ever be one of us. And it's going to be me. As long as she lives, I will, too."

We all shared an uncomfortable silence, each lost in our thoughts. After a few moments, Avery stepped forward and looked into each of our eyes before speaking.

"There is only one way to guarantee safety for all of us—we must work together," her jaw clenched. "If we are going to fight and restore balance to the world, then we need to deal with each other for now. I don't want to bother with any of the rest of your issues until after we're done what we need to do. Now heal me."

He placed his hand on her chest, a faint light emanating from his hand. "Happy?"

"Very much so."

"Can we go home now?" I asked, suddenly missing my brothers and my babies.

"Yes." We stood in a small circle, and Avery focused on taking us out of the dream and back home. Landing with a smack on the grass outside, I rubbed my backside.

"Why did you land us outside? I'd have preferred the bed." I groaned.

"Because I don't want him near the babies. He can stay out here, where he belongs."

"Good point." I conceded.

"I am not a dog. You cannot just leave me out here." Osric growled.

"Yes, actually, I can, and I will."

I laughed at the strong will of my beautiful mate, "You heard her. After she has seen the babies and we are rested, we will call you in for a strategy meeting."

Before he could utter another word, Avery dragged me inside.

"Finally! My Goddess, you have been gone forever!" Roman said dramatically.

"Only two days," Gabe chided.

Both men rushed up to her and smothered her with kisses, a babe in each of their arms.

"Whose daddy's little princess?" I cooed to Aurora, delighting in how her little finger wrapped around mine. "And there's daddy's handsome man!" Onyx was solemn as he stared up at me.

"Give them to me!" Avery demanded, finally untangling herself from Roman and Gabriel's excited onslaught.

I reluctantly handed them over.

"Oh, my sweethearts, mommy's home. I missed you both so very much, and boy, do I have a fantastic bedtime story for you tonight. I will tell you all about your Auntie Sapphire and your Auntie Alara and how strong and brave they were." Tears pricked behind her eyes as they turned red.

"And I am going to tell them how beautiful and smart their mother is," I said, quietly wrapping my arms around her middle, gazing into the faces of perfection.

"Hello? Are we just chopped liver? Nik, you hogged her for two days; make yourself useful and make us some damn coffee. I swear to Goddess. Selfish asshole," Roman mumbled, pushing me off Avery and taking my place.

Watching her love on those kids made my heart swell. How is she everything all at once? Perfect and serene, motherly and fierce. My dream come true. Her eyes locked onto mine as she smiled, quietly mouthing for me to do as Roman asked. I nodded and started making coffee while my mate enjoyed her time with my brothers and the twins.

4: Roman

A very had been gone for so long that I had been growing restless. Cooped up with Gabriel and his perfectionist persona. "No, don't hold them like that," "No, you have to burp them now," "No, Roman... just give them to me!" He had gone from anal-retentive asswipe to asswipe extraordinaire in a matter of HOURS. It was exhausting. Then, we had a momentary heart attack when Nik and Avery's bodies vanished before they appeared at the door. Man, if Avery never leaves my side again, it would be too soon for the rest of her life.

"They're finally asleep," she said, pulling her shirt down, "all fed and happy. My little angels."

"Excellent, now we can do the hanky panky," I wiggled my eyebrows up and down as Nik snorted from the corner he had been banished to. No more touching Avery for him. It was my turn.

"Roman, seriously? I'm exhausted..." Avery whined.

I put my arms around her and felt the tension leave my body. "I just want to hold you," I whispered, "we don't have to do anything else." She melted into my embrace, and I held her tightly, feeling her warmth and softness against me. It felt like it had been ages since I could smell her scent on my skin.

I leaned down to kiss her gently, and she responded with a sigh. We pulled apart and looked into each other's eyes with love and longing. "I missed you so much," I said, my voice hoarse.

"I missed you too," she fluttered a kiss on my cheek. "Being away from you and the babies was so hard. I am so happy to be with you again. Now, if only we can do what we must and get home. I'm tired of the world."

"Shhhh, no more dooms talk. I want to snuggle into you silently and hold you while you sleep."

I lifted her and carried her to the bed, gently laying her on the sheets. I kissed her again, and our lips locked in a passionate embrace. Her skin was like silk as I traced lines down her body, rediscovering all her curves and contours as if for the first time.

"I thought you were going to let me sleep?" She said quizzically.

"Yes, but that doesn't mean I can't touch you first," I said with a grin. Avery laughed and pulled me closer, wrapping her arms around me. Her lips found mine, our tongues entwining, passion growing along with my cock. I pushed my hips against hers, feeling the heat rise.

Suddenly, Nik's voice interrupted us from the corner. "Do you guys need anything? Water, a towel, me…"

I cut him off with a glare, silencing him instantly. "No, we don't need anything. Thank you. Can you just get back to your corner? We're busy."

He snorted but fell silent. I turned back to Avery, nuzzling her. "Where were we?"

Avery smiled and pulled me close. "That's all for right now, Roman, I'm serious. I am exhausted, and a giant, ancient Lycan is pacing angrily outside. I need some rest, please."

I sighed, "Okay, babe," I wrapped my arms around her as Gabriel hopped in to spoon her from the other side.

She smiled in contentment and quickly fell asleep. As she slept, my mind raced about what she had experienced while away. The world had become dangerous, but I couldn't imagine being able to dream-walk and experience even more despair. I watched her chest rise and fall, noticing the bags under her eyes; pride washed over me. She was handling everything that was being thrown at her like a champ.

I lay there, lost in thought, my legs itching to move. Gabriel's breathing deepened as he drifted off to sleep. Untangling myself from her legs, I slipped out of bed to check on things outside. I tiptoe to the door, trying to miss the creaks in the floorboards so I don't wake anyone.

"I wouldn't go out there if I were you," Nik said as he sat like a statue in his corner, only a dim light showing his face.

"I just want to see him..."

"He's not safe to be around, Roman, especially not without Avery. He can't kill her, but he can kill you."

I paused for a moment, considering his words. He was right, of course. Osric was dangerous, and with all the chaos in the world, it wasn't easy knowing who to trust. But there was this feeling that I needed to see him, even just for a moment. I just couldn't shake it.

"I'll be careful," I said, slipping out the door before Nik could protest further. The night air was crisp and cool, causing goosebumps to prickle my skin. The sky was lit with stars which illuminated the clearing, casting everything in an eerie light.

I stalked towards the edge of the woods, pausing as the massive form of the ancient Lycan came into view. He was pacing back and forth, muttering in a low growl. As I got closer, he must have sensed my presence because he abruptly turned around and locked eyes with me. I froze in place, unsure of what his next move would be. The Lycan's eyes flickered with recognition before they went blank. Was he wary of my presence? I took a cautious step forward, hoping to bridge the gap between us.

"Stay where you are, wolf," Osric warned, his voice deep and menacing.

Instead of listening, I took another step closer.

"I am in the middle of trying to tame the beast that wants to rip everyone to shreds. I suggest you heed my warning."

I hesitated momentarily, but my curiosity got the better of me. "Can I help?" I asked him, trying to sound confident and strong.

Osric sneered at me. "You? Help? Don't make me laugh. You are a mutt. And besides, I don't think Avery would be too pleased to see you here. I know how she gets all protective of you three like she would a pet. Like a cat or something equally sad and pathetic."

But the distraction worked; he was calming the longer he spoke to me.

"I wanted to ask you about the prophecy. I thought you would know about it.

"Ah yes, that garbage. It doesn't exist. The only prophesy that rings true is the same one that always has. Light and dark must balance. Where one exists, so must the other."

"But why would the witch tell us we would have to make a sacrifice to save the supernaturals?" I asked, confused. We'd based most of our journey on the notion that we were tasked with this gargantuan task of saving everyone.

"Because you will have to make a sacrifice at some point. What did you think? We could just walk into hordes of demons, kill Belial, and walk out in time for supper?" He laughed.

My nails bit into my skin as my fists clenched; I felt foolish and embarrassed. Of course, it would be challenging. I had been hoping that all of us could see the world as it flourished, but Osric was right... it wouldn't be easy, and one of us may die.

Suddenly, his expression changed, his eyes glinting with a thought. "But that doesn't mean we can't try. I make no promises that you will come out of this alive, but I have my vendetta against the big bastard, and I want him banished just as much as you do."

My heart quickened at the thought of facing Belial, of taking on such a task. I had always known the journey ahead would be shitty, but hearing Osric's words somehow solidified the reality of it all. We were actually going to face him. My girl was going to fight a lord of the Underworld. What in the actual fuck? How was this our life?

But I couldn't back down now, not when so much was at stake. "What do we do?"

Osric smirked. "We'll need a plan, *Alpha*. And some heavy firepower. The Seraphina is young and inexperienced, but perhaps I can call on some old friends to join us and make it a real party."

"You have friends?" It just slipped out before I could filter it.

His head snapped back as his eyes shot daggers at me. "Yes, I have friends. They won't be the cute little pets you boys call your pack. These boys are the ruthless ones who hunt Alpha's like you for sport. We had a blast back in my day."

"Yeah? Killing innocents and destroying lives?" I said sarcastically.

"It wasn't always like that. We all co-existed peacefully for quite some time before I started taking matters into my own hands. Only after Selene repeatedly denied my request for her intervention did I become... full of rage."

"I see." Really, I didn't.

"Anyway, we will have to travel to their packs and recruit them. Numbers, boy, numbers. Belial has his army. We need ours."

"Roman? Roman, where are you?" Avery's worried voice called out.

"Coming!" I yelled as I turned from Osric and ran back to the cabin as fast as I could.

5: Belial

The scent of brimstone hung heavy in the air as I stood atop the precipice, gazing down upon the sprawling landscape below. A desolate wasteland stretched out as far as the eye could see, a testament to the devastation I had wrought upon this realm. For centuries, I had hungered for freedom.

The world of mortals had become a prison, an insipid cage that restricted our malevolent essence. We demons yearned to roam the Earth again, to sow chaos and despair amongst the humans. The time had come to unleash our dark legions upon this realm and reclaim what was rightfully ours. Power.

The portal, a gateway to the mortal plane, lay dormant, concealed within the depths of the ancient ruins. Centuries of planning and sacrifice had led to this pivotal moment as I stood there, preparing to awaken the dormant energies that would rend the very fabric of reality.

I extended my clawed hand towards the abyss, calling upon the primordial forces that coursed through my veins. A surge of power emanated from deep within, resonating with the very essence of darkness. My infernal energy crackled and danced around me like serpents writhing in anticipation.

The air shivered with an eerie vibration as I began the incantation. As my voice took on a haunting chorus of whispered words, it seemed as though a weight lifted off me; it was the weight of untold ages and forbidden knowledge held by my speech alone. The ground trembled beneath my feet as my words grew louder, resonating with ominous power.

Like writhing shadows, dark tendrils slithered from my outstretched hand, snaking towards Earth below. They dug deep into their earthy destination, piercing its core. A rumbling reverberation echoed through the landscape, signaling what was about to become a cataclysmic transformation.

The dormant portal stirred, coming to life from its age-old slumber. A vortex of swirling darkness materialized before me, an entrance to the forbidden realms beyond. The sweet anticipation of victory could be tasted as my eyes fell upon the opening maw, beckoning me closer.

With a surge of unholy power, I stepped through the threshold, crossing the barrier between realms. The sensation was exhilarating, a rush of energy coursed through my veins. I emerged on the other side into a desolate plane of eternal night, a domain fit for demons and their infernal desires.

There, in the heart of darkness, I gathered my demonic brethren. They appeared from shadows, their twisted forms illuminated by an ethereal glow. With eyes burning with malice and hunger, they pledged their loyalty to their Lord and Master.

I raised my hands high, commanding their attention. The time for the final onslaught had come. Together, we would descend upon the mortal realm, an unstoppable tide of malevolence. We would shatter their feeble illusions of safety and plunge their world into an eternal abyss of despair.

As I led them through the portal, a sense of triumph filled my being. The taste of victory was almost tangible—so close that I could savor it on my forked tongue. The mortals would tremble in fear, their futile attempts to resist us only fueling our insatiable appetite for chaos. A God I would become.

I took one last look at the swirling abyss—the portal through which our liberation would be achieved. A wicked grin curled upon my lips as I stepped forward in this new land, leading my legion towards the final conquest. The Earth would tremble beneath our unholy might, and the name of Belial would be etched in annals of history, forever synonymous with darkness and damnation.

As we surged through unfathomable numbers to mortal minds, a tempest of despair engulfed their realm. The skies darkened as though mourning the impending doom that approached. The fabric of reality began to warp and twist under our presence, distorting their familiar landscape into a grotesque reflection of our desires.

Cities crumbled in our wake, reduced to smoldering ruins, engulfed by our fiery fury. Terrified screams of mortals filled the air, creating a symphony of anguish that invigorated us. We reveled in their fear, feeding on their angst for their suffering fueled our infernal power.

I stood at the forefront of the infernal horde, my eyes ablaze with dark-lit fire. My wings unfurled, casting a shadow that engulfed the land, shrouding it in my wake.

We descended upon the weak, helpless, and righteous. No corner would remain untouched by our wrath. We rend the very fabric of their feeble existence, tearing apart their illusions of safety and order. Chaos reigned supreme as their futile attempts to resist us crumbled beneath our relentless onslaught.

The world trembled beneath our dominion's weight, acknowledging its rightful rulers. The skies crackled with thunder and lightning—a storm mirroring the destruction raging within our blackened hearts. Earth rebelled, unleashing torrents of fire and brimstone to consume lands we traversed--to wipe itself clean of any memory of us.

As I witnessed carnage unfold before me, a twisted smile spread across my face, revealing rows of sharpened fangs. This was the culmination of centuries-long longing—the manifestation of insidious ambitions we harbored. We had returned to claim what was unjustly denied to us.

But amidst chaos and destruction, whispers of resistance emerged. Mortals—defiant and resolute—rallied against our onslaught. Their futile efforts only enraged ours further. We relished in their desperation, a testament to our power.

Yet there flickered a doubt within me questioning the price of our conquest. Weren't we prisoners ourselves, slaves to our own insatiable hunger? The very existence that we sought to dominate reflected the darkness within our souls.

The ancient Lycan bearer of primal strength and the last Seraphina imbued with celestial grace were said to possess power enough to unite their disparate worlds against our onslaught. If these two forces were to align, it could shatter the fragile balance upon which our triumph rested. There was a reason I had kept him locked behind cloak and dagger.

In the darkest recesses of my mind, a sliver of doubt crept in. The thought of such a formidable alliance threatened to erode my confidence. Could they genuinely wield enough power to challenge our reign? Ancient prophecies had been dismissed as mere folklore, but a whisper of uncertainty lingered.

I summoned my most trusted minions, those who had stood faithfully by my side through ages. In the flickering light of infernal fires, we convened, made sacrifices, and shared blood, discussing growing rumors weighing the possibility of a united front against us.

"The Lycan and the Seraphina," I growled, lacing my voice with disdain and trepidation. "Their bloodlines converge, bringing with them the potential to unravel all we had achieved. We can't dismiss this as mere folly—we must be prepared."

A murmur of agreement rippled through the assembly; their eyes gleamed with anticipation and caution, understanding the implications well.

"I will dispatch my most cunning agents," I decreed, echoing authority in my voice. "They shall scour the realms seeking their haven—we must know their intentions, alliances, and depths of their powers."

With nods of compliance, minions dispersed, leaving me alone in contemplation. Fear—a sensation long repressed—tugged at the corners of my consciousness. I had reveled in chaos and destruction, basking in the glory of triumph, but now faced a formidable opposition that filled me with dread unanticipated.

In the depths of my darkened sanctum, I delved into ancient tomes and forbidden grimoires, seeking knowledge and spells to defend against their convergence. Flickering candlelight cast eerie shadows upon worn pages as I delved into incantations and rituals long forgotten by the mortal realm.

Time was of the essence for their union drew nearer with each passing moment. I had to prepare my demonic legions for a battle unlike any we had ever faced. Our fate rested upon my shoulders, and I had to ensure balance of power remained tipped in our favor.

6: Alara

A vision unfolds from my celestial perch in Selene's Garden—an alternate future. My descendant and her sturdy partners steel themselves for an impending battle. A pang of yearning pulses within me, wishing I could stand beside them. But the ties between my celestial entity and this realm bind me. Oblisk, the ancient dragon, rests beside me, his eyes holding centuries worth of wisdom.

"Oblisk," I breathe softly, "See them? Our champions, facing the darkness with unyielding spirit."

The dragon raises his head, emerald scales gleaming under Selene's delicate light. His gaze meets mine, locked on the mortal world beneath us.

"Yes, Alara," Oblisk's voice rumbles, "I see them. Youthful, with a strength born of their beliefs. Their hope burns brighter than the shadows closing in."

I watch Avery's eyes, filled with both resolve and doubt. She carries an amalgamation of generations of legacy and my celestial essence within her power. But it's not enough. The darkness in her, Belial's ancient demon legacy tainted by Osric's infection, threatens to envelop her. My fragment within Nik should guide her through the treacherous road ahead.

"I hope that my soul piece within Nik is sufficient," I murmur. "That it will give him the strength to control the darkness and guide Avery towards her destiny."

He regards me with knowing eyes. "You have done all you can, Alara. Now, we must trust their resilience and unified strength."

I am longing to be present, to provide comfort and protection. Yet, as Seraphina, I am bound by duty to this realm. My sacrifice has tethered me here.

"I wish I could be there," I confess. "To lend my strength... shield Avery."

He gazes at me, his eyes filled with empathy. "Your essence dwells within her, Alara."

My dragon, my fierce and loyal protector through the Centuries. He has guided and walked the plane with many of us, choosing to tether his soul with mine. A bond of kinship, but something much more. His words resonated deep within my being, stirring the embers of hope in my heart. I watch as Avery clasps the hands of her mates, their bond unyielding, their determination unwavering.

A soft breeze rustled the leaves of the celestial trees as if Selene herself offered her blessings upon our cause. The moon casts its silvery glow upon the mortal realm, illuminating the path ahead for Avery and her comrades. The vision is as clear as the night sky above it.

"I will believe. Believe in their strength, their love, and their bond. They are my legacy, and I have faith that they will succeed."

Oblisk lowered his massive head and stared at me. "And I, too, have faith in them, Alara. They will. They must."

Together, we continued to watch, our gazes fixed upon the mortal realm. The battle draws near, and the clash of steel and magic echoes in the distance. Avery and her mates stand united, their hearts ablaze with courage.

"I will be with them in spirit," I whisper. "May my light guide them, may my love surround them, and may they emerge victorious against the forces of darkness."

And so, we remained in Selene's Garden, two souls bound by duty and love, watching as the vision unfolded. Will the course of fate change? A mere shift in the winds can throw the vision in another direction. It is vital they stay the course. Wavering could prove deadly.

My gaze shifted from the battlefield, my thoughts drifting towards another source of concern. "Oblisk, what do you know of Osric, the Lycan God? Will he honor his promise to aid Avery in her quest to defeat Belial?"

Oblisk's eyes narrowed. "Osric is a force unto himself. His allegiance is fickle, driven by his own agenda. While he may have pledged his support, they cannot rely solely on his word."

A heavy sigh escaped my lips, contemplating the ramifications of an unruly ally. The Lycans possess a power that could tip the scales in favor of our cause, but if Osric were to falter or turn against us, it could spell disaster.

"I fear that his ambitions may cloud his judgment," I confess, my voice laced with concern. "He has always harbored a thirst for power, and if his desires supersede the greater good, the consequences could be catastrophic."

The dragon nods. "We must prepare for the possibility that Osric may not keep his word. Avery and her mates must be aware of this uncertainty; they are wise."

I turned my attention back to the mortal realm. Avery and her mates stand tall, their weapons gleaming in the moonlight, ready to shift or cast off energy at a moment's notice. I offer a silent prayer, a plea to the celestial forces that guide us that they may be granted the strength and wisdom they need to emerge victorious. The vision must be seen through to its end. It is the precursor to what might come to be. What should come to be if they stay on the path, narrow and true?

"Our champions," I whispered. The fight was long, as it was brutal. A pang hit my chest as I watched Nik fall. My Goddess, they are dying. Alone stands our Seraphina. Her aim is steadfast and true as she strikes light into the heart of darkness, shattering him from within. As she collapses, no strong arms envelop her in love—only despair as she shouts at the skies. No, no, this cannot be.

Oh, ancient Gods who rule above,
Please hear my plea.
Our Seraphina needs your guidance,

With eyes that can truly see.
Wrap your arms around them,
Make them truly whole.
Take away the threat of death,
Let them keep the breath you stole.

Oblisk's rumbling voice joins mine in a sacred prayer, our hopes intertwined as our hearts broke. We will watch over them, protect them as best we can, and pray that their journey leads them to triumph.

A small flame blossoms within me as I implant the seed of fear into one very erratic Lycan. May the flame grow until a mighty fire changes the course of the vision. It must.

7: Osric

The moon's pale light cascaded through the thick canopy, casting haunting shadows upon the ancient forest where Ulric, the Alpha of the rogue pack, my comrade in chaos, and I met in secrecy. The crisp night air carried a sense of anticipation as if the elements held their breath in anticipation of the impending darkness we sought to unleash.

Ulric's piercing yellow eyes locked onto mine as I approached him, a mix of wariness and curiosity flickering within their depths. His rough, scarred muzzle curled into a snarl, displaying a formidable set of fangs. He was a creature of primal beauty, honed by centuries of survival and the merciless battles we had fought together.

"Osric," he growled, his voice a low rumble that echoed through the night. "To what do I owe this unexpected reunion? And who are these new beings that the trees whisper of in the night? For surely that is why you come."

I met his gaze with an air of calculated dominance, revealing a glimpse of my true intentions. "Ulric, my old friend, how nice to see you after all this time. To answer your question, these beings, Avery and Nik, are more than mere mortals. Avery is the last

Seraphina, blessed with a connection to the divine, while Nik is the last of the Lycans, a force to be reckoned with."

Ulric's ears perked up in intrigue, a flicker of recognition crossing his eyes. "Ah, the Seraphina," he mused, his voice tinged with a mix of curiosity and malice. "The light that dances in the darkness. And Nik, the last of his kind, an Alpha in his own right, of course, he is no longer last now that you're back."

A shadow of a smile played on my lips as memories of our past battles flooded my mind. "Yes, my friend. Do you remember the battles we waged, the chaos we unleashed upon those who dared to defy us? We were a force to be feared, our dominance unchallenged."

Ulric's gaze hardened, his voice a low growl. "Those were the days, Osric... when our pack ran rampant, sowing chaos and fear in equal measure. The supernatural realm trembled beneath our claws."

"Indeed," I watched as his mood shifted. "And now, with Belial's hold weakening, we have an opportunity to reclaim our rightful place. To reshape the supernatural realm according to our own desires."

His lips curled into a sinister grin, his fangs gleaming in the moonlight. "Tell me, old friend, how do these creatures factor into our grand design?"

"They possess power. Avery, with her power, holds untapped potential. She carries a piece of my essence within her. She thinks it is gone, but there it lingers, waiting... growing, and it is through her that we can further our ambitions. Nik, the last

Lycan, is a formidable force. I aim to bring him under my wing, harnessing his strength and loyalty."

Ulric's eyes glowed with a mix of greed and anticipation. "And what of their defeat of Belial?" he questioned. "How does that serve our purpose?"

A chuckle escaped my lips as I outlined my plan. "Belial's demise will send shockwaves through the supernatural realm," I explained. "We shall seize the opportunity to strike, to manipulate Avery and Nik in their moments of vulnerability. Once we take everything from them, they will break. With their defeat, and their hopes shattered, they will be ripe for our control. Fear and dominance will become our greatest weapons."

He grinned. "I relish the chaos, the suffering. To see them crumble, their spirits broken beneath our relentless assault. It shall be a lifetime of torment."

"Indeed, my old friend. We shall exploit their weaknesses, manipulating their desires to suit our whims. Through terror and domination, we shall reshape the supernatural realm to bow before us."

As we delved further into our plans, strategizing and reminiscing, I reveled in the hatred. The world would tremble beneath our combined might, its denizens consumed by the terror we would unleash. And when the time came, Avery, Nik, and the other two, should they survive, would awaken to a new reality—one where they would serve as slaves in our grand design.

As the night wore on, we enjoyed our discussions, exploring the intricacies of our plan. We recounted tales upon tales of our past conquests, reveling in the memories of battles fought and enemies vanquished. The air crackled with an electric energy, a palpable anticipation that resonated between us.

"Remember the time we decimated the rival werewolf packs?" Ulric reminisced, his voice filled with a mix of pride and sadistic delight. "Their screams echoed through the night as we tore their territories apart. It was a bloody mess."

Ah, yes. Their futile attempts to resist our control only fueled us. We were unstoppable, an unstoppable force of darkness. What a beautiful decade that was."

Ulric snarled. "And now, we shall reignite that flame. I have been awaiting your return. With those two under our control, the realm will cower before us. We will be unmatched, once again."

Little did our heroes know of the darkness that awaited them. They slumbered, oblivious to the fate that we weaved. The stage was set, and the players are ready.

In the heart of the night, the moon cast its ominous glow upon us; as Selene watched as she always does, we solidified our alliance and brought back the bond of old. The shadows whispered their approval as if relishing the pact we had forged. With every step, with every rumored plan, the tendrils of darkness tightened their grip around my heart. I had been chained, and now I was free. Free to finish what I was started all those years ago.

I halted as we reached the rogue pack's territory's outskirts. I glanced back at Ulric, his eyes gleaming with a feral hunger. He was not known for his patience. "Wait here," I commanded. "I shall speak on your behalf and gauge their receptiveness. Not that they have a choice. Death awaits those who disagree."

"Do not keep me waiting too long, Osric," he growled. "The moon wanes, and time presses on."

With those words, I melted into the shadows as I became one with the darkness. Swiftly and silently, I moved through the underbrush, my senses attuned to the sounds and scents of the rogue pack. The smell of damp earth mingled with the musk of unwashed fur, a familiar aroma that brought forth memories of a bygone era.

Approaching the outskirts of their encampment, I observed their crude yet efficient setup. The rogues, driven by their primal instincts, had created a stronghold that exuded an air of lawlessness. Their mangy forms prowled the perimeter, their eyes gleaming with both hunger and aggression.

Slipping into their midst, I made my presence known. Their eyes narrowed, a mix of curiosity and wariness flickering in their gaze. These rogues had long lost their way, disconnected from the pack hierarchy and thriving in the anarchy they had embraced. Ulric was a leader, but a leader in chaos. They won't be in disarray much longer.

"Osric," one growled. "To what do we owe the honor of your presence?"

My hand glanced his arm before giving it a tight squeeze. "I have come with a proposition. A chance for redemption, for the restoration of our dominance. Ulric has already given his approval."

Their ears perked up, the flicker of interest igniting within them. They were wolves, after all, creatures drawn to the allure of power and the thrill of the hunt. They hungered for purpose, for a leader who could guide them through the darkness.

"There is a war brewing. Belial, the demon God, has reigned for far too long. He weakens, and our time to strike is nigh. Join me, and together, we shall ensure his defeat and establish ourselves as the true masters."

"The Seraphina. Avery, the last of her kind, possesses powers beyond imagination. She and her mates aim to defeat Belial, but they lack the cunning and ruthlessness that we possess. We will help them defeat him, allow them to rest while we lie in wait. Once they no longer suspect we are a threat, we will strike. I want Avery alive and Nik, as he is the last Lycan and my charge. You can kill the other two. I've no use for weak wolves."

The rogues exchanged glances. They were intrigued but also knew they had no choice.

"And what of Nik?" one of the rogues questioned. "Why should we trust him? What does he bring to our cause?"

My patience was wearing thin. My choices are not ones to be questioned. Quelling the anger that rose within me, I smiled. "Nik possesses a raw power that can be honed and guided. Under my guidance, he will become a formidable weapon, a force that will strike fear into the hearts of our enemies. With his loyalty firmly secured, we will have an ally whose strength knows no bounds."

"But what of Avery, the Seraphina?" another rogue inquired, his voice tinged with curiosity. "She is the last of her kind, possessing divine powers. How do we ensure her compliance? What reason does she have to comply?"

"Avery's powers are indeed formidable," I replied. "But she is burdened by her own humanity, her compassion and desire for righteousness. We shall exploit these weaknesses, manipulating her emotions and desires to serve our own agenda. With the right incentives and calculated persuasion, she will become a puppet in our hands."

Wicked delight danced in their eyes. They reveled in the idea of controlling such a powerful being, of twisting her noble intentions to suit their darker purpose.

"And once Belial is defeated?" He continued his line of questioning. "What will become of the realm?"

Irritating mutt, this one. Perhaps I should destroy him. "Once Belial is vanquished, the realm will be thrown into chaos. After relief will come fear. They will look for a leader to protect them from further threats. This is where we come in."

A roar went up as excited mutts howled at the moon.

The era of the Lycan was beginning.

8: Avery

As the first rays of dawn painted the sky in hues of gold, the tranquil atmosphere inside the cabin began to stir. Slumber gradually released its hold on our weary bodies, and we emerged from the realm of dreams into the embrace of a new day.

With the twins still nestled in their slumber, their tiny chests rising and falling rhythmically, I turned my attention towards creating a mishmash of breakfast from whatever I could find in the cupboards. Soon, the aroma of freshly brewed coffee mingled with the scent of breakfast.

Nik was the first to join me, his towering presence filling the room. His eyes gleamed with a mix of mischief and exhaustion. "Morning, love," he murmured, kissing my temple softly. "What's on the menu?"

I grinned, flipping a pancake with practiced ease. "The usual—pancakes and some canned fruit. Simple but satisfying. Just like I'd be making back home."

Roman ambled into the kitchen, his tousled hair and goofy grin instantly brightening the room. "Ah, the smell of victory!

Or is it just pancakes?" He winked playfully, eliciting a chuckle from Nik and me.

Gabriel soon followed; his warm eyes sparkled with a blend of excitement and concern. "Avery, have you sensed anything unusual? Anything that could give us an advantage against Belial? I thought I felt something strange last night, but I can't be sure."

I paused mid-flip, and a feeling of unease traveled through me. "Actually, last night, I felt a ripple in the fabric of the realm. It was brief, but it felt like a portal opening somewhere nearby. I fear he is growing stronger, and time is running short."

The jovial ambiance began to fade, replaced by a weighty silence that settled over the room. We had known that our day of battle would come, but the reality of it was sobering. Roman broke the silence.

"So, what's the plan, Avery? How do we go about defeating him and saving the world?"

I exchanged a glance with Nik. "We need to ask Osric for help. He claims to have ties with a pack of rogue werewolves who have their own score to settle with Belial. With their help, we may have a chance at victory."

Gabriel frowned, his gaze fixed on the table. "Rogues? Are they trustworthy?"

Nik's voice held a note of caution as he spoke. "They are a wild and unpredictable bunch, driven by their own thirst for power and revenge. But if we can channel their energy and focus it on Belial, they might prove to be formidable allay."

A silence hung in the air, pregnant with the weight of our decision. Nik jumped down from his seat on the counter, beckoning us to gather around the table. "We need to discuss this further with Osric. Avery, can you call him in?"

I nodded as I slid the last of the pancakes onto a plate. "Eat."

I stepped outside, inhaling the crisp morning air, and summoned Osric with a wave of my hand. Moments later, he materialized before me, looking pretty pissed off.

"I was just about to have breakfast. Why would you do that?"

"I don't really care what you were doing. Come inside, it's time." Truthfully, teleporting was exhausting, and I only did it when I absolutely had to. I technically didn't *have* to teleport him, but if I could find a way to irritate him as much as he irritated me, I was going to do it.

"Alright, so, we need a strategy," Nik began once we made it inside. "We don't know much about Belial, just that Avery and you are needed. So... what can you bring to the table that makes your presence worthwhile?"

His lips curled into a sly smile. "Indeed, my dear Nik. But first, let us break our fast together and discuss our plans in detail."

As we savored the simple yet comforting breakfast, Osric's piercing gaze roved over each of us, making me uncomfortable. There was no small talk, no jokes, no laughter. Just silence and the occasional chewing. The twins began crying, and Roman took off to tend them.

"You may go as well." Osric motioned for Nik and Gabe to follow.

They remained rooted to the spot.

"I'd like a word, alone, with her. It will only take a moment. I promise not to bite." His attempt at a smile was grotesque.

I nodded, and they reluctantly left to follow Roman down the hall.

"So, Avery," Osric began, "tell me more about your issue with Belial. What is it that drives you to see him defeated? I'd like to know what type of person I'm getting in bed with. As far as I can tell, you can just walk away and let him do his thing. You don't *need* to do anything."

I swallowed hard, meeting his intense gaze head-on. "He is a menace to both the human realm and the supernatural world. As the last Seraphina, it is my duty to protect the balance and ensure the safety of all beings. But more than that, I have seen the devastation he leaves in his wake—the pain and suffering he inflicts upon innocent souls. I cannot stand idly by while innocents die. You know this."

Osric nodded. "I do know this. So why bring in Nik? He's your mate, so why not just do this by yourself? He could die. Is that what you want? Do you want him to die? How does he fit into this grand scheme of yours?"

"He is more than just my mate. He is the embodiment of strength and loyalty. Together, we are bound by a love that transcends time and circumstance. With his abilities, he possesses the power to turn the tide of battle. We are tied together. The four of us."

The ancient Lycan God's lips curled into a smirk. "Ah, Nik, a powerful creature indeed. It seems that fate has intertwined your destinies for a reason. How fortunate for you, Avery. You not only have one man, but three, ready and willing to die for you. You do know they will die, don't you?"

I narrowed my eyes. "This is a fool's errand. You know nothing of value, clearly, or you wouldn't be wasting time talking about things that don't move us forward. What is it you truly want, Osric?"

He coughed, quickly sipping some water before leaning back in his chair. "Belial may have imprisoned me for a century, but my desire for dominance and control remains unquenched. I aim to restore my rule over the supernatural realm by aligning myself with you and your mates. We shall claim victory together, and I shall rise once more."

Ah, so that's exactly what I thought. Osric's motives were veiled in darkness, his thirst for power insatiable. Yet, if joining forces with him was the means to an end—the end of Belial's reign of terror—then we would have to. We will worry about the rest later.

"Nik," Osric commanded. "Join us. We must discuss our strategy in further detail. The other two can stay or go. I care not."

Nik nodded as he cast me a reassuring glance before he took his place at the table. The air grew dense with anticipation as they delved into the intricacies of their plan, the web of alliances and strategies woven with precision.

Listening intently, I marveled at the intelligence and strategic prowess that unfolded before me. Osric outlined a multi-faceted approach, exploiting the weaknesses he said Belial had while minimizing the risks to our allay. It was a careful dance, a delicate balance between manipulating dark forces and harnessing the power of light.

As the morning wore on, the sunlight cast longer shadows across the cabin floor, a reminder that time was not our ally. Osric's voice grew more urgent, emphasizing the need for swiftness and precision. Each of us offered suggestions, debated tactics, and sought the most effective path forward.

Finally, we reached a consensus—a plan that intertwined our skills, our strengths, and the dark forces Osric would bring to bear. It was all laid out. Now, all that remained was to execute the plan and face Belial head-on.

As we rose from the table, reality set in. Fear crept into my heart and gripped me. This was really it. The moment had come.

With the morning sun blazing high in the sky, we stepped outside, ready to enjoy our last days before we tried to meet Belial head-on. The winds whispered secrets of ancient battles; the trees swayed in rhythmic harmony, and the promise of a future teetered on the precipice.

Roman stood beside me quietly, "What of the twins, Avery? What are we going to do with them?"

I looked up at him, "We need to take them to my parents."

9: Avery

The sun cast a golden hue over the forest as we began our journey, our steps deliberate and measured. The anticipation of reaching my parents' house hung in the air, mingling with a touch of nervous excitement. The atmosphere was charged as the guys bantered. I hadn't seen them in ages. Excitement tore through me at seeing them again.

Roman glanced at me, a mischievous twinkle in his eyes. "So, are your parents going to interrogate us like we're spies on a covert mission?"

I laughed, rolling my eyes. "Oh, you have no idea. They have a whole arsenal of embarrassing childhood stories ready to be unleashed."

Nik chuckled, his voice filled with mock concern. "Great. Just what you need—your past exposed for all to hear. I can't wait to hear how adorable you were as a tiny cherub."

Gabriel chimed in. "Don't worry, Nik. We'll all be in the same boat, relishing in her beautifully blushed skin and attempting to control our animalistic urges. I'm sure her parents will appreciate your charm and quick wit, though."

Nik exchanged a glance with Roman, both of them feigning nervousness. "Charm and wit, huh? We'll need all the help we can get."

As we walked, the forest unfolded before us, revealing a breathtaking tapestry of natural beauty. Sunlight warmed my skin. Birds serenaded us from their perches, their melodic songs filling the air with a sense of tranquility.

Aurora and Onyx looked around fervently, their curiosity brightening the path ahead. We took turns carrying them, enjoying the warmth and innocence of their presence. Their joy acted as a soothing balm, easing the nervous tension that lingered within us. Such beautiful babies, so full of life. Leaving them would be a difficult pill to swallow.

Roman glanced at me; a slight smile tugged at his lips. "Are you sure your parents won't mind that I'm a were-wolf?"

I squeezed his hand reassuringly. "No, Roman. My parents have always been open-minded. They understand that love transcends boundaries. Plus, they raised me in a pack, remember?" Thankfully, their house was on the outskirts of the pack. It made coming and going much easier. And there was no risk of running into anyone I knew.

Nik nodded. "Avery's right. We're a family bound by more than just our devilish good looks and wild charisma. Love will always triumph. Plus, being a wolf is normal to them; wait until they find out I'm a damn Lycan."

Calm and composed, Gabriel added, "Besides, we've faced far more daunting challenges than meeting the in-laws. We'll handle this with grace and charm."

We continued our journey through the forest; the pace slowed as we soaked in the beauty around us. The air was scented with moss's earthy fragrance and wildflowers' delicate perfume. The melody of a nearby brook soothed me, its gentle babbling serving as a beautiful backdrop to our conversation.

As the sun began its descent, casting shadows across our path, the conversation shifted to lighter topics. We shared stories and jokes, our laughter blending harmoniously with the sounds of nature. It was a respite, a moment of peace in the face of the challenges that awaited us.

Nik's voice carried a note of reflection as he turned somber. "Remember when we faced the Wendigo in the icy caverns of the North? We thought we wouldn't survive that night, but together, we conquered our fears and emerged victorious."

Roman laughed as he recalled the memory. "And what about the time we infiltrated the Forbidden Citadel to retrieve the ancient scroll? It felt like every trap in existence was set against us, but we outsmarted them all. That scroll ended up being nothing but the butt end of a joke our dad's played on us."

Gabriel's gaze grew distant. "Those were trying times, but they shaped us into who we are today. We've faced countless battles, and we've always come out stronger on the other side."

Nik nudged Roman with an elbow. "So, Roman, any tips for impressing Avery's parents? You know, since you've done this with Cassie."

Roman scratched his chin, pretending to ponder the question. "Well, be sure to mention my impeccable table manners and my ability to juggle silverware while reciting poetry."

I snorted, unable to contain my amusement. "Oh, yes, because that's exactly what my parents will be looking for in a son-in-law."

Gabriel joined in. "Don't forget to mention your extensive knowledge of fine cheeses, Roman. I'm sure that will seal the deal."

He feigned offense as he placed a hand over his heart and gasped dramatically. "Ah, yes, my cheese expertise! How could I forget? I shall regale them with tales of the finest Gouda and the most exquisite Camembert! I cannot help that cheese is the entire point of eating!"

Our laughter woke the twins, and I had to pass Aurora to Gabe because it gave me a stitch in my side. These were my men; gotta love em.

We stopped when we found a small clearing bathed in the soft glow of dusk. It seemed like a sign, a natural sanctuary where we could rest and prepare for the meeting with my parents.

With practiced efficiency, we set about creating our camp. Gabriel gathered firewood, arranging it skillfully in a circle, while Nik and Roman worked together to gather some fallen branches for a crude shelter. I joined in, tending to the twins, ensuring they were comfortable and content.

The crackling fire came to life. It cast dancing shadows on our faces as the warm glow enveloped us. The air grew cool, and we huddled close to the fire's embrace, drawing comfort from its warmth.

Sitting together, we shared a simple meal, savoring the taste of canned beans and spam. It felt like a delicacy after days without a proper home-cooked dinner. Conversation flowed effortlessly, a mix of playful banter and moments of quiet reflection. We reveled in the magic of the evening, our worries and nerves momentarily set aside. Laying under the stars that had awoken across the sky, we fell silent as we allowed the moment to last just a little bit longer.

Nik's voice broke the peaceful silence. "You know, this reminds me why we're fighting so hard. It's not just about defeating Belial—it's about preserving the beauty and joy that still exist in this world. About love. Family."

Roman nodded. "Absolutely. We are the reason we fight. It's always been for us."

Gabriel's gaze drifted to the starlit sky above. "Tomorrow, we'll face a new challenge—the meeting with Avery's parents. But tonight, let's cherish our family. The one we built. The one we chose."

As the fire crackled and the night deepened, a sense of unity settled over our camp. We nestled into our makeshift beds, cocooned by arms and legs and the sounds of baby coos.

10: Gabriel

The night was heavy with stillness as I paced around the camp, my thoughts spiraling into a tangled web. Sleep evaded me as anxiety kept my mind alert and restless. I glanced at the peaceful figures of Nik, Roman, and the twins, their steady breathing a stark contrast to the turmoil within me. Wait, where's Avery?

A rustling sound caught my attention, and I turned to see her making her way towards me, her eyes heavy with sleep. She moved with a grace that mirrored the moonlight's caress, her presence calming the storm raging within me.

"Gabriel," she whispered. "Are you having trouble sleeping?"

I exhaled deeply, my shoulders slumping as I met her gaze. "Yeah. There's a restlessness within me, an unease that keeps my mind spinning. I'm seeing things. I'm feeling things I can't explain. It terrifies me. I can't seem to find peace tonight."

She stepped closer and wrapped her arms around me. "You don't have to face this alone, Gabriel. Share your burdens with me."

I sighed. I hated being vulnerable. Exposed. "Sometimes I worry, Avery. I worry about the challenges we'll face and the dangers that lie ahead. And most of all, I worry about keeping you safe."

She reached down, her delicate hand finding mine, intertwining our fingers. "I understand your concern, my love. But I have faith in us, in our strength. Our bond. We've overcome so much already, and we'll face tomorrow just as we have today."

Her words were a balm to my troubled soul, slowly extinguishing my fear. I pulled her gently towards a fallen log, where we sat side by side, her presence grounding me.

She rested her head on my shoulder, her voice filled with tenderness. "Gabe, you don't have to carry the weight of the world on your shoulders. We are a team, and I am here for you, just as you are here for me."

A soft smile tugged at my lips. "I know. Sometimes it's just nice to hear you love on me."

As the night wore on and the gentle quiet of the forest enveloped us, a melody began to form in my mind. A lullaby was born from the depths of my feelings for Avery, a song that whispered of all the things I loved about her.

I cleared my throat, my voice gentle and hushed as I sang the lullaby to her. "In the darkest night, our love takes flight like stars that blaze across the sky. Through trials, we'll stride by each other's side with a love that will never die..."

Her breathing slowed; her body relaxed against mine as the melody faded on the wind. The breeze carried our whispered promises, the essence of our love, into the ethereal realm of dreams. Just as my troubled mind eased, sleep found me.

Hours later, the morning sun greeted us with its golden rays, illuminating the forest in hues of warmth and feelings of new beginnings. Avery stirred in my arms, her eyes fluttering open and a smile gracing her lips.

"Good morning, babe," she yawned.

"Good morning, my love," I gently kissed her forehead. The world around us seemed to fade away, leaving only the two of us in this delicate moment.

We rose from our spot, stretching and shaking off the dirt and leaves. Sleeping against a log wasn't as comfortable as I'd hoped it would be. Roman and Nik were already up, attending to the twins getting us ready to walk.

Her parents' home loomed closer with each step, a mix of anticipation and nerves pooling in my stomach. I had no doubt that they would welcome me with open arms, but the weight of their expectations weighed heavily on my mind. Would I be enough? Would they see the love and devotion I had for their daughter? Would they be weirded out that there are three of us?

She must have sensed my inner turmoil as she squeezed my hand. "Gabe, my parents will love you, just as I do. They will know how much you mean to me and see the goodness in your heart. You are the glue that holds us all together."

Her words brought comfort and strength, which allowed me to push past my worries and enjoy thoughts of what was to come. After the battle, after the healing. The life after. I wove dreams of a future filled with hope. One where the twins grew to be strong, and we grew old together.

I marveled at the beauty around us, the way nature reclaimed what had been taken by Belial's darkness. Decimated villages gave way to vibrant wildflowers—Nature's way of righting his wrongs.

As the hours passed, we stumbled upon a small brook, its crystal-clear waters cascaded over smooth rocks. We paused, taking a moment to dip our hands in the cool water, finding solace in its touch. Grateful for the moment of rest during the long trek.

Finally, the trees began to thin, revealing a clearing ahead. Avery's childhood home stood before us, nestled in a haven of greenery and tranquility. It really was the perfect house. It exuded a sense of warmth and familiarity. A tremor of excitement passed through me as I imagined her growing up here, surrounded by love.

We paused at the start of their yard, the weight of the moment settling upon us. Avery turned to face me, trailing her hand down my face.

"We're here, Gabe," she whispered. "Are you ready?"

"I'm ready, my love. With you by my side, I can face anything. Including meeting your parents."

11: Roman

As we approached the house, a mix of excitement and nerves fluttered in my stomach. Meeting the parents was always a milestone, and no matter how many times I had done it, a sense of uncertainty always lingered. But being the goofball that I was, I'd be able to inject some humor into the situation to ease the tension. Poor Gabe, though. He looked a bit green around the gills. I don't blame him though. He is a bit stuffy. I'd be nervous too if I didn't have a host of awful joked at the ready.

Avery's parents, Helen and Richard, stood on the porch, their smiles wide and welcoming. It was hard to miss four people ambling towards their front door. Helen wore a wide grin while Richard stood and watched as we approached. They were clearly excited to meet us and to meet their grandchildren.

We stepped onto the porch, and I gave them a sweeping bow, a playful grin plastered across my face. "Greetings, esteemed parents of the magnificent Avery. I am Roman, the bringer of bad jokes and awkward moments. Pleased to make your acquaintance!"

Avery rolled her eyes, trying to hide her amusement, while Nik chuckled beside me. Gabriel stood still as a beanpole. What a stick in the mud. That was clearly hilarious judging by her parents' reaction. They exchanged bemused glances.

"Roman, it's a pleasure to meet you, finally," Richard replied, extending his hand. "And you can save the bad jokes for later. We have plenty of time to endure them."

I shook his hand with a dramatic flair. "Ah, a man who appreciates my humor. We'll get along just fine, Richard. Wait, what do you mean finally?"

Helen laughed, "did you think Sapphire did not keep us updated about Avery? My dear, I know more about you all than you would think. We also have connections, my dear." She teared up as she glanced at her daughter before hugging her fiercely. "Oh, my girl, it's so wonderful to have you home. And these little ones!" She gently touched Aurora's soft cheek, her eyes shining with love. "Welcome to our family, little angels."

Avery beamed, radiating joy as she introduced us one by one. "Mom, Dad, this is Nik, my mate and the last Lycan. And this is Gabriel, the one who grounds us all, another one of my mates. And finally, this goofball here is Roman, as he so aptly introduced himself, the resident comedian... another mate of mine."

Richard extended his hand to Nik, a glimmer of admiration in his eyes. "Nik, it's an honor to meet you. Sapphire has told us so much about you. Same about you both."

Nik shook his hand and nodded. "Thank you, Richard. It's a pleasure to meet you both."

The conversation flowed effortlessly as we settled into the cozy living room, surrounded by the warmth of family and love. Helen couldn't contain her excitement as she peppered us with questions, eager to learn more about our adventures and the connection we shared with Avery. She was in her element, and I was content to sit and watch her interact with her parents. What a loving home to grow up in.

The steam from the pot of bubbling stew drifted throughout the small kitchen, making our mouths water. Helen was a God-damn good cook. I could get used to this. Avery held Aurora, and Gabe cradled Onyx as we ate. Their gurgles brought joy to the table. Richard was drawing Gabe out of his shell by asking him lots of questions, and Nik engaged Helen in a conversation about her recipe, leaving me to watch. This is what I wanted. This was family.

As the evening drew to a close, Avery's parents hugged us and told us how grateful they were that we brought her here. They expressed their joy in having us as part of their family. They even had a nursery set up for the twins during our stay.

Before retiring to our rooms, Helen pulled me aside for a chat. "Roman, I have a feeling you'll be the one to keep this family on their toes with your jokes and pranks. Just promise me you won't drive poor Avery crazy."

I grinned. "I can't make such promises, Helen. But I promise to keep the chaos within reasonable limits."

Helen chuckled as she patted my arm. "That's all I can ask for, Roman. Just take care of my girl, will you?"

As I made my way to the guest room, I felt a sense of contentment. They embraced us with open arms, genuine warmth and love laced every interaction. It was clear that they welcomed us not just as guests but as part of their family.

The night was calm and peaceful as I settled into bed; my mind buzzed with the events of the day. But one thing weighed on my thoughts no matter how many jokes I'd told—leaving the babies. Despite the lightheartedness of the evening, the gravity of what we needed to do haunted me. The more I became entwined with Avery and her family, the more fear gripped my heart at losing it all.

I couldn't shake the growing sense of urgency. Each passing day meant Belial continued to kill innocent people and grow stronger. I wanted so badly to enjoy this and being here, but the truth was, I just wanted to go, kill, and raise our family in an environment like this.

The door creaked as Avery tip-toed to bed. I smirked at the thought of her choosing to sleep with me. Clearly, I was the favorite. Or wait, maybe I was the least favorite because if her dad caught us...

"We are just sleeping, Roman, relax."

"Did you read my mind?"

She giggled, "No, your butt clenched, so clearly you were worried about something. I presumed it was my parents finding me in here, which they won't because they aren't intrusive. But even if they did, we're all adults."

I relaxed; such a perceptive one she was.

"Now sleep."

I held her close, her warmth and soft breathing pulling me into bliss. Tomorrow would bring new challenges and obstacles to overcome, but this was everything for now.

The following day, the sun's rays filtered through the curtains, filling the room with light. Avery stirred beside me, her eyes fluttering open, and a soft smile graced her lips as she saw me watching her.

"Good morning, my love," she whispered.

I brushed a strand of hair away from her face. My fingers lingered against her cheek. "Good morning, babe. Did you sleep well?"

She nodded. "Better than ever. Being home feels right, you know?"

Slowly, we untangled ourselves from the warmth of the bed and prepared for the day. The scent of fresh coffee wafted from the kitchen, mingling with the aroma of a delicious breakfast. The rest of the house was already up, their laughter echoing through the halls.

As we ventured into the kitchen, Helen and Richard smiled broadly.

"Come, come! Coffee is over there, and breakfast is on the table! The twins are lying on the carpet in the living room. We bought them a mat thing. Oh Richard, was is it called?"

"How the hell should I know? It's a mat with toys."

"Oh, you. You could at least try to be helpful."

Richard sat at the table, "Can we eat, please? I'm grumpy when I'm hungry."

Over breakfast, our conversation flowed effortlessly once again, the previous night's humor resurfacing as we resumed our light-hearted chatter. The nervousness of meeting Avery's parents had dissipated, replaced by a growing sense of familiarity and acceptance.

As we prepared for the day, Richard piped up. "You men are quite large. We need firewood. Later today, we will get some. Now," he clapped his hands together with a boom, "what's on the agenda for today?"

12: Avery

The decision I was about to make carried the weight of uncertainty, but it was one that needed to be made. The twins cooed and wriggled in my as they searched the world around them.

Taking a deep breath, I walked towards my parents, their faces etched with warmth and love, and the time had come to have a serious conversation that would shape our immediate future.

"Mom, Dad, may I talk to you for a moment?" I asked.

Mom's eyes crinkled with curiosity, and Dad set aside the newspaper he was reading. "Of course, dear. What's on your mind?"

I shifted the weight of the twins, feeling their tiny bodies snuggled against me. "I've been thinking... With everything that's happening, I need to keep the twins safe, I... Would you be willing to take care of Aurora and Onyx while we do what we must?"

Silence hung in the air for a moment as my parents processed my request.

Mom reached out, gently caressing the soft cheek of one of the twins. "Avery, you know we adore these precious little ones.

We would be honored to care for them. But are you sure you want to leave? It's a big responsibility, this war you're waging, and we want what's best for all of you."

I nodded, tears welling up in my eyes. "I know, Mom. And I trust you both. This is the best decision for the twins. They'll be safe and loved here."

My dad cleared his throat. "We'll do everything we can to keep them safe, Avery; you know we will. Don't worry, my girl. They'll be in good hands. But what about you? We are worried about you."

Relief washed over me, mingled with a tinge of sadness. It was bittersweet to think I had to part with my children, even temporarily, but I knew it was the right choice. Taking a deep breath, I composed myself and focused on the next part of our conversation.

"But there's something else, a favor I need to ask. We need time to rest and regroup. We've been on the move, battling Belial's forces, and we could use a few days of respite."

Excitement buzzed. I'd have to reign it in. You give them an inch, and they'll take a mile.

Mom spoke first, her voice filled with compassion. "Avery, my heart aches at the thought of you going out there. You all need time to recharge and find strength. Please, stay here and rest as long as you'd like, forever, ideally. Let someone else take care of this, please, my child. We'll take care of everything."

Dad's gaze softened, his love for me evident in his eyes. "We insist, Ave. We want to support you in any way we can. Stay here; let us take care of the twins and regain your strength."

I held back a flood of tears. I wanted nothing more than to stay here where it was warm and safe. Where my babies would flourish, but I couldn't. Not yet. "We can't stay for an extended period. Maybe three or four days, max."

The room grew quiet, tension thick in the air as my parents absorbed my words. Mom started crying, and Dad's brow furrowed. They were struggling to balance their desire to protect me with the knowledge that nothing would stop me from doing what I had to.

"But, darling," Mom started, her voice quivered, "we just want you all to be safe. Is there no way to postpone your mission, even for a few months? We could all spend time together as a family to rest and heal. You need to be here with your little ones. They need you."

I understood their plea, their yearning for a sense of normalcy and togetherness—something we hadn't had in a long time. The weight of responsibility pressed heavily on my shoulders, and I longed for a reprieve, a chance to be enveloped in the warmth and love of my family.

Tears welled up in my eyes as I grasped my parents' hands, the need for understanding palpable. "I wish we could, Mom. I truly do. I desperately want to be here and watch my children grow, but I can't. The darkness will spread. It will cover everything we've ever known. It will affect the way Aurora and Onyx grow in this world, and I can't that thought. We have to go."

Dad sighed heavily, his gaze fixed on the floor as he wrestled with his conflicting emotions. "I understand, Ave. But it's difficult to let go, to watch you go back into danger. Understand my heart."

"I do, dad. We can stay for a few days, but then we have to go."

Dad's expression softened, a smile tugging at the corners of his lips. "You always were a spitfire. Three days to rest, recover, and reconnect as a family. It's a compromise we can make. I wish it were longer; we've missed you so much."

A surge of gratitude washed over me as I grabbed them both in a tight embrace. "Thank you, Mom and Dad. Your support means everything to us. These three days will be a precious gift, a chance to gather our strength and make memories."

The tension in the room dissolved, replaced by a sense of warm love and understanding. We spent the rest of the morning planning, discussing the logistics of our stay, and my mom busied herself with preparing a feast fit for a small army. Cooking had always been her first love.

Midday approached, and the scent of home-cooked food wafted through the air. My stomach growled in response. Laughter echoed from the kitchen as we all pitched in, each contributing our unique touch to the preparations.

The hours slipped by, carrying with them a sense of joy. Unbridled joy. We sat together in the living room, wherever there was room. I just wanted us all to be together, it didn't matter where. Our plates were loaded—everything from pigs in a blanket to taquitos to various salads. Mom even made French Onion soup, my favorite. The twins gurgled happily from the living room floor as their dads surrounded them, making funny faces and cooing at them, blissfully unaware of the weight that rested upon our shoulders.

We savored each bite, relishing the simple joy of being together. The tension of the past days melted away, replaced by simple moments that made our family whole.

We found home in those fleeting moments surrounded by love, compassion, and the mouthwatering flavors of a home-cooked meal.

Outside, the world continued its relentless march, unaware of the respite we had carved for ourselves. But within those four walls, time seemed to slow, granting us more than we'd ever thought we'd have.

The sun began its descent as plates clanged in the kitchen. Mom and Dad washed and dried respectively, allowing us some privacy of our own. The twins, tuckered out from a day of play, nestled contentedly in their cribs, their peaceful slumber a testament to the peace that surrounded them.

13: Nikolai

As I stepped into the study, the weight of anticipation settled upon my shoulders. Richard sat behind his desk, a stern expression etched upon his face. I could sense his protective nature, the underlying concern for his daughter's well-being. He had requested a chance to speak with us about taking care of Avery.

The room was filled with an air of formality, the walls adorned with shelves of books and mementos. Richard motioned for us to take a seat, his eyes lingering on each of us with a mix of scrutiny and curiosity. I understood his desire to ensure his daughter would be cherished and protected. After all, I knew firsthand the depths of my love for Avery and the lengths I would go to keep her safe.

"Thank you for meeting with me," Richard began. "Let's get down to it. I'm not one of those shotgun dads, but I do love my child. This is just our chance to get to know each other more personally. Avery is my only daughter, and as her father, it has always been my responsibility to ensure her happiness and well-being."

Roman and Gabriel nodded in agreement, their expressions serious and respectful. I held a deep respect for this man. He was in the room with monsters who could destroy him at any moment, yet he had no qualms about telling us what was what. Not that we would ever do that. I'm just saying.

"I've watched the three of you interact with Avery," Richard continued, his gaze shifting between us. "And while I admit it took some time for me to fully grasp the complexities of your relationships, I can see your love and devotion for her."

I straightened in my seat, meeting Richard's gaze. He must know our commitment to Avery and that we were prepared to protect and care for her for the rest of our lives.

"I understand your concerns, Richard," I replied. "But please know that we would never take her well-being lightly. We are fully aware of the responsibility we bear as her mates, and we will do everything in our power to support and protect her. We would die for her. Over and over again. There is nothing we wouldn't do."

Richard's eyes softened, his gaze shifting to a photograph of Avery on his desk. A mixture of emotions flickered across his face.

"I have spent countless nights worrying about her safety," he confessed, his voice tinged with vulnerability. "But seeing the love and care you have shown her, I can't deny the bond that exists between you. It may not be what I had envisioned for her, but it is evident that you bring happiness into her life. I don't quite fully understand why she has three of you, though I won't complain. More of you to keep an eye on her. She's quite the handful, isn't she?"

Roman and Gabriel nodded in agreement. "She certainly is," Gabe said with a smile.

"I accept you as Avery's mates and guardians," Richard finally said. "Not that you needed or wanted my approval; I just felt it necessary to give. I remember when I met Helen's father. His approval meant a lot to me. She clearly loves you, and I trust that you will always put her first."

A wave of relief washed over me, a weight lifting from my shoulders. We had gained Richard's acceptance and trust.

"Thank you, sir," I said as I stood to shake his hand. "We will honor your trust and protect Avery with our lives. She means everything to us."

"Take care of my daughter, you three. Make her happy, keep her safe. That is all a father could ask for."

We rose from our seats, a new understanding and connection forged between us. As we exchanged a final nod, I knew that our path was aligned. Richard had entrusted us with his precious daughter, and we would honor that trust. I left the study and a sense of relief washed over me. That was a pivotal moment, one that solidified our place as Avery's mates and guardians.

Walking through the hallways of the house, I found Avery waiting for me, her eyes filled with curiosity and hope. She had undoubtedly sensed the weight of the conversation that had just taken place. I took her hand in mine, intertwining our fingers, and gave her a reassuring smile.

"He accepts us, Avery," I said. "Your father accepts us as your mates."

Avery's face lit up with a radiant smile, a mix of emotions dancing in her eyes. "I knew he would. My dad is the best dad in the world. He only ever put my happiness first."

I pulled her into a tight hug, cherishing the feeling of her in my arms. "He sees the love and happiness we bring into each other's lives," I whispered. "And he trusts us to take care of you."

She nodded against my chest, her voice muffled. "I've never doubted your commitment or the bond we share. But knowing that my father accepts us, it means everything to me."

We stood there for a moment, wrapped in each other's arms, and I wanted to whisk her upstairs and have my way with her, but I couldn't. Not right now, at least.

As evening approached, Avery and I found ourselves sitting by a crackling fire in the living room, basking in its comforting warmth. We watched as Roman and Gabriel entertained the twins.

Avery leaned against my shoulder, her fingers tracing gentle patterns on my hand. "This feels like a dream," she whispered, her voice filled with contentment. "Having my family and mates together is more than I could have ever hoped for."

I kissed the top of her head. "We've been blessed, Avery. Richly blessed."

At that moment, as I looked around at the smiling faces and felt the love radiating from every corner, I was grateful for the journey that had brought us here. Our bond had grown stronger. We'd seen the life we wished to live.

"Come, my love, let us go to bed."

"I'll be right there. I'm just going to help Roman put the twins down, and then we will join you," she said with a wink, purposefully swaying her hips.

"Oh, I can't wait."

14: Gabriel

Once the twins were in bed and we had all brushed our teeth and showered, the three of us piled into Avery's room and waited like anxious puppies for her to leave the bathroom. It was worth the wait. She looked incredible. She had on a soft, white silk nightie that barely hit her knees. Nik was practically clawing at his pants to get them off, and Roman sat there, gazing at her in awe. As she made her way across the room to us, her hips swayed seductively, and her long hair cascaded down her back in perfect waves. My heart raced at the sight of her, and my cock sprang to attention.

Without a word, Roman reached for her hand and pulled her down onto the bed beside him. Nik wasted no time and crawled onto the bed on the other side of her. I sat back and watched as the two of them vied for her attention, each wanting to be the first to explore her body.

Avery let out a low laugh at their eagerness, running her fingers through their hair and teasing them both. Her touch had always been electric, and I could feel the heat emanating from the bed, even across the room. I couldn't resist any longer and approached them, slipping my hand under Avery's nightie and feeling the soft skin on her thigh.

Her breath hitched as I leaned in to kiss her neck, my hand slowly moving higher. Nik and Roman looked up at me, their eyes dark with desire, and I loved it. All I could think about was how badly I wanted her. How badly they wanted her. She was the epitome of sexy.

She moaned softly as my fingers reached her panties, teasing her through the silky fabric. Nik and Roman slid their hands under the hem of her nightie and ran their fingers across her hips and over her stomach.

"I can't wait to taste you," Nik growled against her neck.

Roman looked into Avery's eyes, "We both can't."

"Well, you are going to have to," Avery said coyly, "We have to wait until he gives permission." I appreciated her giving me control.

All three of them looked at me, waiting for my signal. I reached out and took her hand, pulling her up off the bed. She winked at me as I bent her over and bit her butt before spreading her cheeks. "I want the first taste tonight," I growled.

"Anything for you, my King," Avery said breathlessly.

Pulling her panties down just enough so I could see her pretty pink lips, I pulled her hips back toward me and pressed my face against her clit. I licked and sucked over and over, her juices flooding the inside of her thigh. She tasted amazing, but I wanted more.

I slapped her ass, leaving an angry red handprint, and she moaned loudly at the sensation. Pressing my thumb against her tight asshole, I slipped my tongue inside her pussy and felt her entire body tense with pleasure. Nik and Roman played with her breasts and nipples as she writhed and pleaded for me to fuck her.

"Please?" She whimpered, "Please fuck me."

Picking her up as if she were weightless, I laid her down, placing a pillow under her so she would feel just how deep I could go. Running my hands down her body, I slipped them under her thighs and pulled her toward me. The tip of my cock pressed against her opening, but I wanted her to want it more.

"Tell me how much you want it, Avery," I growled, "tell me how you want my cock inside you."

"I want you to fuck me, please Gabe, I need this," she moaned. "I want you to fill me."

I pushed into her, filling her inch by inch until my cock settled firmly inside her. Her eyes fluttered closed, and all I could see was the look of pure ecstasy wash over her face. My cock lodged inside her tight walls, and I could hold out no longer. I wasn't nearly as good at this teasing thing as Nik was.

"Please," she whispered, "please, please, fuck me."

I pulled back, almost leaving her before pushing in again and again. Roman knelt on the bed and bent over, sliding his cock between her lips as I watched.

"Fuck my mouth," Avery growled, "harder."

He pushed down and made her gag, waiting a few seconds before pulling out and letting her breathe. Her muffled moans were so sexy, flooding the room with a white noise that edged me closer to the edge of my own climax. She pressed her head back against the bed, her breath hit hed as Roman grunted quietly as he thrust for the last time. Hot, white ropes of his cum shot across her breasts and face, painting her skin.

Her back arched as her body bowed with her orgasm; her screams made my body tense, and my cock twitched inside her clenched walls. The feel of my cum flooding into her drove me wild. Placing my hands on her hips, I picked her up and placed her so that her thighs were on either side of Nik's legs. She took his cock in her hands and guided it inside her mouth, sucking hard around the shaft as it slid along her tongue. His cock began to twitch inside her, and she hummed softly around it. "I can taste it," she mumbled, "I can taste his cum already on my tongue."

I pulled her off of him and turned her over, my cock still hard as I reached down and turned to the table beside us. I grabbed the bottle of lube that had been sitting there, wanting to be used for her, and drizzled it over her ass.

"Mind if I go?" He said with a devilish grin.

"I want both of you in my holes," Avery said as she turned to Nik, and he picked her up and slid her down his cock. Her ass was waiting for me. "I want both of your cum inside of me," she said, turning and looking at me with a devious grin that made my cock twitch with hunger for her.

"I'm going to fuck you so hard," I said as I slowly slid my cock around her asshole and leaned over and kissed the nape of her neck as I began to push in. Her gasps as she tried to push me out heightened my arousal. "Easy, babe, just breathe; give it a sec."

Nik grabbed her hips and began thrusting, pushing his cock into her at the same time as me. The tightness of her ass was incredible, and she moaned loudly as he increased the speed of his thrusts while I hit it rhythmically inside her backside. She was panting from pleasure, and I could feel she was close as I increased my speed.

Roman watched us, his hand pumping his semi-erect cock, as Nik pumped into Avery faster until she screamed out in pleasure, coming hard around our cocks. Both of us released deep within her. My dick twitched as it came.

Her legs trembled as we slid out of her; Nik caught her before she dropped.

"Damn... you boys did a number on me this time." She said sheepishly.

"Let me go grab a washcloth," Roman said, quickly running to the bathroom.

She looked at me and smiled as she reached down and stroked my cock. It instantly tried to come back to life, which made her giggle. "I guess I know how to handle you, Gabe. Didn't know you had enough juice to go again."

"For you? Anytime, anywhere, any place." I wiggled my eyebrows, "and I do mean any place. Except maybe a bit later... I'm a bit milked right now."

"Lay down, Avery, let me clean you and tuck you in. Your mom said we are going to the beach tomorrow, so let's get a good sleep," Roman said, slipping into a caregiver role while Nik snuck off to shower.

She yawned, "good idea." Before he had finished gently wiping her, she was already fast asleep.

15: Avery

As we walked along the sandy shoreline, the sound of crashing waves was music to my ears. We picked a spot with a nice big tree and set up our blanket. The twins were safely nestled inside an open box, their tiny hands reaching out to touch the colorful feathers of seagulls soaring above.

Roman, Nik, and Gabriel splashed in the water before dunking under and swimming. They played like carefree children, their banter getting lost in the rhythmic sounds of the ocean. I watched them, a smile playing on my lips. They needed this. Sometimes I forgot that they also had feelings of fear or anxiety. Sometimes, I got so caught up in my own head that I became selfish and demanding of their emotional energy. Making a mental note to try to be more mindful, I snagged a bottle of water and downed it.

Beside me, my parents watched the scene unfold with adoring eyes. They marveled at the joyful energy radiating from our little family.

"They grow up so fast," my mother remarked, her voice tinged with both nostalgia and pride as she looked at the babies.

I nodded, my gaze fixed on the twins as they excitedly kicked their tiny legs. "Yes, they're little bundles of energy. It feels like just yesterday they were born."

Dad chuckled. "Well, you were quite the bundle of energy yourself when you were their age."

We laughed, reminiscing about my childhood adventures and the trouble I used to get into. Like the time I cut my own hair. That was a riot.

As we chatted, the guys emerged from the water, laughing at some joke Roman probably told. They plopped down on the sand beside us, their wet hair sticking to their foreheads.

Roman couldn't resist. "Did you miss us, ladies? We bring gifts of seaweed and sand in our hair."

Nik leaned in closer. "I think the seagulls mistook Roman's hair for a cozy nest at some point."

"Ah, boys, you are all equally beautiful, but yeah, Roman, you need a trim."

I turned to my parents, a soft smile on my lips. "I'm so glad you could witness this. This is what family means to me."

Mom's eyes shimmered with tears of happiness. "And we're grateful to be a part of this journey. Our hearts burst with pride and joy for you and the beautiful family you've created. You have grown into a fine young woman."

Dad cleared his throat. "Speaking of family, guys, let's go for a swim. I want a chat between fathers."

My heart skipped a beat, warming at that my father took such a liking to them that he'd want to impart his parenting wisdom onto my handsome men. I exchanged a glance with the guys as they stood.

As the men walked together a short distance away, I turned my attention back to the twins. They babbled happily, as they always did. Onyx grabbed at Aurora while she kicked into the sky.

"Looks like they're enjoying the beach," Mom observed.

I nodded. "Yes, they're taking it all in, experiencing the wonders of the world. I want them to cherish every moment, just like I cherish the moments I spent with you both."

Mom reached over and squeezed my hand. "You're doing an incredible job, Avery. We couldn't be prouder. I couldn't be prouder. You're not only an amazing woman but an amazing mother."

Our conversation continued; I spoke of a world filled with possibilities, where they would be free to choose their paths, guided by love and supported by family—a choice I had until my world was yanked from under me.

"I want them to know that they can be anything they want," I sighed, thinking back to my own choices, " I want them to pursue their passions and live a life that brings them fulfillment."

Mom smiled warmly, her eyes shimmering with pride. "You've always been a dreamer, Avery," she held my hand. "And I have no doubt that you will instill those dreams in your children after you slay the evil demon lord. Until then, our little cherubs get to be spoiled by Grandma and Grandpa."

Hooting, hollering, and splashing water distracted us as Roman, Nik, and Gabriel emerged from the ocean, carrying my dad like a bride between them, their bodies glistening. They gently put my dad down, and I relished the joy on his face.

Roman plopped down beside me, his wet hair clinging to his forehead. "What's the discussion about, future dreams for the little ones?"

I chuckled, brushing away a few grains of sand from my arm. "Yes, I was just sharing my hopes and aspirations."

Nik and Gabe joined us, sitting on the other side of my mom. "And what exactly are those dreams, Avery? I don't know that we've ever discussed them outside of just trying to keep them safe." Nik asked, curiosity sparkling in his eyes.

I took a moment to gaze at the twins. "I want them to know the power of love and unity... I want them to understand the importance of family and the strength that comes from supporting one another. I want them to know peace."

Gabriel leaned forward. "We will do everything in our power to guide them, to protect them, and to show them the beauty of this world."

Nik placed a hand on my shoulder. His touch grounded me. "And we will ensure that they have the freedom to explore, to learn, and to grow into the best versions of themselves."

We sat there quietly,, each of us bringing our own unique strengths to the table.

The sun began its descent, cueing us that it was time to start getting our things together. We watched in silence and embraced the serenity of the moment. As the sun finally dipped below the horizon, we all stood up to head back home. The twins cuddled up in the arms of Gabriel and Nik, and my mom walked arm in arm with my dad. Roman took my hand, interlocking his fingers with mine. He leaned in and whispered into my ear, the warmth of his breath sending shivers down my spine, "You know, Avery, I have a dream for us, too."

I turned to look at him, my heart skipping a beat. "What's that, Roman?"

"I want us to face adversity together," he said, "but mostly, I want us to love each other and grow in that love every day."

I smiled at him. "I share that dream," I said, feeling my voice crack with emotion. "I want to experience everything with you, to face Belial, to face Osric, to face whatever else unknown catastrophes await us because that's what we do. We fight tooth and nail for each other. Always."

He leaned in and brushed his lips tenderly against mine, the sweet gesture making my heart flutter.

16: Avery

Today was the day we said goodbye to my parents. I gazed down at my beautiful babies, and my heart did a flip-flop. I didn't know if I'd ever see them again. My heart clenched at the thought, but knowing my parents would protect them with their lives also brought me a sense of peace and comfort. As I hugged my mom and dad tightly, tears flowed freely. I tried to hold back the sob that was building up in my throat. My heart shattered, but I had to be strong for my babies. Images of them growing up without us there ripped and tore at my mind, threatening to force me to stay. This just wasn't fair.

"I promise to come back to you soon, my little ones," I planted a tender kiss on each of their foreheads.

My parents took the twins into their arms as they bid me goodbye. There were no drawn-out accolades, just words of comfort as they made us promises of safety, of love. They knew that no amount of despair would change the outcome. The look on their faces showed a mixture of sadness and hope. I knew they wanted to keep me there with them. Safe. Warm. They swallowed their words with a sigh and watched as we fawned over our children one last time.

"Avery... we have to go. Osric just mind-linked. The rogues are ready." Nik said.

"Just give me more time," I wept.

"We can't, Avery. I promise we will be back here to be with them as soon as possible. You can count on it," Gabe whispered. "I'm so sorry, baby."

I watched as Roman kissed the twins, followed by Nik and Gabe before they gave my parents hugs and helped me walk out of the front door.

The sun shone brightly in the sky, highlighting the beautiful scenery of our home. But none of it registered. It could have been snowing for all I gave a fuck. As we walked away down the dirt path, I turned around once more and waved goodbye to my parents. The sting of farewell was alive, working its way deep into my skin as it tried to force me to crumble.

My legs were numb as I walked through the thick brush and around tall trees until we reached a brook. It didn't hold the same allure as it did before.

"Let's take a break." Nik glanced at Roman and Gabe, worry etched into his face.

"Nature will ground her, I think." Roman wrapped his hand around mine and pulled me to the side of the path.

We stopped to catch our breath as I tried to take in all of nature's beauty around us. The sweet smell of wildflowers, the soft chirping from birds, and the rushing water calmed my nerves slightly as I stepped closer to the brook. The coolness of the water soothed my feet, and I closed my eyes for a moment to take in the serene surroundings. To breathe deeply, holding the crisp air in my lungs before I exhaled. Maybe this was a good idea, after all. I allowed myself another moment of grief before my heart closed and blocked all the pain I held. Despair would have to wait.

"This isn't goodbye, my love; it's until next time."

Gabe scoffed. "Next time needs to be soon. I already miss them."

"Me too," Nik said quietly.

"Block it off," my voice wavered ever so slightly, "it's the only way."

It wasn't long before we heard the rustling of leaves and snapping of twigs in the distance. Nik immediately stood up and got ready to shift while Gabe and Roman followed his lead.

"Avery, you have to stay behind us," Gabe said as he pulled me behind them.

I nodded, feeling the adrenaline rush through my veins. Footsteps crackled against the ground before a tall man walked into the clearing.

"Hello, Avery," he said.

"Who are you?" Nik stood in front of me protectively.

"My name is Sion, and I have come to give you news of Belial."

My heart skipped a beat, and my skin prickled.

"What news?" Gabe asked, "And why?"

"Belial has returned. He's been gathering an army in the North, preparing for war," Sion said nonchalantly. "I know of Osric and his rogue army. You should be careful."

"How do you know all this?" I asked.

"I know all, see all. It was a gift from Belial to me for enabling him to retake his form."

"So why are you warning us now? We already knew he had reopened a portal." Nik said sarcastically.

"Because something of mine has vanished. A young woman named Emma. I would like her back. If you'd be so kind as to fetch her and bring her to me, I will aid you further."

Nik growled, his shoulders tensed. "We don't work for you, Sion. And we certainly won't help you find someone who probably doesn't want to be found."

His eyes narrowed, but Nik's aggression didn't seem to threaten him. "I can offer you something in return. Information about Belial's plans. I have spies in his army and can give you details about his weaknesses."

Gabe stepped forward. "We'll consider it. But first, what do you want with her, and why do you think we have anything to do with her."

"You found her and took her in," Sion said with a grin, "I would just like my property back."

"Why? Why is she so special?"

A slow, dark chuckle escaped his lips. "Emma is no ordinary human, my dear. She possesses something that Belial desires greatly. She is the key to something far greater than you will ever understand, even as the last Seraphina. Emma's bloodline is pure and has not yet been tainted by interspecies breeding... or mates," he smirked at me.

We exchanged a look, contemplating what he could mean. If what he said was true, then Emma was in grave danger. But could we trust him to keep his end of the bargain?

"No deal." I said firmly, "If what you said is true, she doesn't deserve to get dragged into this by you or anyone else."

His eyes narrowed into slits as he stared at me, his expression dark. "You underestimate the danger, Seraphina. Belial will stop at nothing to get his hands on Emma. He knows she has the power to unlock the gates of worlds you don't even know exist. He even knows of your children. I suspect it won't take him much longer than I took to find where they are."

A chill ran down my spine. He might actually be a more dangerous enemy than the demon lord. If what he was saying was true, then Emma could be the key to fixing all of this entirely, but does she deserve to get thrust into the middle of all of this chaos? I couldn't bring myself to make a deal with another devil; one deal with the devil was enough anyone should be making for a lifetime, and Amrin made that for us.

"We'll find her," Nik said, his voice tight.

"No. Nik. We won't." Mine was firm as I tried to push him out of my way. "She needs to stay safely within the compounds of the pack. If Sion is here, then that means he can't get to her there; that's all that matters. She deserves to live a life of peace, and if we have to go to war to protect her and whoever else out there that's like her, then we do so. Alone."

Nik's eyes flickered with a mix of anger and pride, but he didn't say anything. Sion just shrugged and turned to leave, his steps lithe and calculated. I knew his own agenda didn't align with ours, but his words had made one thing clear - Emma was in grave danger, and we needed to find a way to keep her safe.

"How are we going to go back home and go to Osric at the same time?" Gabe sighed. "He threatened the twins, Avery."

"I... I could dream walk... I could go to our pack and whisper to someone to protect her. I've never dream walked on our plane before, but I'm sure it can be done..."

"Tonight, then?" Roman said.

"Tonight," I confirmed, wondering just what in the hell Sion was up to and what species Emma was.

17: Nikolai

"Ahhh, there he is," Osric said from the shadows, "I was beginning to think you wouldn't show. Where are the others?"

"They're... busy," I said. I'd told them I would meet with him and discuss the plans for infiltrating Belial's main camp. The demons were reported to have started spreading from the initial portal contact, so it was going to be an uphill battle getting to it.

"Busy?" He asked, shocked, "What could be more important than this? Is your little angel girlfriend backing down now?"

"No. She's busy. We will discuss our point of entry, and I will relay the message back to them." I snarled.

"You need to get a reign on her. She dictates too much. Anyway. The new plan is simple. There is a camp over yonder; these were sent to track and destroy you. So, in my own interest, we need to take it out. I will go in with the rogues and destroy the wanderers, you will flank from the side, and then we will retreat and regroup for stage 2, which will be the actual battle. Good?"

"You want me to flank... by myself?"

"Sure, you're a Lycan, are you not? You should have grown enough in strength that taking down a few demons shouldn't be an issue."

I shifted uneasily on my feet. He was testing me. There was something off about Osric's plan and his demeanor. He was more cautious and calculated in his earlier strategies, but this time, he seemed reckless and eager to jump into action.

"Osric, is everything alright? Why are you so eager to attack the demons head-on right now?" I asked, trying to keep my voice even.

He didn't answer me, instead taking a step closer and as he grabbed my arm. "Don't question me, pup. You'll do as you're told or suffer the consequences."

The threat in his words sent a chill down my spine, but I backed off, "Fine. When do we begin?"

"Now. His forces are swarming towards your camp, and I suspect they won't take much to break through and make their way down to your little girlfriend, so time is of the essence. If you care for her, that is."

I took in a deep breath, steadying my nerves and focusing on the task ahead. I could do this. After all, I had trained for this moment. My entire life had been one giant training camp. With one last flex of my muscles, I signed my fate as I stepped forward toward the fray that awaited us.

The darkness of night shrouded us as we ran through the dense forest towards the stench of sulfur. We moved quickly and stealthily, careful to avoid any potential detection. Finally, we arrived at an open clearing where we were met with an army of demons numbering close to a hundred. Fear filled me momentarily as their glowing eyes settled on us, but I straightened my spine and prepared for the fight of my life.

Osric signaled for me to flank to the right as he and the rogues charged forward to attack. I nodded, taking in a deep breath as my heartbeat quickened. My body moved on instinct as I transformed into my Lycan form, my claws elongating and my fur bristling. Sharp fangs sprung from my gums, and I could feel their movements through the trembling ground.

My appearance caught The demons off guard, and I took full advantage of their momentary confusion. I tore into one's flesh, ripping and gnawing as chunks of flesh fell from its body. The monster retaliated, its talons raking across my back, but I barely felt the pain as adrenaline took over. I really was powerful. The thought made me high.

We fought fiercely; my human strengths worked together with my Lycan as we took down demon after demon. Screams of pain and fury filled the air. But amidst the chaos, I caught a glimpse of Osric, his eyes locked on me, a look of intense satisfaction on his face.

Suddenly, I felt a searing pain in my side, and I stumbled back, realizing too late that I had let my guard down. A demon had managed to land a direct hit, and blood poured out of me. I lunged forward again with a snarl, determined to take down as many as possible before I was overrun. I roared, and they paused their advance, fear-stricken on their faces. Taking advantage of their hesitation, I allowed my darkness to take over, willing me to move faster, hit harder, and attack with force. Moving with lethal precision and speed, I charged through the hordes of demons, taking them down one by one. With every slash of my claws and the roar of my voice, their numbers decreased as they scattered in all directions in an effort to flee from me.

"Fucking weaklings!"

I turned my head and saw a giant demon lumbering towards me, his twisted grin splitting his face. Growling, I stood and bared my fangs, poising myself to strike. The demon's laughter echoed through the night, a garbled, strangled sound that mocked me. Rage surged through my veins as I sprang at him, shredding into his grotesque body. But this one was tougher than the others, and he hurled me off with a powerful blow. Swaying back, I realized I had misjudged my target, his legs oozing blood from the wounds I had inflicted. Yet, I wouldn't let him live to retaliate. I charged again, closing my jaws on his throat. His eyes widened in terror as I brutally tore him apart, my claws penetrating deep into his flesh.

As his life force drained away, I watched as his soul spiraled up into the air above us. The world seemed to blur, yet it shone brightly in the same instance, and a warm, tingling sensation invaded my limbs.

"How do you feel, pup?" boomed Osric's voice as he ripped the last demon in two. "Feels good, doesn't it? Unleashing the darkness in you."

The answer eluded me because, indeed, it did feel good- more than good...it felt liberating. Power surged in my veins, and an urge to confront Belial alone overcame me.

"In due time, lad. We're done here for now. Fetch Avery first thing tomorrow morning. No excuses about being occupied. We have a demon God to annihilate, and he isn't dawdling for your whims." He gestured dismissively around himself, "Do you really think these are all of them? This is but a fraction of his army while he keeps creating more portals as we squander our time."

Nodding in agreement, purpose kindled in my heart. The power radiating from Osric filled me with such confidence it felt like I could achieve anything. I would be invincible if I could possess even a part of his strength. Without another word, he pivoted and disappeared into the shadows. Feeling at peace, I started my journey back to camp.

The walk back was serene, the luminous moon casting its silver glow upon me like a comforting cloak. Each step brought me closer to a sense of tranquility. My Lycan seemed in sync with the nightly energy around me, as if nature itself sensed my presence and welcomed me back in its understanding embrace. For once, he wasn't tormenting me.

Approaching the camp, I saw Avery, Roman, and Gabriel resting soundly under the stars- smiles on their sleeping faces reflecting their contentment despite being oblivious to the night's event. As much as a part of me craved rest, my adrenaline was still high from the battle.

"Hey..." her melodious voice wafted through the air, "I saw you return. Are you okay?"

My voice abandoned me as I sunk down next to her and enfolded her in a tight hug. Time slipped by before I managed to regain my voice, and when I did speak, I said, "I'm okay. For the first time, I feel complete- as though I'm finally becoming who I was meant to be."

"What does that mean, Nik?" she asked.

"I just feel... potent and resilient and capable of restraining myself."

Looking at me intently, she asked," Should I be worried? You were gone for quite some time tonight with Osric..."

"No need to worry, sweetheart. Battling those demons proved that I can harness power even in my darkest moments."

"Isn't it scary that you have to depend on your darkness instead of your light?"

"Not at all. It shows me what I can be and what I need to be to deserve someone like you."

She rested her head on my muscular chest, the rhythmic beating of my heart soothing her. Looking up at me, she said, "Darling... you don't need to be anyone but yourself- someone I'll love unconditionally no matter the circumstance."

I simply nodded and kissed her before we drifted off to sleep, cradled in each other's arms.

18: Avery

I woke up to the gentle caress of sunlight that shone directly into my eyes. The warmth of Nik's body against mine was a comfort, but my heart clenched with worry. I had unsuccessfully tried to dream walk back to pack lands last night to check on Emma and the rest of the pack. But no matter how hard I tried, I couldn't breach the veil of dreams that separated us. It was as if Alara's death had cut me off from everything. I was stranded here, and I didn't know what to do.

Fear clutched at my insides as I thought of Emma, alone and vulnerable, not knowing what was coming. Dream walking had become my connection, my way of protecting and guiding those I loved, of learning what I needed to know. But now, when they needed me the most, I was powerless. It felt like a betrayal, a shattering of the very essence of who I was.

"Nik," I whispered, brushing a strand of his dark hair away from his face. "I couldn't reach them last night. I'm scared for Emma and the others. I should be there with them, protecting them."

His eyes fluttered open, and he fixed his gaze on me. "Avery, baby girl, you can't blame yourself. You're doing everything you can. We knew the risks when we left. Emma is strong, and she has the pack to support her. We'll find a way to reach them, I promise."

I sighed, feeling the weight of his words seep into my bones. I knew he was right. I had to do my best to trust that our pack was a safe haven. As I mulled over my fears, the ache of longing for my twins and the gnawing worry for our future rolled into the pit of my stomach. My parents had agreed to care for them, away from the escalating conflict, and yet, in my selfish humanity, I wanted them here with me. They were with family, but the separation felt unbearable. I yearned to hold them close, to protect them from the dangers in this war-torn world. The gaping hole in my soul over not being the one to defend them ate me from the inside out. Goddess, I was a mess. A blithering mess.

"Babe, I just... I miss the babies so much. I wish they were here with us," I cried out. "I'm struggling to gain perspective right now, and I know I'm selfish, but this is just so hard."

His arms tightened around me, offering comfort and strength. "I miss them too, Avery. But we made this sacrifice for their safety. I promise we'll find a way to reunite our family. Until then, we have each other and'll keep fighting for a better future. Roman and Gabriel will protect you, too, baby girl. Once all this is over, we can be with our babies again."

As always, he was right. My chest heaved as I sucked in a breath of air, slowly releasing it and feeling the anxiety began to lift.

"I know. You're right. I can't keep looping. I'll spiral. So... what is the plan today?"

His lips pressed against my forehead. "That's my Seraphina, always finding strength in the darkest of moments. We can do this. As for the plan... I don't know."

We untangled ourselves from our embrace, and a sense of urgency built in my chest. Time was slipping away. We had taken such a long break to enjoy each other that we couldn't delay much longer. Who knows how much damage Belial was reaping. I needed to tap into the depths of my powers to find a way to reach Emma. So much to do and figure out. There just wasn't enough time. If dream walking was no longer accessible, I had to discover an alternative.

"Babe, I need to find another way to connect with Emma and the pack." I sighed. "There must be another method, another pathway to guide and support them. I don't see how they would just leave me with no way to connect with my power. Ugh, this is so frustrating. I wish Alara were here, Aunt Sapphire, anyone. Anyone who could guide me. I think I just need some space to think."

He nodded as he stood. "I believe in you, babe. You have a gift, a strength that goes beyond dream walking. Trust in yourself, and you'll find a way to bridge the distance. Don't go outside of earshot."

Without another word, I turned away from him and walked into the woods. His eyes followed my every move as I stepped into the shadows of the trees. As soon as he was out of sight,

I exhaled deeply and allowed myself to slip into a meditative trance. The air around me hummed with life, wind rustling through leaves, birds chirping in the distance. My eyes fluttered shut, and I cleared my mind of all extraneous thoughts, allowing an inner peace to settle over me. My breathing grew shallow and rhythmic as I opened myself up to divine guidance. *Is anyone there? Can anyone see me? Where have you gone?*

My heart leaped when images came flooding to my mind's eye - a beautiful landscape filled with nature's bounty that shifted into a brilliant array of colors, swirling gold and purple that bridged together like connecting links in a chain. A text beneath the colors scrawled before me, and suddenly, it all fit together perfectly. Without reading the scribbles, I just knew what it meant.

It came to me in a moment of quiet introspection—the whisper of ancient wisdom that echoed within my soul. My powers were not limited to dream walking alone. There were other realms to explore, different ethereal pathways to traverse.

Hope pulsed through my veins, I hurried back to Nik, eager to share my discovery. I found him immersed in training, honing his Lycan abilities to perfection. His eyes gleamed with ferocity as he embraced his primal strength. He paused, panting as he stared at me.

"Nik, are Roman and Gabe up? I've got it!" I exclaimed, breathless from excitement. "I've found it, a way to connect with Emma and the pack. It's not dream walking, but something more."

He smiled. "I knew you would figure it out. Tell me, babe. What did you figure out?"

Taking a deep breath, I explained my revelation—a path called "Soul Linking." It was a powerful technique that allowed me to form a deep spiritual bond with those I wished to connect with. It transcended the limitations of physical distance and bridged the gap between our souls.

"I believe that I can reach Emma and warn her through Soul Linking. It will require immense focus and energy, but this is it."

His face lit up with a mix of pride and adoration. "Avery, you never cease to amaze me. You are truly incredible."

I paused, "I just don't know how to like... access that..."

Nik took my hand in his, his touch sending a wave of warmth through me. "Let me see if I can guide you," he whispered. "Close your eyes and breathe deeply; let the vibration of your soul guide you."

I did as he instructed, feeling my body relax in his grasp. His presence was a comfort, a grounding force that tethered me to reality. Slowly, I let go of all doubts and allowed myself to be swept away in the tide of his energy. A chain snapped in place, holding my soul to his, allowing me to roam the Soul Link without fear of losing myself in it.

After a few minutes, a spark within me ignited a flame of pure energy that burned brightly in my consciousness. It was unlike anything I had ever felt before, transcending physical sensation.

It was a connection to something otherworldly, something sacred and divine.

With Nik's tether, I honed my focus, pouring all of my energy into this ability. The colors and shapes in my mind's eye intensified, swirling within me like a whirlpool of pure energy. I could feel my consciousness expanding, waiting to reach out to those I wished to connect with.

Suddenly, I felt a tug on the strings of my soul, and I knew that I had succeeded in establishing a connection. Emma's face appeared before me, her blue eyes filled with wonder as she gazed upon me.

"Hello?" she whispered, her voice tinged with disbelief. "Who is there?"

"Hi, Emma. Don't be afraid. I'm Avery..."

"Avery? THE Avery? But how?" She said.

"Listen, girl, I don't have the time to explain everything to you, but Sion is coming for you. Do not, under any circumstances, leave the pack, okay? For some reason, he can't get in there; stay there!"

Emma's eyes widened in fear as she whispered, "Sion? What does he want with me?"

"I don't know exactly," I replied, as energy drained from my body, "but it's not good. Please, promise me you'll stay with the pack."

"I promise," her voice shook. "But what about you? Are you going to be okay?"

I tried to speak, but the connection was fading. "I have to go, Emma. Just please be safe." And then the link was gone.

I opened my eyes to see Nik looking at me expectantly. Concern etched on his face. "Did you make the connection?" he asked, his voice a low murmur.

I nodded, wiping sweat from my forehead. "She's going to stay inside the pack walls. I hope to the Goddess they keep her safe."

"Me too."

Roman yawned from behind me. "What'd I miss?"

19: Avery

I faced Roman, my shoulders sagging. That had been exhausting. "Roman," I stammered, "we need to get ready. I've made contact with Emma and warned her, but who knows what will happen. We need to move on Belial, as fast as we can."

With furrowed brows, Roman looked serious. "Sion is a damn bastard. So is Belial. God, these guys are something else." He sighed heavily before adding, "We can start packing right now."

Gabriel approached us, his brows equally furrowed. "I overheard," he began grimly. "Avery, I'm glad you were able to establish a connection. Hopefully, your warning is enough. I agree, though, the only way we can start ending this is by killing the demon."

Strong arms encircled my midsection from behind in a warm embrace. "I am so proud of you," the voice assured me. "I know you're tired, but do you think you're okay to travel?"

Nodding into his chest, I offered a thin smile. "Let's do this," I agreed quietly. "Sleep can wait."

Soon after, we took off towards Osric's camp—a flurry of bustling activity and anticipation surrounding us. Wolves dressed in battle gear marched forward in unison, their eyes squinted in grim determination.

As we arrived at the armory, I gasped at the sight—countless rows of gleaming weapons and armor lined up neatly, ready for battle. Along with awe came an immense wave of dread and apprehension that gripped me tightly as I pushed away my doubts and focused.

Greeting us with a nod was the werewolf armorer - obviously, a seasoned warrior with scars etched across his weathered face that told stories of past battles won and lost – casually challenged us to "Pick your poison."

My heart pounded in my chest as I glanced at the assortment of weapons and armor. This was it—the moment where we would equip ourselves for a war that would decide the fate of our world. Each piece held the weight of destiny, the potential to protect and to destroy.

Taking a steadying breath, I selected a sleek yet sturdy armor designed for mobility and protection. As I strapped on the pieces, I could feel the weight of responsibility settling on my shoulders. This armor was more than just a physical barrier; it symbolized my commitment to the fight, a tangible representation of the sacrifices I was willing to make.

Beside me stood Roman and Gabriel, their own battle gear gleaming in the dim light of the armory. Roman dressed himself in a set of heavy plate armor, his expression focused and determined. Gabriel opted for lightweight attire designed for swift movements.

Roman's voice cut through the silence, preparing himself for a pep talk. "We've faced many battles together, brothers, but this one..." he paused briefly to collect himself," This one is different. Belial is a threat unlike any we've encountered before. We need to have each other's backs."

Gabriel stepped up and continued. "This fight is not just about winning the battle; it's about winning the war. Today, we fight for those who cannot fight for themselves."

As I tightened the straps of my armor, the metal pressed against my skin roused me from my thoughts; the pinch of the plates made me feel alive. "I love you all." There were no other words to be said.

Nik stood beside us, his battle gear adorning his powerful frame. His eyes met mine, and in them, I saw the world. "Avery," he began gently, "my baby girl, you're a force to be reckoned with. Don't doubt yourself. Let your power flow through you. Don't overthink or hesitate. They won't be. We've got your back."

I reached out to him, taking his hand in mine, drawing strength from his unwavering support." Thank you, Nik," I whispered, "you always know exactly what to say."

As we stepped out of the armory, motivation filled my being like a wave crashing over me. The time for hesitation was past us; it was now a time for action. We would fight for what we believed in, the people we loved, and a future free from darkness.

"Osric!" Nik called out as he clapped him on the back, grinning mischievously all the while, "What's with all the armor? You know we're shifters, right? Super healing and all that."

"It's so that you don't go down in the first 30 seconds of battle from the harpies he is bound to have flying everywhere." Osric retorted without missing a beat as he turned around, a grimace etched onto his features, "If you get surrounded, it will protect you long enough to pull them off."

He scoffed before adding mockingly, "Dipshit. You guys look like you came out of a box set. Pathetic."

"Would you rather do this alone?" I countered calmly but firmly," Oh wait, you can't. You need us just as we need you."

He laughed and rolled his eyes. "I don't need anyone." He declared defiantly as he turned his back to us, his gaze scanning the surroundings as if looking for a way out. "I can handle myself just fine."

I sighed heavily, shaking my head at his stubbornness. Osric had was headstrong, never wanting to show any vulnerability. But in a battle like this, we needed to trust each other; to depend on each other. There wasn't any room for ego.

"You might be able to handle yourself," Roman countered, "but we need each other. We're stronger together than we ever could be alone."

Gabriel stepped forward, his face almost touching Osric's as he glared at him. "We are a team. That's what our pack stands for, and that's what we're fighting for. Find what you're fighting for and drop the asshole act, alright? We get it. You're the big bad, ancient Lycan, but we have to focus now. So cut the bullshit."

He scowled darkly at Gabriel's words, but his shoulders dropped slightly as if resigned to the fact. "Fine," He muttered grudgingly, "I get it. We stick together. But don't expect me to thank you."

Nik placed a hand on Osric's shoulder, offering a small smile. "We don't need your thanks, bud. All we need is your loyalty and your strength in battle. If you choose to betray us after, well, that's going to be a consequence you face. Let's go."

We all set out, the weight of the impending battle heavy on our shoulders. As we approached, the enemy army gathered in large numbers. Their eyes glinted ominously, and their teeth sat in jagged rows - their cruel smiles promising nothing but pain and suffering. Demons were everywhere, surrounding us from all sides as they gathered at the forefront of the clearing. The scent of sulfur filled the air, making my stomach churn uncomfortably. I could sense the worry and fear among my mates, but we couldn't let that hold us back. This was it. Do or die.

Nik caught my gaze then and nodded in understanding; a silent promise passed between us. We had all been through so much, but this was different. This was the battle for our existence.

With a deep breath, I channeled my energy. The uneven ground pressed under my feet as I ran forward with my mates, ready to face whatever hell the enemy had in store for us.

As expected, the demons charged at us with full force, their blood-lust evident on their faces. We met them head-on: fangs bared, claws unsheathed, and energy sparking. The sickening sound of bones crunching and flesh tearing echoed around me as we fought tooth and nail.

A group of harpies appeared overhead, just as Osric said they would, their wings flapping menacingly as they aimed their talons at us. Without a second thought, I leaped into the air; unsheathing my wings and rocketing towards them. The scent of their burnt feathers filled my nose revoltingly as I crashed into them - my energy raking through their ranks mercilessly.

Below me, I heard the sounds of struggle; the distinct sounds of my mates fighting for their lives kept me grounded despite the chaos surrounding me. As long as they struggled, they breathed. Osric's snarl cut through the fray, and he was in the thick of it, his massive form throwing demons around like rag dolls, defying their monstrous size. It would have been impressive if he weren't such a dark force himself.

But our enemies were numerous, an endless swarm of grotesque beings that kept coming wave after wave. As I touched down, the sting of a demon's claws raked across my back, and I screamed at the sudden surge of pain, turning around quickly to face it. The demon growled, baring its gruesome teeth at me defiantly, but it didn't stand a chance against my power. My hands rose, unleashing a blast of light and incinerating him where he stood. Easy.

We fought tirelessly for what felt like hours until the sun began to dip below the horizon. I was covered in blood - both mine and our enemies' as the battlefield turned into a crimson mess. But somehow, we were still standing, still fighting despite our exhaustion.

Suddenly, two massive shapes appeared on the horizon: Wyverns. Belial had summoned more of his monstrosities to fight us, to terrorize us. He knew we were growing tired.

They were enormous creatures - dwarfing even Osric, arguably the most formidable being I'd ever seen. Their red eyes bored into mine, filled with nothing but contempt. These were destroyers; they would not be stopped easily.

I knew what had to be done.

The swell of power deep inside of me rose to the surface slowly, holding the air around me in an invisible grip as anticipation built within me. This would take everything I had, but I knew without a doubt that I could do it.

Without any hesitation, I released a concentrated blast of air aimed at the two wyverns, sending them tumbling backward abruptly. They screeched loudly in response, the sound piercing through my ears painfully as they righted themselves nonchalantly - ignoring the gaping wounds in their chests blatantly. What the hell? Blasting them again, their gazes fixed upon me, gaping mouths revealing forked tongues.

With effort, I dropped to my knees, panting heavily from exhaustion. I had used everything, and I could feel my will slipping slowly. There was nothing left to give. "W-we're done,"

I whispered hoarsely; despair settled deep in my heart, "There's too many."

With a roar, Osric turned around abruptly and took off into the darkness - the rest of his pack on his heels, leaving behind nothing but echoes of their howls. Despite everything, a small smile found its way onto my face as I felt myself slipping away slowly, exhaustion finally taking over completely. Finally, I will know peace. *Live well, my babies. I am so proud of you.* The last thing I saw was Nik's worried face staring down at me in concern against the backdrop of the ashen sky.

20: Avery

I felt a jolt of sudden movement, and my eyes fluttered open to find Gabriel crouched beside me, urgency etched on his face. "Avery, we need to move. The demons are closing in. We have to get out of here."

Groggy from my deep sleep, I struggled to regain my bearings. The last thing I remembered was the weight of my exhaustion pressing down on me, pulling me into a restless darkness. But now, the fear in Gabe's voice snapped me back to reality. I could hear the distant growls and snarls, the unmistakable signs that our enemies were fast approaching.

With Gabriel's help, I managed to push myself up, my limbs heavy with fatigue. My body protested every movement, but I couldn't afford to succumb to weakness now. We were on the brink of danger, and every second counted.

As I struggled to steady myself, Roman and Nik sprang into action. They positioned themselves at the forefront, readying themselves to defend us as they scanned the encroaching army. Terror pricked at my heart as I willed my legs to listen.

"Stay close, Avery," Nik called out, his voice cutting through the chaos around us. "We'll cover your escape. Gabriel, get her on her feet. We can't let the demons reach her."

Gabriel nodded, his strong arms wrapping around me, supporting my weakened frame. "Lean on me, Avery. We're getting out of here."

As we stumbled forward, I felt the ground trembling beneath us. The deafening roars of the demons echoed in my ears, threatening to consume us. Adrenaline surged through my veins, heightening my senses, as we weaved through the maze-like forest, desperate to evade our pursuers.

But just as it seemed like the demons were about to descend upon us, a brilliant light illuminated the sky. I shielded my eyes, barely able to comprehend the celestial beauty that unfolded before me.

A figure, ethereal and radiant, descended from above. Her presence exuded power and grace as she commanded the very forces of nature. Roots weaved a shield around us, forcing the advance to a halt. Recognizing her, I sighed. She had come to our aide at last.

The demons recoiled at the sight of her, their snarls turning into whimpering retreats. Selene's voice, gentle and yet commanding, rang through the air. "You shall not harm them. They are under my protection. One more step, and you shall no longer be of this plane."

She extended her arms, and an otherworldly energy enveloped us. It was as if time stood still, the chaos frozen in a moment of divine intervention. I felt a warmth and tranquility wash over me, the weariness and pain melting away.

The world around us transformed, the darkness giving way to vibrant colors and lush foliage. We found ourselves in the heart of Selene's enchanted gardens, a sanctuary teeming with life and serenity. Flowers of every hue bloomed in radiant splendor, their fragrances filling the air. The trickling water soothed my senses, a gentle reminder of the healing power surrounding us.

Selene's voice was like a gentle breeze. "Rest, dear child. You are safe now."

I sank down onto the soft grass, the weight of my exhaustion lifting as her energy enveloped me. Her presence was soothing, a balm for my weary soul. It was as if she understood the burdens I carried, the battles I had fought, and she offered respite from the storm.

My eyes closed, and I allowed myself to be embraced by her healing energy. It flowed through me, mending my physical wounds and the deep-seated exhaustion in my spirit. It was a feeling of renewal, of being reborn amidst the chaos.

When I opened my eyes again, I found her kneeling before me, her silver eyes filled with compassion. "You have faced great trials, Avery," she said, her voice a gentle melody. "But know that you are not alone in this fight. I am with you, and I shall guide you. Most importantly, I am so proud of you. Alara sends her regards."

Tears welled in my eyes as I reached out, my trembling hand touching hers. "Thank you, Goddess," I whispered, my voice filled with gratitude. "I am honored by your presence; your help humbles me."

She smiled, and the radiance warmed my heart. "Rise, Avery. The battle is not yet over, but you are strong. The darkness shall not prevail if you have the light within you."

Pushing myself up from the grass, my limbs responded in kind, and I felt renewed. The warmth of Selene's energy lingered within me, taking up space in my soul. Roman, Gabriel, and Nik gathered around as I stood, their eyes filled with concern and relief.

"Is she alright? Is she healed?" Roman asked, his voice laced with worry. "Will she be able to continue?"

Selene turned her gaze toward me, her silver eyes shimmering with wisdom. "Yes, she is healed. She knows what she has yet to do."

Gabe placed a reassuring hand on my shoulder, his eyes meeting mine. "Thank you, Goddess."

Nik smiled. "We are eternally grateful. But if I may... we need to know how to defeat Belial, how to put an end to this darkness once and for all."

Selene's expression grew solemn as she considered their words. "He is a formidable adversary, a master of deception and manipulation. But he has a weakness, a chink in his armor. In his desire for power, he has become consumed by it. His own hubris blind him."

If we can find where his power ends and his weakness begins, we stood a chance. The cogs in my mind began turning. Osric and I completed the circle of balance. His need for control consumed Belial. If I could figure out how to use my bond with my mates, along with the darkness in Osric, we'd be able to fragment Belial's resolve, weakening him. Then we can destroy him.

"What is his weakness? How do we exploit it?" Nik ran his hand through his hair.

She peered at me with a smile. "You have the right idea, Avery, but that will only banish him back to his realm. To truly defeat him is another matter. He draws his strength from the corruption he spreads. To weaken him, you must sever his connection to the dark energies that fuel his power. Seek out the Celestial Crystals, fragments of divine energy scattered across the realms; your ancestors placed them there, Avery. You have a natural affinity towards finding them. When brought together, they have the power to banish darkness and restore harmony. Once you have them, they will find their counterpart and reunite with them. Once they are whole, he will be destroyed as light and dark restore themselves. There is a stone that would be of particular interest to your Lycan mate. Another bearer resides within your pack. That is all I can tell you."

Roman's brows furrowed in thought. "But where do we find these Celestial Crystals? How do we even begin?"

"The path will not be easy, but it is within your grasp. Seek the Oracle of Elysia, a wise witch who holds the knowledge you seek. She resides in the Celestial Citadel, a place hidden beyond the mortal realm. She will guide you and provide the answers you need. You may even see those you have parted with."

My heart raced. Finally. Answers. It had only taken almost dying to get them. *But why now? Why are you telling us this now? Because, child. I cannot watch my children suffer any longer. I will receive any punishment for my insolence with grace.*

I looked at my mates. "We'll do it."

Gabriel squeezed my hand as he smiled. This may add days or weeks onto our goal, but if it would protect the future, it's what we'd do.

"But why are you helping us?" I turned back towards the Goddess, giving her a moment to explain herself further.

"I should not be, I confess, but I can see the heart of Osric is dark. It has no shred of light left. Once you defeat Belial, he will do whatever he can to take control of the realm. I cannot let that happen... this is my safeguard. Nik will become his replacement in your dance with light and dark. But only if you gather the Crystal. With them... you can defeat the darkness. You already have one fragment inside of you—the Spirit Stone. I was lucky enough to have it gifted to me by your ancestors. The rest have been hidden from even me. A way to ensure I stay neutral. Given the time constraints, I could not wait any longer to tell you. Please, you must hurry. I have saved your body, but you are not safe. You must go and go now. I cannot kill his demons as much as I want to. It will upset the nature of the realm too much. I can shroud you for a time, though. Please." She was urgent.

"Thank you, Selene."

Without another word, I was ejected from her garden, slammed in the middle of body parts, and oozing black blood.

21: Gabriel

The deafening roar of battle faded into the distance as Selene's energy enveloped us, transporting us back to the field overrun by demons. The sudden return to chaos caught me off guard, and confusion washed over me for a moment like a tidal wave. But I snapped back into focus after seeing Avery lying there, drifting in and out of consciousness. The landing must have jolted her.

We were hidden from sight under the protective shroud Selene had cast upon us. Thank the Goddess for that. Demons roamed, looking for any trace of us.

"We need to move quickly, grab her." Nik moved forward to scout ahead.

With Avery's weight resting on my shoulder, I guided Roman and Nik through the shadows. We weaved between hulking forms and gnashing teeth, our movements swift and deliberate. Sulfur and decay hung heavy in the air, threatening to choke us with its noxious fumes.

Finally, we reached a small cave nestled behind a majestic waterfall. It was a hidden sanctuary, shielded from prying eyes.

The rush of cascading water masked our presence, adding an extra layer of protection to our fragile refuge.

We lowered her gently onto the cave floor. Her brow furrowed with fear, even in her unconscious state. Roman and Nik collapsed next to her, sighing in relief. We were battle-weary, battered by the relentless onslaught, and betrayed by those we once tentatively considered an ally.

As the others caught their breath, I set about gathering dry wood, preparing to start a fire. The cave's entrance was concealed by dense foliage, providing us a momentary respite from the outside world. The flames danced and crackled as they grew, casting flickering shadows across the rough stone walls. It's warmth began to thaw the chill that had settled into our bones.

Nik leaned against the cave wall, running a hand through his disheveled hair. "What happened out there? Why did Osric abandon us? I don't understand. He wanted him dead just as much as the rest of us."

I sighed, my gaze fixed on the dancing flames. "I don't have all the answers, Nik, or any at all, really. I don't know any more than you do... but of all of us, you should know him best."

Roman clenched his fists in frustration. "How could he betray us like that? We were on the same side. Even if it was a temporary truce."

A wave of anger washed over me, but this wasn't the time to lash out. "We'll confront Osric in due time. But for now, let's focus on what we can control. Avery and the Crystals."

Nik nodded, his eyes reflecting a mix of exhaustion and re-solve. "You're right. We can't let Osric's betrayal distract us from our mission. Avery is counting on us."

I was lost as the task of yet another journey crushed my soul. Would this ever end? Before I could spiral into an angry rant... a spark of mischief flickered in Nik's eyes. "Hey, Gabriel," he said with a mischievous grin, "remember that time we went swimming in the pools beneath the waterfall back home? My dad told us about the gold that was supposedly down there. God, that was wild. We just dove in. Remember the one? The one that has all those boulders at the bottom."

A smile tugged at the corners of my lips. "How could I forget?" I replied, a hint of nostalgia creeping into my voice. "Those were simpler times, weren't they?"

Nik stood, brushing off his pants. Not that it did any good; he was covered in blood and muck. "Well, why don't we take a moment to reclaim a bit of that simplicity? The water is right there; we can go see if there's gold at the bottom."

Roman chuckled. A quick dip wouldn't hurt. Checking on Avery before we left, I tucked what was left of my shirt around her shoulders. It was tattered, but it was something.

"We'll be right back, my girl."

We shed our shredded clothes and waded into the calm waters at the base of the waterfall. The rushing cascade enveloped us as the chill of the water bit into our skin. For a few fleeting moments, we allowed ourselves to be lost in simple joy, splashing and laughing like the children we once were.

As we swam and played, the weight of the world momentarily lifted, replaced by a sense of camaraderie and friendship. We were not just warriors but individuals who had forged a bond through shared hardships and a common purpose.

"Hey Nik, remember that time you stole Ms. Black's apple pie from the kitchen window?" Roman laughed.

Nik grinned, his eyes crinkling with amusement. "How could I forget? She chased me down the street, waving a rolling pin and swearing like a sailor."

"Yeah, but you, Roman, you put Alpha Blackburn's shoe soles on backward, and he was walking with a funny limp all day but didn't have the guts to call anyone out on it. Do you remember that?" I said, joining in on the memories. Roman chuckled, his eyes twinkling with mischief.

"Oh, how could I forget? I thought I was being so clever, but Alpha Blackburn wasn't amused."

"Hey Nik, remember that time you stole Ms. Black's apple pie from the kitchen window?" Roman laughed suddenly.

Nik grinned, his eyes crinkling with amusement. "How could I forget? She chased me down the street, waving a rolling pin and swearing like a sailor."

"Yeah, but you, Roman, you put Beta Blackburn's shoe soles on backward, and he was walking with a funny limp all day but didn't have the guts to call anyone out on it. Do you remember that?" I said, joining in on the memories. Roman chuckled, his eyes twinkling with mischief.

"Oh, how could I forget? I thought I was being so clever, but Blackburn wasn't amused."

Those were the days. Carefree and filled with joy. How different those memories are from the ones we are creating now. We'd grown, as men, brothers, but more importantly, into our role as Avery's mates.

When we first realized we would be sharing her, I wasn't sure I'd be able to. But then I watched her come to life and realized that we were all just pieces that fit together to make a whole. The water lapped at my hands as I drew designs on its surface. As much as the memories of days gone were heart-warming, and these times were trying, I wouldn't change them. Everything we had accomplished until now was for a reason. One of those reasons slept in a cave, and the other two were safe with their grandparents.

"I'm freezing," Roman whined, "can we go back now?"

After a few minutes, we returned to the cave, damp and rejuvenated. Huddling around the fire, we warmed our wrinkled skin.

"Look how beautiful she is."

"Yeah, I just wanna bend her over my knee and leave handprints on her ass," Nik's gaze turned feral.

"Calm down there, cowboy." I chuckled, "I can see your tent from here."

Roman hollered, causing Avery to stir.

"You boys talking about me again?" she said, her voice tinged with sleep. She sat up against the wall, her hair tumbling in wild waves around her shoulders. Her eyes were heavy-lidded and drowsy, but there was a smile on her lips as she looked at us.

"Always," Nik said, getting ready to swoop her into his arms and carry her away, no doubt.

There was a moment of silence as tension built. Then she rose to her feet, stretching her arms towards the ceiling of the cave, a slip of her stomach showing. I groaned. Ever since she fixed my dick, I couldn't control the beast.

"Well, I don't know about you guys, but I'm starving. Who's up for some dinner?" She winked at me.

"Yes... but where are we going to find dinner?"

"You're all wolves, and you can't go hunt us something to cook over this amazing fire? For shame!" She cried playfully.

Roman and Nik howled in unison, and I couldn't help but chuckle at her humor. She rolled her eyes, but the smile on her lips betrayed her amusement.

"Alright, alright, let's not wake up the whole mountain," Avery said, her voice softening. "Go find us something to eat, but be careful. Who knows what else is lurking out there. The demons..." She trailed off.

We nodded in agreement. In a matter of minutes, we were ready to venture out into the night.

The air was crisp and biting as we stalked through the dense foliage, our noses quivering at the scent of potential prey. We moved in silence, each of us attuned to the night around us. Suddenly, Roman held up a hand, halting our progress. He crouched down, pointing at footprints.

"There," he whispered, pointing towards a small burrow in the earth. "A family of rabbits. Easy."

The rabbits were fast, but we were faster; Nik missed his, but Roman and I each managed to grab one before they scurried away. We made our way back to the cave, carrying our prizes with pride. They were just rabbits, but still. We caught them. With our bare hands.

Avery prepared the meal expertly, cooking the rabbits over the roaring fire. The scent of sizzling meat filled the air, and my stomach growled in anticipation. We ate in silence, our hunger sated by the flesh. It wasn't enough, but it took the edge off. We can find more tomorrow.

As the night wore on, we took turns keeping watch. The hours passed in comfortable silence, broken only by the occasional crackle of the fire or the rustle of leaves outside.

"Hey, boys... I know it's late, but I need to go rinse off..." Avery's small voice came from behind us.

"I don't know, Avery..." Roman said.

"I'll be quick, I promise." She said as she walked outside of the cave and stood, basking in the moonlight.

Slowly, she stripped off her clothes, throwing them into the water to clean as she took one backward look at us before diving off the rockface.

22: Roman

She was beautiful as the water glittered off her skin. I looked at my brothers, who nodded as they watched from the rock ledge. I dove in, relishing in the icy shock that hit my skin as I came from underneath Avery and grabbed her.

"Oh!" She yelped, turning to face me before putting her arms around my shoulders, "Hi, babe." The world around us seemed to fade away as we stared into each other's eyes, lost in our own little world.

"I love you," I whispered, feeling a lump form in my throat.

Avery's eyes widened before a smile spread across her face. "I love you too," she replied softly, leaning in closer to me.

Her lips parted as my tongue danced with hers as her fingers knotted in my hair.

"Make love to me," she whispered in my ear as I wrapped her legs around my waist.

"Always," I whispered as I held her tightly. "You're beautiful, Avery, so perfect for me in every way."

We stayed like that as the water rocked us, just holding each other. Her skin was smooth to the touch, and I glided my hands across her body with ease. Her sighs and gasps as I played with her breasts spurred me on. I flicked her nipples and drew out her pleasure. I ran my finger between her thighs and felt her slick warmth. My finger traced the outline of her lips, and then slowly, I pushed inside of her.

I felt her body shudder beneath my touch as I moved my finger in and out of her, pushing her to the brink. My tongue caressed the curves of her neck as I thrust in and out with increasing speed. She began to moan louder, her hips bucking against my hand as her pleasure built. I could feel her tremors and knew that she was close.

I continued to finger fuck her until she could no longer contain herself and came apart in my arms. Her orgasm shook through both of us, setting off a series of aftershocks that lasted for a few moments afterward. When it had finally subsided, she looked at me.

"More."

I led her towards the edge of the pool, pushing her upper body so her ass was perched nicely just above the water line and her chest rested on the rock ledge. Gently spreading her legs, I began to work my cock inside of her.

"Oh God," Avery cried out as I went deeper, her pussy clenching around me. God, she was so tight, it was impossible to try last with her.

"I want you," she whispered, "I want you to fuck me until I scream your name."

I drove my hips into her, pounding into her with everything I had. She groaned, pushing her ass against me to meet my thrusts.

It was then that she almost undid me. "Fuck me, baby, fuck me hard."

Before I came, I pulled out, turning her around so she had her legs wrapped around my core. I kissed her deeply while our bodies started moving again, slowly and rocking up and down as she found her rhythm. Her fingers eagerly clawed at my back until they latched onto my shoulders.

"Yes," she moaned, "oh God, yes, Roman, yes."

She kissed me, and I felt her pussy quiver. My cock ached as I watched her ride out her orgasm, slowly coming down from the heights of bliss she had just found.

Her hands slid down my chest until they rested on my waist. She looked up at me with those big eyes and whispered, "Keep going."

So, I did. My pace was slow and deliberate, seeking that sweet spot as she reached down and gently rubbed her clit.

I groaned as I thrust deep into her and let go, releasing inside her. Our breathing was heavy, and our bodies were covered in a light layer of sweat. Avery's head was resting on my chest, and I could still feel her heartbeat.

"Holy Hell," she giggled, "you are a machine. But that thin g... where you slowed down... I liked that. You guys are always pounding me hard, and don't get me wrong, I love it, but that was... something else."

"To be fair, it's hard to go slow when you're screaming, 'fuck me harder, Roman.' Or 'faster, Roman, faster.'" I grinned as I held her to my chest.

"Truth," she laughed. "Thank you."

"For what?"

Avery looked down at the water and cleared her throat. "For saving me today."

"That wasn't just me, babe, we all did. I guess we can thank Selene because she did most of the work."

"Yeah, I suppose, but you three lay your lives on the line for me, again and again... I feel overwhelmed with gratitude, I guess." She said, gently pushing her fingers through my hair.

"What do you think she is talking about..." she whispered, "the Celestial... stones?"

"Crystals. Celestial Crystals. Well, she said you have one inside of you, which makes sense since, you know, you absorbed it and all, so that's one down. Though... we need to find out what the others are so, I guess we have to go to the... Celestial... palace?"

"Citadel." She said, laughing.

"See? This is why we are perfect together. We remember what the other doesn't." I laughed with her.

She started shivering. "Come, let me carry you back to the fire."

"That would be nice," she sighed.

Before I even stepped foot inside the cave, she had passed out.

23: Avery

I woke with the dawn; my eyes adjusted to the dim light, and I smiled as I watched the guys getting ready for the day. A mix of emotions swirled in my gut—excitement, apprehension, determination. Today, we would begin our journey to the Celestial Citadel. To the crystals that supposedly would help us.

"Morning, baby girl."

"Morning, Nik. You're all up early."

"We had to get ready to go or we would never leave. Fucking you in the waterfall was as close to paradise as I'll ever get, and I've half the mind to keep you here and damn this whole thing."

Gabe snorted, "You'd miss the kids."

"Yeah, sure, we can get Helen and Richard to bring them here."

"Okay, okay. I love that, but... are we ready to go?" I said, trying to refocus them. The last thing we needed was more sex to distract us, although I can't say I would mind.

"The Celestial Citadel awaits," Gabe said, brushing the dirt off my butt. "Let's not keep it waiting any longer."

We trekked through dense woodlands and across rocky plains, the terrain becoming more treacherous with each passing day. Massive trees with gnarled branches loomed overhead, their shadows dancing across the forest floor. An eerie quiet had settled over the land as if the creatures were holding their breath in anticipation of our journey. I don't know when, but we had crossed from our realm some time ago into something much different.

An owl hooted softly in the distance, breaking the silence. I glanced up at the sky, but nightfall was still hours away based on when we left. So why was it so dark? Something about that call felt off, as if it were a warning rather than a greeting. I narrowed my eyes, searching the trees for any signs of movement.

"Do you sense that?" Nik asked quietly. He had also picked up on the strange energy in the air.

"We're being watched," Roman said. His hand drifted towards mine, covering it protectively.

I whispered a quick incantation, allowing my aura to spread out and analyze the area. I was learning at a rapid rate now, almost as if there were no more barriers between me and my capabilities. There were no immediate threats, but dark magic lingered here. "We need to move quickly," I said. "Belial knows we've left the earth realm... he's shifting his course."

Gabe groaned, wiping the sweat off his brow. "As if this quest wasn't difficult enough already."

"If it were easy, they wouldn't have fated us to do the job," Roman said wryly.

This new journey that Selene had put us on... it was amazing. The chance to maybe see my family again, maybe learn some new things, but quite frankly, I just wanted it to be over. I missed my family. My babies.

I shook my head, pushing those thoughts away. No use dwelling. It is what it is.

"Remember when we faced that dragon in the Shadowfen?" Nik asked suddenly. "I thought we were done for, but you came up with that crazy plan to get it to set fire to itself. Still can't believe that actually worked!"

"As I recall, you were the one who provoked the beast in the first place," Roman said.

Nik shrugged. "Minor details."

I laughed.

"We've come a long way since then. That dragon seems like child's play now compared to what we've faced." Nik adjusted his shirt, or what was left of it anyway. Too bad I wasn't in the dream realm, I could have just whipped us up some less homely-looking clothes.

"And yet we're still here," Gabe said. "Stronger than ever. Brothers in arms, the sharers of the angel."

"Sharers of the angel? Really?"

"Don't be pouty, Avery, it was quite funny. For Gabe anyway."

As night fell, we set up camp in a secluded glade. That owl hooted softly in the distance. Creepy little bugger must be following us. Or maybe it was a different one, and I'm just being paranoid.

Just as we sat by the fire, a flash of light darted through the trees, illuminating the forest for a brief moment. We jumped to our feet, bodies positioned for battle, but the creature that emerged was not a threat. A pixie fluttered into view, her delicate wings shimmering like stained glass.

"Greetings, travelers," she said in a voice like tinkling bells. A small owl sat on her shoulder. "I am Luna, guardian of this part of the forest. I come to offer you guidance on your journey."

I bowed low, motioning for the others to do the same. "Hello, Luna. Did Selene send you?"

Luna nodded. "The fate of all hangs in the balance. But do not lose hope. As long as there is light, there will always be those who stand against the darkness."

"Are we going the right way?" I asked.

"Continue until you meet an old foe, then continue some more. Do not stop until you can feel it," Luna said before promptly disappearing, leaving that damn owl behind.

Silence reigned as we returned to our seats by the fire. "What on earth does that mean?"

Gabe sighed, "I don't know. Why the fuck is everything so cryptic around here?"

"Right? I thought the same thing. Even Selene waited for the tenth hour before telling us what the hell to do. It's like she waited until we almost died to give us what we actually need to do."

"That's literally what she did, Roman. Like exactly what she did." Gabe half-chuckled.

These Gods of Old enjoyed their games. Who knows what other things they'd spring on us before we got there? Many challenges surely awaited us in the Celestial Citadel; nothing so far had been easy, so why would finding the crystals?

"Who knows anymore, but I do know I'm kind of fed up, not even going to lie," Roman continued.

Nik smacked him upside the head, "Quit your bellyaching. We do what we came to do so we can go home. Nothing more, nothing less. And once we're done, I'd live a happy life if I never saw Selene again." Darkness crossed his face.

I gasped, "Nik! You don't mean that! She has been helpful!"

"No, Avery, she really hasn't. She's the one that started all of this because instead of killing Osric and restoring balance, she tied him to a demon lord and then allowed your ex-mate to summon him."

"I guess, in a way, she actually started it," Roman said unhelpfully.

"I'm going to bed. You guys can be assholes to each other, but I need to rest. Night." I sniffled as I rolled onto the soft grass. It wasn't that I was protective over Selene. It was that I needed this to matter. I needed all these sacrifices to matter. If they were saying Selene didn't matter and that she's at fault, they're basically saying none of this matters anymore. Fuck it. Fuck it all.

I awoke as the first rays of sunlight filtered through the trees. The fire had died down to embers, my men still asleep.

I stood and stretched my arms overhead. The air felt fresh and alive, scented with pine and dirt. Somewhere in the distance, a bird trilled a cheerful song. Finally, the owl was gone. I don't know why, but that thing gave me the heebie jeebies.

"The day promises to be fair, my lady."

I turned to find Roman gazing at me, eyebrows wiggling.

"As do our fortunes," I replied with a smile.

"You seem chipper this morning."

"Should I not be? Being angsty has clearly not won me any awards."

"True." Roman sighed. "But you are allowed to feel angsty, as you so eloquently put it."

"Yeah, but I'm done now. Time to focus on other stuff, like finding the Citadel in a place we don't know and figuring out the Crystals that we don't have images of. That kind of stuff."

He managed a wry smile. "Spoken like a true Seraphina."

I stuck my tongue out at him. He chuckled, the tension easing from his face.

The others began to stir. I clapped my hands, calling them to action. "Up and at 'em! Adventure awaits!"

Gabe yawned and peered up at the sky. "Does adventure have to start so early?"

24: Nikolai

"Do you feel that?" Gabriel asked as Roman narrowed his eyes.

"Yes," I said. "We're being watched. Again." What the fuck else was new?

I slowed my pace, scanning the dense foliage for any signs of movement. There. A flicker of shadow shifted behind an oak tree, disappearing as quickly as it came.

My blood ran cold. "We have company."

Before I could react, a dozen or so demons emerged from the underbrush, their gaping mouths revealing rows of teeth, their red eyes glowed as they advanced on us.

"Ambush!" Gabriel shouted, shifting into his wolf. Roman launched himself forward, striking one of the demons in the chest. It squealed in pain, black blood oozing from the wound.

The demons charged at us, gnashing their sharp teeth. I shifted without hesitation, stepping forward to shield Avery.

"Get behind me," I ordered. Sure, she was a Seraphina, but she was my mate, too.

The battle was swift and bloody. Roman, Gabriel, and I cut down the demons in a flurry of slashes and parries. Their corpses littered the forest floor—an easy win.

Breathing hard, I turned to Avery. "Are you hurt?"

She shook her head. "I'm fine. Thank you for protecting me."

I clasped her hand and pressed a kiss to her knuckles. "Always."

"But you know, I can protect myself. I can even protect you." She pulled her hand away from mine.

"I know, baby girl. I can't help that my instinct is to put myself in the line of danger first. Next time, you can take the lead. Is that better?" I knew full well that wasn't going to happen.

She beamed, "Yes, actually, that is better." She grabbed my hand, and we went on walking.

The demon attack reminded me of our very first challenge together when we were young and inexperienced. We were tasked with dispatching some demons that had slipped through from the other side. We were to kill them and then allow our witch to close the portal. Minor battle, but it was our first, and boy, did we almost fuck that up.

"Remember our first tangle with lesser demons in the Silverwood?" I asked Roman and Gabriel. They chuckled, sharing a look.

"We were but naive youths," Roman said. "You rushed in headfirst as always, Nik, nearly getting yourself killed."

"And you followed right behind me," I retorted, elbowing him playfully. "If I recall, you were the one who nearly lost an ear that day."

"My thanks to Gabriel for his inability to control himself," Roman said, clapping him on the back. "Else, I'd be half the man I am today. Literally. I'd be earless if you weren't such an intolerable smuck."

"I mean, an ear isn't half of you, but..." Gabriel grinned. "What are brothers for?"

"The demons made a grave mistake in ambushing us," I said confidently. "They won't get another chance. Now we know that what Avery said is true, not that I ever doubted you, babe, but Belial has definitely shifted his path."

We had gone far today, and Avery was tired. Noticing this, Gabe offered to set up camp and start a fire while Roman went to find some food. I wanted to snuggle my baby girl, so I hung back until they were back. As the fire crackled, she rested in my arms, her head on my chest. I wrapped my arms around her, holding her close. In the dancing light of the flames, I could see the weariness etched into her delicate features.

"Are you okay, love?" I asked softly, brushing a strand of hair from her face.

She nodded, a small smile gracing her lips. "Just tired. It's been a long day."

I pressed a kiss to her forehead. "Get some rest, my sweet. I'll keep watch."

Avery snuggled deeper into my embrace, her breathing steady and calm. I held her close, my eyes scanning the darkness beyond the reach of the firelight. The forest was silent but for the chirping of crickets and the occasional chittering of the squirrels. Before I was even aware of my unconsciousness, I had fallen into a slumber alongside my love.

The following day, we set off once more into the forest. An unnatural chill hung in the air, raising the hairs on the back of my neck. Something felt weird.

My instincts proved correct when we came upon a small hut in a clearing, smoke curling from its chimney. An old man sat outside, puffing on a long wooden pipe. He was old and wrinkly, basically a bag of bones. A long black cloak hung off of his back. The hood pushed roughly around his neck.

"You seek the Celestial Crystals," he said, his voice a raspy croak.

I tensed. How did he know?

The hermit waved a wrinkled hand. "Peace, warrior. I mean, you no harm. I have guarded this wood for centuries, and little escapes my notice." His gaze turned inward, clouding with sorrow. "The crystal's power is not meant for mortal hands. Should it fall into the wrong ones, eternal darkness will reign. They are not what you think they are."

"We must have them," I said. The hermit's eyes narrowed as he peered into my soul.

"The path ahead is not for the faint of heart," he intoned. "The Citadel is both protected and sought after by forces beyond your imagination. Turn back now or face almost certain death."

I stood tall, meeting his piercing stare with my own. "That is our concern."

He sighed slowly. "So be it. But heed my warning, warrior, and steal your heart for what's to come. The trials ahead will test the bounds of your courage and whether you have the strength to do what must be done."

His cryptic words meant little to me. At this point, all these weird fucks can take their riddles and shove them. I'm done investing energy into trying to figure out what they mean and how it applies to us. It probably doesn't. He's probably forgotten to take his medication and needs a sleep. Or a dirt nap; he looked pretty shaky.

We moved on, leaving him to his ramblings. After a few hours of hiking, we came upon a clearing filled with the most dazzling wildflowers I had ever seen. Vibrant colors blanketed the meadow as far as the eye could see, dotted with butterflies drifting on the breeze.

Avery squeezed my hand, her eyes shining with wonder. "It's beautiful."

I smiled, wrapping an arm around her waist and pulling her close. "Yes, it is."

"We should stop here for lunch," Roman suggested, already unpacking the leftovers from yesterday's hunt. Gabriel was busy trying to tickle Avery while she ran through the flowers.

We sat in the fragrant field, basking in the warm sun as we ate. A profound stillness settled over the clearing as if time itself had stopped. I closed my eyes, letting the tension ease from my body. This was nice. The knots in my shoulders were slowly releasing as Avery came over and began to work them out using her fingers in all the right places. My girl always knew when I needed a hand. Except sometimes when I *need a hand*. Like now.

I pulled her around and plopped her in my lap, pushing my boner into her as she giggled.

"We should really get-"

The ground began to shake violently beneath us. A massive fissure split the earth, unleashing a noxious green mist. An enormous worm-like creature emerged, snarling and snapping its razor-sharp teeth.

"What in the blazes is that thing?!" Roman cried. The beast let out another bone-chilling shriek, rearing back to strike. "Where the hell are we that there are so many weird creatures?!"

My heart pounded as I got ready to shift. The hermit's warning echoed in my mind. Maybe he wasn't a loon after all. "It's obviously not a realm on earth, dipshit; now get ready to run, or fight, or both."

I gripped Avery's hand tightly, refusing to let go.

"Stay behind us," I ordered.

"Not this time, babe." She rubbed her palms as they began to glow. Damn, she was beautiful.

Roman and Gabriel flanked me, their beasts snarling and snapping angrily. The worm screamed in rage, writhing away from their strong bites. Acidic venom spewed from its gnashing jaws, sizzling against our skin, but we refused to yield.

"Aim for its eyes!" I shouted.

"Which one? The thing has like a hundred!"

Oh my God, really, Roman? "Any of them, obviously." If we could blind the creature, it would lose its advantage. Gabriel ducked beneath its thrashing body, plunging his claws deep into one of its eyes. The monster wailed, convulsing in agony.

Roman darted forward while it was distracted, piercing another one. Slowly but surely, we picked at it until it was a bloody mess. The ground oozed with acid, but as it burned us, we just healed. Blinded and enraged, the beast thrashed wildly. Its tail whipped around, knocking Roman off his feet. He tumbled across the ground, dazed from the blow.

I raced to intercept the creature before it could crush him. "Over here, you sweaty meat stick!" I yelled, slamming my body against it. It reared up, following the sound of my voice. I rolled away just as it struck the spot where I had been standing, its teeth snapping shut on empty air.

The ground shook again as more fissures formed, unleashing a swarm of lesser creatures. My heart sank at the sight - we were being overrun.

"Nik, look out!" Avery cried. I whipped around, raising my arm just in time to deflect a glob of venom from one of the creatures. It splattered across my arm, sizzling angrily.

We were surrounded, outnumbered, and fighting for our lives. Again. A lesser beast lunged at Avery, knocking her to the ground. Rage filled me as I ripped it in two, pulling her back to her feet. "Are you hurt?" I asked, scanning her for injuries.

She shook her head. "I'm fine. Look out!" She shot behind me with a blast, exploding the creature into pieces. Chunks of flesh rained around us.

I spun around just as another tail whipped towards us. Throwing myself over Avery, it bounced into my back. It let out an angry hiss, advancing with jaws agape. Turning to face it, I began to advance.

Before it could strike again, an arrow whistled through the air, piercing its open mouth. It gurgled and collapsed, revealing the hermit standing behind it, bow in hand. He flashed us a toothy grin, already lining up another shot.

A loud roar shook the cavern, drawing my attention. The blinded meat sack was thrashing wildly, snapping at anything that moved. It was only a matter of time before it started trampling its own allay.

I gripped Avery and Gabriel's hands, pulling them back just as the Earth groaned, splitting apart. "Fall back! We need to regroup."

Roman stumbled over to join us, clutching a bleeding arm. I tore a strip of cloth from my shirt, hastily bandaging the wound. It would heal, but it looked pretty bad.

The ground rumbled ominously. More fissures were spreading, fracturing the ground beneath our feet. It was now or never.

"Run!" I screamed as I grabbed Avery, and I shifted, carrying her on my back until we had left the beast writhing and struggling against the ground it had fractured.

25: Avery

"That was close," Gabe said, side-eyeing me.

"It was, but we made it. The ground probably swallowed it or something. Haven't seen it come after us or heard it screech." I shrugged, not letting on that this place terrified me. The magic pulsated here. My lungs expanded with it and exhaled as it wrote itself into my body. We left our own realm long ago, and that thought filled me with apprehension. Leaving meant I also left my babies behind. What if we die here?

My footsteps crunch on fallen leaves and twigs as we weave between gnarled tree trunks older than memory. Shafts of golden sunlight filter through rustling branches above, pouring life into me.

Roman brushed a spider's web aside with a hand. "How much farther, Avery?" His voice is tense, impatient. "I really just want to get there, get the crystals, and bounce. This place is freaky. I miss home."

"Not far," I said, hoping I sound more confident than I feel. I really had no idea, it's not like I had a map or anything. The Celestial Crystals could be leagues away for all I know.

Her voice echoed in my mind once more, a whisper of guidance amidst the rustling leaves: *The light will guide your path...Have faith, Seraphina*.

I square my shoulders and press onward into the dense wood. Behind me, Nik stumbled on an exposed root but caught himself before he fell. Gabriel reached out a steadying hand, his eyes full of concern.

"There's something strange about these woods," Nik said. His hand grips his belt, knuckles white with tension. "I sense a presence here, like the forest is watching us, or something, it's weird."

"Maybe Luna?" I said, hopeful that she is looking over our journey, keeping us safe from the unknown.

"Probably not, I think her territory ended where the hermits began. This one seems to be unguided," Gabe scratched his chin, deep in thought.

A rustle in the undergrowth made us freeze in our tracks. Gabriel and Nik exchanged a guarded glance, a wealth of meaning conveyed in that single look. They could smell something.

I stopped walking and watched intently. The rustling grew louder, and more persistent, and my heartbeat quickened. Suddenly, a low growl reverberated through the forest, and I realized that the forest wasn't the only thing watching us. We stand still. Waiting.

Out of the undergrowth emerges a massive beast, its fur matted and its eyes glowing with an otherworldly light. I recognize the creature immediately.

Osric. An old foe. Just as Luna had said, we were on the right track.

My heart restricted at the sight of him, a surge of anger lighting me on fire. I strode forward, hands clenched into fists, and confronted the betrayer who abandoned us to our fate.

"You," I spat out. "How dare you show your face here after what you did."

Osric held up his hands in a placating gesture, but I saw the truth in his eyes. Could it be? Remorse and regret warred with indignance, a hint of resentment at my accusation. "I understand your anger," he said, voice rough. "But there are things you do not know, reasons I could not intervene."

"Reasons?" I scoffed, disgust twisting my lips. "What reasons could possibly justify abandoning us when we all agreed on the goal?"

"There is much you do not know, young Seraphina," he said, not without a hint of distaste. "Our fates have been entwined since the beginning of days. I could not interfere without disrupting the weave of destiny and ensuring our defeat."

I stared at him, torn between rage and a flicker of pity for this fallen God. Once, he had been a champion, a beacon of hope in a world falling into darkness. Now, only a shadow remains, a wisp of his former glory.

"The prophecy demanded a sacrifice," Osric continued, his gaze grew distant. "And honestly, I was willing to let you take the fall. But then I had an... issue with my rogues. Selene turned them all to ash after we fled, so basically, I need you again. She then tied our fates together. Yours, mine, and Belials. To ensure we see this through."

Beneath the betrayal lay a deeper purpose, a destiny woven into the fabric of time itself. The Goddess chose this path, and we must walk it. The truth still stung. She was willing to let me die.

Still, resentment lingered. "You should have told us," I said. "We deserved to know the truth."

"You will know what I allow you to know. No more, no less. It doesn't even matter anymore. Selene has forced my hand. I must submit to her, or I will lose my soul. This time, it wouldn't be banishment; I would be obliterated."

I swallowed hard against the lump in my throat, blinking back angry tears. If my fate was tied to his and Belials... and we are trying to destroy Belial... that means....

Osric's gaze softened as if understanding the turmoil in my heart. "You have grown into a formidable leader, Avery, and your mates are loyal to a fault. But there are forces at work here beyond any of you." His voice dropped, threaded with pity. "If you want a future for your children... you will complete the task she gave you. Then you will be released from this curse she has placed on all of us."

The anger bled from my pores, leaving behind quiet acceptance. Osric is right. We had no choice. Clearly.

I met Osric's gaze, and a flicker of understanding passed between us. We have walked different paths, he and I, but we faced similar trials. There is truth to be found even in deception and meaning in the sacrifices we will come to make.

"The prophecy will be fulfilled," I said softly. "As the Goddess wills it, so shall it be."

A ghost of a smile brushed Osric's lips, deepening the lines that creased his weathered face. "And so, we shall prevail."

"Woah, woah, woah, wait a damn minute," Nik said explosively, "you mean to tell me that because you betrayed us, Selene tied Avery to you? What the actual hell?"

Osric sighed, "Young Lycan, you grate on my nerves. Belial was never supposed to be unleashed, but Sion exploited a loophole. He, too, seeks the crystals for his own gain. Belial was always a stepping stone for him. Sorcerers can never be trusted."

"What is the end game here?" Roman demanded.

"I don't know. I am not privy to everything, nor do I want to be. I am tired, wolf. I am tired of holding the hatred in my heart, hatred that has been so engrained I cannot be rid of it. All I know is that if I want a resting place in Selene's Garden, or God grant it, the Citadel, I will follow through with this task. The rest is not up to me. Nor will it be up to you." He said, running his fingers through his hair.

I watched their expressions shift from wariness to anger. Gabriel's eyes met mine, a silent question in their depths. I give a slight nod, and tension released from his shoulders. Roman folded his arms, leaning against a tree with a scowl, though he offered no protest. Only Nik remained unreadable, his face a mask of indifference belied by the sharpness of his gaze.

They understood, as I have, that we cannot afford division. Not now, when the fate of our world hung in the balance. Whatever misgivings they harbored must be set aside for the greater good. For now.

Osric fell into step beside me as we resumed our journey. The forest embraced us once more; a sea of green stretched endlessly before us. Somewhere in the distance, the crystals called out, their light a beacon to guide our path. The steady hum of magic ebbed and flowed between us—a strange ragtag group of various species, all bound by the same fate.

Gabriel and Roman walked ahead, their quiet voices carried over their shoulders. Nik brought up the rear. An uneasy peace settled over the group as we went in silence.

The Goddess' presence surrounded me, a mantle of comfort against the unknown road ahead. *Have faith*, her voice whispered. And so, I shall. Victory will be ours should we stand united against the darkness.

The forest whispered secrets not yet revealed, trials to come, and sacrifices to be made. But we will face them together, bonded by love and guided by destiny. The light of the crystals will shine through, lighting our way to a new dawn.

I glanced at Osric, wondering what his end game was. He has always been an enigma, his allegiances as fickle as the wind. And yet I sense a change in him now, a purpose that echoed my own. Perhaps we are not so different, bound as we are by the threads of fate.

Roman and Gabriel came to a stop ahead. I quickened my pace, a flicker of unease stirring. "What is it?"

Roman nodded at the ground. A series of markings were etched into the soil, unfamiliar symbols and runes glowing with power. The magic they contained thrums in time with my heartbeat as though in recognition.

"A ward," Osric said, studying the markings. "Placed here to guard something...or keep something in."

Dread pooled in my stomach. "The Oracle, perhaps? Are we close?" The name whispers through the trees, carried on a breath of wind.

"Perhaps. We shall encounter many more along the way. The closer we get to the Citadel."

Gabriel stepped forward, his hand reaching out to touch the glowing runes. His fingers brushed against the magic, sending sparks flying in all directions. With a start, he pulled his hand back, a surprised look on his face.

"Gabriel, what happened?" I asked, concern lacing my voice.

"I... I saw something," he said, his eyes haunted. "A vision."

"What did you see?" Osric said, his voice low.

Gabriel took a shaky breath. His eyes remained unfocused. "It was... a woman. She was chained in a dark room, her eyes flashing with anger. There were guards around her, and... I don't know. It was just a flash."

"Could that be the Oracle?" My heart skipped a beat.

"It's possible," Roman said, his expression grim. "We need to keep moving. Every moment we waste here is one more that we don't have the crystals."

26: Gabriel

The thick canopy of branches overhead obscured the sky, shrouding the forest in shadows as a fog rolled in. An uneasy chill crept down my spine as we trekked deeper into the woods, my werewolf senses on high alert. The path slowly wound upwards as the air thinned, my lungs working hard as they expanded and contracted.

Up ahead, Avery navigated the curving path with quiet confidence, her footsteps sure and steady. But beneath the facade of composure, I could sense the tension radiating from her in waves. The weight of our quest bore heavily on her shoulders--on all our shoulders--but she wore the brunt.

I quickened my pace to walk beside her, lowering my voice. "How are you holding up?"

Avery glanced at me, her eyes clouded with doubt and determination in equal measure. "As well as can be expected." Her lips curved into a smile, but it didn't quite reach her eyes. "I miss Aurora and Onyx, to be quite honest. I don't even want to imagine that once this is over, they will exist, and I..."

She left the thought unfinished, but the unspoken fears lingered between us.

I clasped her shoulder, hoping to provide some measure of comfort. "We'll get there. You're not in this alone, remember? We're a team. A pack. You're the love of my life; where you go, I will follow."

The tension eased from Avery's posture; this time, her smile held hints of warmth. "I don't know what I'd do without you all."

The sounds of laughter and friendly banter drifted from behind us as Roman and Nik walked with Osric, who had quickly warmed from his previously cold personality. It was peculiar to watch, and I didn't fully trust him. I didn't understand why they did.

"Do you want to stop for a while? I think I saw a small brook a bit backward... we can go there and rest?" She looked tired. Not the young woman she was when we first met. Older, somehow... wiser.

"Let's keep moving. The Celestial Citadel awaits. The faster we get there, the less chance of meeting some gross worm thing or something equally as disgusting."

Gripping her hand, I strode forward to take the lead. "Then we have a date with destiny to fulfill."

The terrain grew increasingly treacherous as we climbed higher into the mountains. Massive boulders and jagged rocks littered the narrow path, threatening to twist an unsuspecting ankle with every step. My senses remained on high alert, scanning the area for signs of danger while also guiding everyone over the hazardous path.

Avery navigated the obstacles with ease, her confidence blossoming as she went over boulders and under fallen logs. Roman and Nik followed close behind, their agility serving them well on the uneven ground.

I placed a steadying hand on Avery's shoulder as she stumbled, her focus broken as she looked into the sky, catching her before she could tumble to the unforgiving rocks below. "Careful. We're not out of the woods yet."

She shot me a grateful smile, brushing a loose strand of hair from her eyes. "I don't know how you do this so easily. It's like you were made for this."

"Comes with the territory. I am a wolf. Besides, you're doing just fine. Stick close. We'll get to the top in one piece. Refocus and balance yourself. You are doing so well, my little mountain goat."

A loud screech echoed through the mountains, followed by a flurry of dark wings in the distance. Corrupted creatures were amassing, drawn like moths to a flame by the power radiating from Avery. They looked like dragons, yet somehow twisted and grotesque. She hadn't stopped glowing since the worm attack. It was as if she was permanently 'on.' Just our luck, they spotted us. First demons, then a damn worm, and now we have some corrupted dragon things. On a cliff face. High... high above the ground. Looking down, I swallowed. This was going to be rough.

Gripping her hand tightly, I picked up the pace and narrowed my focus to the path ahead. Her hand was hot in mine, her energy pulsing through my veins. The deafening roar of screeches grew louder as the creatures drew closer. We were outnumbered, but we were not going down with a fight.

Roman and Nik took the lead, their movements fluid and coordinated as they engaged the creatures head-on. I could hear the sickening crunch of bones as Roman shifted into his wolf form, snapping jaws tearing through flesh and bone. Nik's claws glinted in the sunlight as he slashed through the shadowy forms, his movements almost too fast for the eye to follow.

Avery let out a battle cry as she fell back, letting her power flow outwards in a wave of golden light. The creatures recoiled, screeching in pain as the light seared against their darkness. I could see the strain on her face as she fought to maintain the connection, her breathing ragged with the effort. Her light began to dim, and I knew I had to step in. We couldn't afford her to faint like last time.

I moved in closer, taking up a defensive stance by her side. "You're doing great, Avery. Keep it up," I said, trying to encourage her. In truth, I was in awe of her power, and my admiration only grew as I watched her fight. Placing a hand on her shoulder like I'd seen Nik do dozens of times, I willed energy to pass from me to her. She began to glow brightly again, and a sense of satisfaction fell over me. Take that, Nik, you aren't the only special one!

The creatures threw themselves at us relentlessly, their dark forms swirling around us like a deadly whirlwind. The smell of blood and the sound of battle filled the air, drowning out the rush of the wind and the roar of the mountains.

I gritted my teeth and fought with all my might; my senses honed to a razor-sharp edge. I could feel the impact of blows against my body, but the pain was distant and remote as if it belonged to someone else.

Another ear-piercing screech rang out, and a shadowy figure emerged on the cliff edge above, snarling down at us with glowing red eyes. More followed, their gnarled wings stirring the air as they swooped towards us.

Leaping forward as one, we intercepted the second wave of attackers, sending them tumbling back with snarls and snaps of our jaws. The creatures shrieked in fury, regrouping for another assault, but we would be ready.

In the lull between attacks, I noticed Avery and Roman exchanging unspoken words, their gazes meeting for a brief moment. Her eyes fell to the open wound on his shoulder. She held out her hand, and the deep wound that tore his shoulder healed rapidly. This was her element—this place. As dangerous as it was, she was... ethereal here.

The creatures swooped down again, shrill cries rending the air, but together, we stood firm against the coming shadows.

A loud horn sounded, and then the battle ended as suddenly as it began. Silence descended upon the forest, the creatures retreating into the shadows from whence they came.

We shifted back to human form, hurrying the last bit of the treacherous path until we found a flat terrain looming ahead of us. In the distance, a large wall reached into the sky.

Stopping to rest, we built a fire and tried to scrounge for something edible. Thankfully, Osric knew this place and could sort out what local fauna was edible and what would kill us. We gathered around a small fire in the moonlit clearing. The flames crackled, casting a warm glow over weary faces. But despite the exhaustion etched into our features, a sense of peace prevailed.

Avery leaned into Roman, his arm encircling her shoulders as if by instinct. Her head rested against his chest, her hair spilling over sun-kissed skin. They did not speak, but in their silence, I felt their connection, a love that needed no words to be understood. She glanced at Nik, then at me, ensuring we weren't injured and in need of attention, before she looked at Osric, hanging in the back, quietly observing our interactions.

"We're close," Avery said softly, gaze meeting mine across the flames. "I can feel it. The Oracle is near."

The fire crackled loudly, sending ash flying, shadows dancing at the edge of light. But in that moment, I glimpsed something more - a fragment of our destiny waiting to be claimed. The path unfolded before me, ethereal and gleaming, leading us to a future of peace not stained by darkness.

I shook off the vision, meeting Avery's expectant gaze. "Then onward we will go. I am so proud of you, Avery. You've really come a long way." Her smile lit my world as she snuggled into Roman's arms. I got up to go for a walk, knowing she was safe.

Alone at last, as moonlight filtered through burnt, gnarled branches overhead, I stilled my mind. A rustle in the underbrush caught my ear, and I tensed - but it was Avery, coming up behind me and wrapping her arms around my stomach. She paused at my side, gazing up at the stars twinkling in the sky, marveling as they danced.

"The night is restless," she said. "Full of threat and whispering shadows. But we have walked this path together before, you and me. Through lifetimes and heartaches and triumphs, we have always found our way. I can sense that we have lived lifetimes before, the four of us."

Her words healed my soul. I wasn't sure if she was saying that to calm my heart, but it worked. Our fates were as interwoven as my love for her.

"The shadows hold no sway over us," I said, meeting her eyes. Determination burned there, bright as the stars above. "We will succeed. Osric mentioned finishing this and the tether being broken. Even if it doesn't, Avery, I want you to know that I won't let you go. I'm yours as you are mine... to the end."

She smiled, slipping her hand into mine and squeezing tight. "To the end," she vowed.

27: Avery

"The air feels charged with energy," Gabriel said softly from behind me. His keen eyes scan the shadows between the trees, watchful as always. We had made it past the plain and entered a dense forest. It was strange how the terrain would change and shift so quickly. As if whoever created this land wanted all the types, all at once, and just scattered them haphazardly. Much like a petulant child.

I nodded, sensing the thrum of ancient power held in the earth and stones. "We're close."

Nik stepped up beside me; his presence steadied my nerves. "This is it, baby girl."

Roman cleared his throat; impatience etched into his handsome features. "Well then, let's not waste any more time. Belial blah blah and all that, let's just go. I'm hungry." He flailed his hands and stalked into the forest.

Gabriel sighed, shaking his head as he followed. "Must he always charge in so recklessly?"

Laughter bubbled in my chest; it had been a good while since we'd had much to joke about. I squared my shoulders and marched into the trees, magic, and mystery that guided my footsteps. The Celestial Citadel held untold secrets, and it's up to us to uncover them.

"This is quite different to the other forest," Gabriel murmured. "I sense ancient magic at work here."

"The hermit did say the forest would test our faith," I reminded him, keeping my voice low. The woods feel hallowed, as if we've entered a sacred space.

Roman snorted, impatience etched into his features. "More riddles and tricks. I grow tired of these games." He stalked forward, "I am tired of creatures, big black birds, and freaking worms. I want to go home." He sounded like an impetuous child. Whining and stomping his feet, but deep down, I felt the same. Those worms were gross.

"I don't think it's much further," Nik states, grabbing my hand.

Silence fell over the group as we ventured further. This place holds the key. The enter culmination of why we came here lay behind those walls. The Oracle awaits. What was she like? Would she help? She has to... right?

The trees began to thin ahead, sunlight spilling into a hidden glen. But there, in a clearing filled with wildflowers, stood a crumbling stone archway. Strange symbols were etched along its surface, glowing with power.

My heart leaped in my chest. We've found it at last—the entrance to the Citadel. Our journey has led us here to the secrets this place holds. Finally. I met my mates' gazes, determination etched into their features, and stepped through the arch into a world of mystery.

A small yelp from behind stopped us in our tracks.

"I... can't get through..." Osric said as he tried to walk through the arch, but a barrier pushed him out.

"Oh, maybe the angels have decided you are not worthy of being in their presence," Nik said with a heavy dose of snark.

"Well, that's just great. Now what?" Osric demanded.

"Now you wait here like a good pup," Roman laughed. "It's not like the Oracle was meant for you anyway. Peace out, dude."

The archway shimmered behind us as we emerged into a massive courtyard lined with columns of marble and alabaster. Strange symbols glowed along the ground, pulsing with magic and power. At the far end of the square stood a towering set of doors, imposing but mysterious, as if daring us to approach.

An uneasy feeling settled in the pit of my stomach. It's too quiet here, too still. As if the entire citadel is holding its breath, waiting to unleash its challenges upon us. Why was it so empty?

"I don't like this," Gabriel murmurs, one hand on his hip. He scanned the courtyard, searching for any signs of danger. "It's too easy."

"A trap?" Roman suggests.

I studied the courtyard, watching and listening for any signs of trouble. My heart pounded but a sliver of peace washed over me. This felt like... home. A home away from home.

"Let's go," I said, "we've got an Oracle to find."

Step by step, we crossed the courtyard toward the towering doors. The strange symbols glowed brighter with each stride; magic thrummed through the air. We were tested the moment we walked through the archway. Osric did not pass. Perhaps we won't pass this either.

The doors loomed before us, ancient wood and metal that have stood for countless centuries. With a deep breath, I reached out and grasped the handles, heaving with all my might. The doors groaned open, and a blast of magic made me tingle as we stepped inside, one by one, nervously trying our hands first before we pushed through in a hurry.

The chamber stretched endlessly before us, shrouded in fog. The strange symbols glowed with ferocity along the walls. Pillars of black stone stood at equal intervals; shadows flickered across their surface. Ancient depictions of angels and demons, wolves howling at the moon, and faeries dancing under the sun were carved intricately along the stone.

My heart pounded as we stepped further inside. The doors groaned shut behind us with an echoing boom, sealing us in. I glanced over my shoulder at the sealed exit, panic threatening to rise in my chest. We are trapped.

No. I took a steadying breath and lifted my chin. We have come this far through trials and tribulations. This is but another test. We just have to figure out what the hell it is.

"The pillars," Gabriel murmured, studying their pattern. His analytical mind is already working to solve the riddle at hand. "There is magic in the sequence."

Nik nodded, brow furrowed in concentration. "It is a puzzle we must solve to progress deeper into the citadel."

We studied the pillars, searching for clues in their shapes and symbols. Each stood easily twice the height of a man, ancient stone weathered by time but still radiating power. There were twelve in all, arranged in a circle with strange runes and grooves along their surfaces.

"The runes correspond to the months of the year," Gabriel said slowly. "But the sequence is jumbled."

"Like the seasons, twisted and tangled to hide the solution," Nik mused. "We must figure out the right order to align them properly."

"Look, there are grooves along the floor," Roman pointed out, tracing a pattern with his boot. "They match the shape of the pillars. We have to slide them into the correct positions."

The pieces clicked into place within my mind. "The runes on each pillar represent a month. We must order them chronologically to reflect the progression of the year. The angels and other beings must represent the eras as they've gone by. Starting with angels and demons, faeries, then progressing through to the era of the wolf."

"Brilliant," Gabriel breathed. Together, we grasped the pillars and began to move them. Stone grated against stone, dust, and grit scattering beneath our feet. Slowly but surely, the runes aligned into their proper sequence.

A tremor shook the chamber as the final pillar slid into place. The runes began to glow with azure light, brighter and brighter, until I shielded my eyes. There was a loud groan of stone against stone and then silence.

I blinked open my eyes to find a doorway in place of the sealed exit. Beyond lay a hidden glade bathed in silvery moonlight, crystal formations glittering throughout. At the center stood a hooded figure, magic thrumming in the air around her.

My heart leaped as I took a step forward. "The Oracle."

She turned to face us, eyes luminous beneath her hood. "You have passed the trial and proven your worth. Now, you can find the truths you seek." Her voice echoed with the weight of wisdom. "Approach, children, and learn of your destiny."

We gather before the Oracle, anticipation swirling within me. What secrets will she reveal? What path lay ahead, fraught with destruction and purpose in equal measure?

I met the Oracle's gaze, searching for answers in her ancient eyes. "You have come far," she began, "faced dangers untold and sacrificed much for the good of this world. Your courage and conviction have led you to this place of knowledge and understanding."

Her words resonated deep within my soul. I stood taller, shoulders squared as she continued.

"Avery, Child of Destiny, the last of your kind," the Oracle stood stoic. "To you falls the burden of leadership, to guide your companions through the dark of night into the dawn. The runes have spoken, the threads of fate now clear - you must find the crystals and drive back the shadows that encroach upon this land. There are five, but only a triad is needed to complete the Trinity."

My breath caught in my throat. Five stones! At this rate, we were going to be sixty by the time we ever saw the kids again. I bowed before the Oracle, a lump in my throat. "Right, Selene said you would know where the crystals a re..."

She nodded, a glimmer of delight in her eyes, but she said nothing. She turns to Gabriel, Roman, and Nik in turn, imparting to each a prophecy and purpose. To Gabe, she gave the task of ensuring that we remain as one. Romans was to keep my heart intact through the darkness, and to Nik, she imparted a cryptic message about Osric and his destiny. This was amazing and all, but I still hadn't received much in the way of guidance.

"But what of the crystals?" I said as she turned to leave. "I appreciate the words of affirmation, but Selene sent us here for the crystals."

"Child, how have you not figured it out by now?" She said impatiently.

"What do you mean?" I asked, puzzled.

"There are five crystals—one for each extinct or almost extinct race. You hold the Spirit Stone. The last Seraphina..."

I scratched my head, "Yes..."

"Oh, child, you certainly are daft for one so powerful."

Nik spoke before I could, "I am technically the last Lycan, but I don't have a crystal."

"But you do. Well, you will. Osric holds yours. Just as Alara gave hers to Selene to give to Avery... Osric must hand you the Lunar Stone, and then you absorb it. Like Avery did."

"But what do these stones have to do with defeating Belial?"

"The forces of the dark have long tried to wipe the most powerful supernatural species from your realm. We ensured they could not fully extinguish them by creating five crystals forged from the ancestor's soul pieces." She took a deep breath. "Come, let's go walk. You will understand if you enter the Citadel."

"I thought we were in the Citadel?"

"Yes. You are in my chamber. The Citadel extends far beyond this. Come now." She clicked her tongue and opened the door.

28: Avery

As the massive doors swung open before us, excitement pooled in my stomach. Roman, Nik, Gabriel, and I stood on the threshold of the Celestial Citadel, our eyes wide with awe and curiosity.

"Never imagined we'd end up somewhere like here," whispered Roman.

"Nor did I; this is something else. Maybe they have a Lycan I can talk to."

Gabriel nodded; his gaze locked on the exquisite beauty that surrounded us.

The Citadel's grandeur was unmatched by anything I had ever seen. Towering walls of white marble stretched as far as the eye could see, adorned with intricate gold filigree that seemed to shimmer in the dimly lit hallways. The ceiling above us depicted a stunning celestial fresco, with stars and galaxies swirling together in a breathtaking dance. Massive stone pillars carved into elaborate statues lined the path, their lifelike features portraying long-lost heroes and legends of the old.

"Look at that," Nik murmured, pointing to a colossal stained-glass window depicting a fierce battle between angelic beings and monstrous creatures. The vibrant colors seemed to come alive in the soft glow of sunlight filtering through it, casting a kaleidoscope of hues onto the polished floor beneath our feet.

"Amazing," I breathed out, my mind raced with questions about the untold stories and secrets hidden within these walls.

"Let's not waste any more time gawking," Roman said with excitement. "We've got so much to explore and learn."

Every step felt like walking further into an ancient world, one filled with mysteries, wonders, and a sense of sacredness that left me humbled. The air itself seemed to hold the essence of the divine, filling my lungs with a purity I had never known.

"Promise me something," I suddenly realized we could get lost here. "No matter what we find here, let's remember who we are and why we came. In a place like this, it would be easy to get caught up in the beauty and forget all about our own realm."

All three chimed an agreement before feasting their eyes on the wonders around us.

The scent of the air shifted as we ventured further into the Citadel, it was a delicate fragrance that reminded me of freshly bloomed flowers after spring rain. I breathed deeply, relishing the smell as it filled my lungs and seemed to permeate every cell in my body.

"Can you smell that?"

"What is it? I can't quite place it, though it smells familiar," Roman replied, sniffing the air.

"Extraordinary," murmured Gabriel, his hand brushing against a petal-like formation on the wall, which emitted a soft glow in response. "I wonder what this flower is."

"Listen," Nik whispered, tilting his head as if trying to catch a distant sound. We all paused, straining our ears, and then I heard it too – a gentle melody.

"Is that... music? But from where?" I shifted and turned to try find the source.

Eager to discover the source of the mysterious song, we followed the sound deeper into the labyrinthine passages, our footsteps echoing softly on the smooth stone floor. As we rounded a corner, a sudden movement caught my eye, and I gasped at the sight before us.

"Look!" I cried, pointing towards a small grove of vibrant, luminescent plants. Amidst the otherworldly flora, several creatures flittered about, their bodies shimmering with iridescent scales and feathers.

"By the Gods," Nik breathed, his face awash with awe. "I've only read about these in ancient texts. They're thought to be extinct. Roman, what are they called again?"

"Rivari birds. And those... those are Essence Drakes!"

I stared at the creatures, the way their wings flittered and danced as if they have not a care in the world. The Rivari birds were small. Their bodies were no larger than a human hand, but their wings shone like delicate stained glass. They had tiny tufts for ears and four little feet that they were using to grab onto each other with. Their melodic trills filled the air as they darted to and fro.

The Essence Drakes, on the other hand, were footlong serpentine beings that weaved gracefully through the underbrush, their scales glowing softly with an inner luminescence. Despite their small, yet formidable appearance, they seemed to coexist peacefully with the smaller birds, their movements almost hypnotic as they navigated the grove.

"Can you believe it? We're witnessing living legends."

"Yes, Avery, we are privileged to be in their presence," Gabriel put his hand in mine.

"Let's approach them slowly," I suggested, desperately wanting to watch them closer. "Perhaps we can learn something from these ancient creatures."

"Yes!" Roman nodded.

As we moved closer, we sat to observe the hypnotizing creatures until they suddenly took flight and left our presence.

"Aw, man! Bummer."

Nik leaned closer to me, "Roman has always had a thing for weird creatures, so long as they're small. Mythics and Legends was his favorite class way back when. Gabe's was obviously the nerdy stuff, like knowing everything about everything."

"What was yours?"

"You don't wanna know," Roman piped up.

As we rounded a corner, we found ourselves standing before a grand chamber lit by a floating orb. Then, we saw them –

ancestral Seraphim and Dark Faeries, their forms as varied and complex as the realm in which they dwelled.

"Welcome, travelers," greeted one of the Seraphim. "I am Lysaria, and these are my kin. You have come seeking knowledge? Ahhh, the last Seraphina. Welcome, Avery."

"Indeed, we have... and yes, I am," I replied, barely able to contain my awe. There were more of me! "We hoped you might share some wisdom with us."

"Ask, and we shall provide what answers we can," said Lysaria, beckoning us forward.

"Please, tell us how the Citadel came to be," Nik asked.

"Ah," she smiled, "the Citadel is a place born from the dreams and hopes of countless beings. It is where we go for our eternal peace. Here, all that once was and might be again converged. Time holds no dominion within these walls."

"Can you explain why extinct species reside here? And not in Selene's Garden?" Roman inquired, his eyes darting towards the Essence Drakes and Rivari birds we had seen earlier.

"Within the Citadel, the forgotten and lost find refuge," one of the Dark Faeries chimed in. "Life's tapestry is a delicate balance, and sometimes, in order for new threads to be woven, others must unravel. And yet, their essence remains preserved within this sanctuary. Selene picks and chooses who enters her realm, mainly wolves, perhaps a favored Lycan or two, but never the ancients."

"Is there anything specific we should know about our own abilities?" Gabriel wondered aloud; his eyes flickered between the Seraphim and Dark Faeries with quiet intensity.

"Your desires and convictions shape your powers," Lysaria said. "But remember, the greatest power lay not in what you can control but in what you choose to let go."

"Trust in one another," urged the shadow-haired Faerie. "You are bound together not only by fate but also by choice – never forget that."

How profound, yet utterly confusing. My desire is to be with my children. So, how does that make sense? We had come seeking answers, but perhaps the true treasure lay in the questions we had yet to ask. As we thanked the Seraphim and Faerie for their time and wisdom, I was pondering what more I could learn from this place.

"Before you depart, allow us to demonstrate our unique abilities," Lysaria spread her soft, white wings wide. As I watched, a soft glow began to emanate from her fingertips, spreading like strings of golden sunlight across the floor.

"Wow," I breathed. "What is that? Can I do that?"

"A manifestation of light," she explained. "We Seraphim harness the power of light and celestial energy, channeling it into various forms. You must have used the light at some point."

"Yes, but never like that."

"It will come in time."

"May we see more?" Roman asked.

"Roman! That's rude!" Gabe admonished him as Roman stuck out his tongue like a child.

"Of course." Lysaria raised her hands, and beams of pure light streamed forth, weaving together to form intricate patterns in the air. As they danced before our eyes, the light seemed alive, pulsing with a vibrancy that left me breathless.

"Amazing," Roman murmured, his gaze fixed on the shimmering spectacle.

"Dark Faeries possess different abilities," the faerie said, stepping forward. She raised her own hands, and tendrils of darkness sprang to life, snaking around her lithe form like a living cloak.

"Darkness is not inherently evil," she continued. "It can be harnessed for protection, concealment, and even healing."

"Really?" Nik asked, his skepticism evident. "How so?"

"Allow me to demonstrate." The faerie glanced at Gabriel, who nodded hesitantly. She reached out with her dark tendrils, which gently wrapped around his arm. He sprung back in pain as a burn appeared on his skin.

"What the fuck!"

"Shhh, just watch," she replied as she reached out again, and within seconds, the burn was gone.

"Remarkable," Gabriel breathed, flexing his healed arm in wonder.

"Indeed," Lysaria agreed. "Both light and darkness hold untold potential, depending on how one chooses to wield them."

"Can you teach us to harness these powers?" I asked, unable to contain my excitement. This was it; this was my moment. Perhaps Nik can learn to control his darkness, too.

"Your abilities are unique to your own nature and lineage," the Faerie replied, her expression blank. "But we can share with you the knowledge of how to tap into your own potential. As a Seraph, you draw from the likes of Lysaria."

"Please do. We seek any guidance that will help us."

"Very well," Lysaria consented. "We shall impart upon you the secrets of the Celestial Citadel, that you may walk a path of balance between the light and dark."

As we listened intently as they spoke of opening pathways to the mind and letting go of inhibition. They spoke of the Shadow Stone and where to find it. The world beyond the Citadel suddenly felt more vibrant, full of possibilities yet unexplored.

Perhaps Selene was right in sending us here. This was exactly what I needed to heal and move forward.

29: Avery.

"Look at that," Roman whispered, pointing to a large tapestry hanging on one of the walls. It depicted a constellation of stars that seemed to move and twinkle before our eyes. "I've never seen anything like it."

"Nor I," Gabriel agreed, his voice hushed as he reached out to touch the soft fabric. He paused, a look of wonder crossing his face. "It feels... alive. Can you feel that?"

I nodded, my fingers grazing the tapestry alongside his. The texture was unlike anything I had ever encountered – warm and smooth, yet somehow also cool and rough, like the dichotomy of light and darkness woven into tangible form. It seemed to pulse beneath my fingertips as if it were breathing.

"Even the air is different here," Nik observed, inhaling deeply. "It smells rich, like spiced wine and honeyed fruit."

"Indeed," I agreed, breathing in the heady scent myself.

"Everything within these walls is infused with magic," Lysaria explained, chuckling at our marvel. "From the stones beneath your feet to the air you breathe, every element has been shaped by those who have called this place home since time immemorial."

"Such power, and to think it lay hidden here, waiting for us to unlock its secrets."

"True power is not so easily grasped, young wolf," a Seraphim with golden eyes cautioned, her voice like a soft breeze. "It requires patience, understanding, and humility – qualities you must cultivate if you are to master the forces that bind this realm together."

"Your journey has only just begun," the Dark Fareie added. "But with each step you take, you will grow stronger, wiser, more capable of wielding the gifts bestowed upon you by fate and heritage. Take care of Emma for me. I look forward to her rising. Goodbye now."

Emma? Emma is a Dark Faerie? But they're extinct... oh my Goddess. She's the third in the Trinity. I can't be sure, but I think she's the key.

As we continued to explore the Citadel, I felt that we were being guided by something greater than ourselves – a force that beckoned us deeper into the heart of this ancient, enchanted place. There was more to discover, and yet our time was running short.

"Look," Roman pointed to a mural on the far wall depicting an ancient battle between Seraphim and faeries. The figures seemed to move and shimmer, their weapons clashing in an eerily lifelike dance of war. As I stared at the painting, I felt a shiver run through me, as if the past were reaching out to touch the present, giving us a warning.

As much as I knew I had a prophecy to fulfill, I wanted to stay here... to continue exploring this realm and speaking with my ancestors.

"Let's go," I said finally, my voice filled with bitter perseverance. "The longer we stay, the more I wish we never had to leave. I can feel a pull towards the Shadow Stone."

The moment we stepped through the massive doors at the end of the room and into another area, the world shifted around us. The air grew colder, and my breath materialized before me in a frosty cloud. The landscape beyond was vastly different from anything I had ever seen. Strange plants and trees stretched towards the sky, their leaves giving off a smoky haze.

"Where are we?" Roman asked, his voice echoing in the stillness.

"It feels different, darker," Nik murmured, his eyes narrowed as he observed the peculiar flora.

"Home is where the heart is, and my heart is back through those doors," Gabriel whined. "Ugh, why are we here?"

I shivered, though whether from the cold or the eerie atmosphere, I couldn't tell. Swallowing my trepidation, I took a deep breath and squared my shoulders. "Because... I feel something pulling me out this way. I don't know how to explain it."

We ventured further into this unfamiliar realm, each step bringing new discoveries. I couldn't help but marvel at the curious creatures that scurried away as we approached: translucent insects with jagged wings and small mammals covered in scaly feathers. Though they were strange, they were fascinating, and I wanted to learn more about them.

"Look," Gabriel pointed towards a clearing up ahead. There, underneath the gnarled roots of a colossal tree, lay a creature unlike any I had ever seen. It was enormous, its body covered in scales that gleamed like polished metal. Its serpentine tail coiled protectively around it, and its fearsome head rested on the ground, eyes closed.

"Is that... an elemental dragon?" Roman whispered.

"Seems so," Nik replied, his voice hushed. "But they're supposed to be extinct."

"Maybe the Citadel brought it back," I suggested, unable to tear my gaze away from the magnificent beast. "Or maybe we've traveled to a time when they still existed."

"Either way, we should be cautious," Gabriel warned. "Dragons are known for their fierce tempers and deadly abilities. I don't know what kind that one is, so best to avoid."

"Right," I swallowed hard. "We'll keep our distance for now."

I was overwhelmed as we continued exploring the strange new world around us. There was so much packed into such a short timeframe that it almost didn't seem real.

"Are you alright?" Roman asked, noticing my frown.

"I'm just... trying to make sense of everything," I admitted. "It's a lot to take in."

"One step at a time, baby. One step at a time."

30: Nikolai

My boots sank into the damp earth as I trudged along. The silence between us was heavy with disappointment - we had been searching for hours yet found nothing but shadows and whispers.

"I'm done," I said finally, feeling strained. "We're getting nowhere. We have to return to the Citadel."

Gabriel's brow furrowed in concern. "But Nik, what about the Shadow Stone? We can't give up so easily."

"Perhaps we need more guidance," I replied, a plan forming in my mind. "I'll seek an audience with the Oracle. She may be able to direct us better."

"Are you sure, Nik?" Roman asked. "The Oracle's words can be cryptic. What makes you think she will tell you anything when we didn't tell any of us anything?"

"True," I admitted, "but it's worth a try. You all head back to the Citadel. I'll meet you there once I've spoken with the Oracle."

As I made my way to the chamber, I felt a shiver run down my spine. The dimly lit room seemed to close in around me, illuminated only by the flickering candles casting eerie shadows on the walls. The scent of incense hung heavily in the air, making it difficult to breathe.

"Oracle," I called out, my voice echoing through the chamber. "I seek your guidance."

Silence. Great.

"Where could she be?" I muttered under my breath, nervously fidgeting with my fingers. "She must know how urgent this is."

"Patience, young one," a voice suddenly whispered from the darkness.

The candles flared up momentarily, revealing the figure of the Oracle as she entered the chamber. She was old, like very old. Wrinkles were etched into her skin, but her eyes really took my breath away. Piercing blue eyes gazed at me without blinking.

"Oracle," I stammered, bowing my head in respect. "Forgive me for my impatience. Time is of the essence, and we are lost without your guidance."

"Time is both fleeting and eternal, Nik. And it is never truly wasted if one learns from their experiences."

"Then teach me," I pleaded, my desperation evident. "We've searched for the stone, but it is nowhere."

"Your journey has only just begun, young one. To find what you seek, look to the land outside the Citadel and find an ancient pillar."

"An ancient pillar?" I echoed. "But where? And how will we know it when we see it?"

"Ah," the Oracle murmured, a knowing smile gracing her lips. "That is a mystery you must unravel for yourselves. Remember, the path to victory is often shrouded in darkness, and only by embracing the shadows can one truly find the light."

The Oracle studied me for a moment. "Nik, your courage is commendable. Yet, finding the Shadow Stone requires more than courage. You must understand the darkness itself."

"What? What do you mean, Oracle?"

"Emma, the last Dark Faerie in your realm, plays a crucial part in this journey. Like a moth drawn to a flame, she will be pulled toward the very source of the darkness. If you do not learn to work with your darkness, how will you teach her how to use hers? There are none left like either of you, yet the same thread binds you."

I furrowed my brow, attempting to piece together the message. Instead of turning and walking away, she stood and watched me as I thought.

"I am afraid your words elude me. Could you please be a bit less cryptic?"

She regarded me with an inscrutable expression. Her wrinkled face remained impassive, giving away no hint of her thoughts.

"Very well," she replied. "Once you find the Shadow Stone, your work truly begins. The darkness will spread, and with it, hope will be lost. You will undergo challenges. Challenges that will test your strength, your courage, and your loyalty. You must be prepared to lose what you hold dear if you are to save this world from darkness. Only on the cusp of hopelessness will you rise in the strength of your power."

"Okay, so... ancient pillar, embrace the darkness, feel hopeless... am I missing anything?"

Her eyes crinkled as she smiled, "Farewell, young Lycan."

With a mind filled with turmoil, I bowed once more and took my leave. A cold wind blew through the narrow passageway leading back to the Citadel, another one of the Oracle's puzzles; the ever-changing landscape to and from her chamber was a bit much. Why can't anything just be simple? I pulled my jacket tighter around myself, attempting to stave off the icy air that seemed to seep into my very core. Is this some kind of reminder? That the future is bleak? If so, I'd prefer some sun before I walked into the belly of the beast.

"Ah, there you are, Nik," Gabriel waited inside the Citadel. "We were starting to worry."

"Tell us what the Oracle said."

"Easy, Roman," Avery chided gently, placing a comforting hand on his shoulder. "Give him a moment."

"Thank you, baby girl. The Oracle... she spoke in riddles and metaphors. But she told us to find the Shadow Stone in an ancient pillar. She also mentioned something about Emma's role as the last Dark Faerie."

"Ah, yeah, I kind of had a feeling Emma was the last one."

"And you didn't tell us?" Gabe asked incredulously.

Avery shifted uncomfortably, "I didn't want to say anything until I knew for sure."

"An ancient pillar?" Roman interrupted. "That could be anywhere. What else did she say?"

"Nothing really, but to be honest, guys, I'm starving. Oh, I forgot, we have to head back into that gross swampy land. She said it would be in the shadows somewhere, and since the Citadel isn't disgusting, it has to be there. Anyway, let's eat and then head back out."

It was strange. I didn't feel tired, and no one else seemed tired either. At least we could feel hunger because I was famished.

31: Gabriel

As we drew nearer to the middle of the Citadel, we were greeted by Lysaria and her Faerie friend.

"Hello." Avery said, "We need to ask for some guidance on what the Oracle told Nik; we must be quick, though, as we've left a companion of ours outside the gate, and we need to fetch him to try to find this stone. Osric, the world's most irritating and dubious Lycan God."

Lysaria gasped. "I know you must have questions. I have answers, but first, I must do something."

"Like what? We're in a bit of a hurry, not to be rude or disrespectful."

"Osric," she sighed, her eyes filled with longing. "I need to see him again. Our paths were destined to cross when I was still in the mortal realm. Our fates were intertwined."

"Intertwined how?" Roman asked.

"Before my ascension into the Citadel, I was his counterpart," she explained, her voice soft and distant. "I was also his mate."

"Sounds more like a curse than a blessing," Nik muttered, crossing his arms over his chest.

"Perhaps," a wistful smile playing on her lips. "But it's a burden I'm willing to bear. I've longed for the day I could see him again; being apart has been difficult."

"Alright," I said reluctantly, knowing how I would feel if I were apart from Avery. "We'll take you to him. But after that, you need to tell us where we can find the Shadow Stone. Avery thought it was outside the Citadel, but we couldn't find it."

"Deal," Lysaria said with a nod.

As we were about to move forward, she put her hand on my arm. "I'll search for Osric on my own. This is something I must do. I'm sure he will scent me anyway. He always did have a good nose."

"Are you sure? We're more than willing to help you."

She shook her head. "No, dear Gabriel, this is my burden to bear. But don't worry, I'll return as soon as I can."

"Be safe, Lysaria, he is not the man you once knew."

"Thank you," she murmured. Then she vanished into the shadows, leaving us with her friend.

We'd hardly a moment to process what just transpired when she started talking.

"Emma's connection to the Shadow Stone is strong, but she has no idea what it is that she is feeling, and without physical possession of the stone, she will continue to grow in discontentment. Her reunification with it will be crucial in your upcoming battle. It will stabilize her, but you must teach her how to wield her power. By the way, my name is Elloria. I don't think I told you before."

"Wait," Avery interjected, her brow creased with confusion. "I'm sorry, hi Elloria, nice to meet you. How has she already connected to the Shadow Stone? I didn't connect with my Spirit Stone until I saw it and felt it against my skin."

She tilted her head, considering her response. "Long ago, a powerful enchantress foresaw a time when darkness would threaten the realms. She imbued the Shadow Stone with a portion of her essence, binding it to a mortal whose heart was pure. That mortal was long past in Emma's bloodline. Today, it is bound to Emma. Our people preordained her lineage."

"Is that why Sion is after her?" Nik asked.

"Indeed," Elloria replied. "Should they obtain the Shadow Stone, the balance between light and darkness would be disrupted, plunging all realms into chaos. If Emma does not absorb her stone and reunite with the part of her that is missing, she will become everything you are fighting against. She will open portals to realms not yet discovered, forcing a convergence unlike anything you could imagine through no fault of her own, but you see, time is of the essence."

"Then why wouldn't you have told us this hours ago?" Avery crossed her arms.

"Lysaria told me not to. She said as the last Seraphina, you would be able to feel it and find it. I see that is not the case. Your path lies within an ancient rock formation," she continued. "Within its depths, you will find pillars of each race and their respective decrees. It is there that you shall uncover the Shadow Stone's location."

"Can you provide us with directions?" I asked, steeling myself for a no.

"Of course," she said, her eyes narrowing as she focused on the doors at the end of the citadel... the doors we had come in from only a few hours before. "Follow the river east until you reach the weeping willow grove. Beyond it lies a cavern adorned with symbols of old. The rock formation lay within. Go further until you see a pillar."

"Let's go," Avery said

"Wait," Roman held her arm, "what about Lysaria?"

"Roman, we really need to go. There's no sense of time here; we don't know how long we've been away. We have to go. Lysaria is a big girl; I'm sure she can handle Osric herself."

"Thank you, Elloria," I whispered, grateful for her guidance. She nodded and waved us off.

I'd thought of getting Osric so he could be part of our stone retrieval, but quite frankly, I still didn't like him. He was an asshole. Besides, we had Nik. Why would we need two Lycans just to fetch a rock? Avery smiled up at me as we exited the doors and started walking back through the swampy shadows. It was surprisingly easy how quickly we got back to where we got lost. Until it wasn't.

"Watch your footing," Roman warned, his voice tense as he helped her navigate a particularly sharp incline. "This place sucks, I don't want to be back here. It's creepy."

"Thanks," Avery murmured, her cheeks flushed from exertion. "I don't know what I'd do without you."

"Probably fall off a cliff," Nik quipped, earning himself a glare from Roman.

"Asshole!" She exclaimed, hitting him in the shoulder.

As if the terrain wasn't enough of an obstacle, we soon found ourselves facing a new danger: creatures swimming in the swampy waters ahead.

"Stay close," my hand instinctively reaching for Avery's. "We can't afford to be separated out here."

"Agreed," she whispered, her eyes darting around warily. "But what are these creatures?"

"Darkspawn," Roman replied grimly. "Twisted beings born from corruption. They're relentless, vicious, and nearly impervious to harm."

"Nearly?" Nik raised an eyebrow. "I don't understand how it's so beautiful back there and like this out here."

"Fire," I answered, recalling the text I read. "It's the only thing they fear. And to answer you, Nik, this is probably where the souls who didn't pass the trials came to reside. Osric will probably land up here."

"Great, fire, got it." Avery ignited a small flame in her palm. "Let's hope we don't need it."

Thankfully, we managed to avoid any further confrontations with the Darkspawn, and after what felt like an eternity, we finally saw it: the ancient rock formation Elloria had described. The cavern entrance loomed before us; its walls were etched with symbols that seemed to glow as we neared.

"Here it is," I squeezed Avery's hand. "The tablets must be inside."

"Let's find out."

As we ventured deeper into the cavern, we found ourselves in a vast chamber, its walls lined with stone tablets, each inscribed with the decrees of a different race.

"Look at this one," Avery whispered, her fingers tracing the ancient script of the Dark Faeries. "I can't read it, but oh! Look!" She pointed at a triangle. At each point lay an image. A Lycan, a Faerie, and a Seraphina.

"How fitting," I replied. "Now, where's that stone?"

"Let's do it, baby. Make that triangle," Roman rubbed his palms together.

"Trinity," I corrected him.

"Whatever," he rolled his eyes.

Nik's sharp gasp drew our attention to a pillar near the back of the chamber. Embedded within its center, a dark gemstone seemed to absorb the light around it.

"Is that...?" Avery's voice trembled with anticipation.

"The Shadow Stone," I whispered. Its surface was adorned with runes, unlike any language I had seen before. Not even my textbooks had anything remotely like this.

"Finally!" Roman pumped his fist in the air.

"But how do we remove it?" Nik frowned.

"Allow me," Avery said softly, stepping forward. Placing her hands on either side of the stone, she closed her eyes and whispered an incantation. The air around us shimmered as the stone began to loosen from its ancient prison.

"Careful," I sensed the immense power emanating from the Shadow Stone. "We don't want to unleash its force accidentally. So don't drop it."

Avery's hands shook slightly as she gently pried the stone loose. As soon as it was released, the runes on the tablet glowed an eerie red before fading away.

"Is everyone alright?" Roman asked

"Fine," Avery replied, clutching the stone tightly. "Just a bit drained. Where are the other stones? She said there were five, but there's only one here."

"Let's get out of here, and we can discuss it on the way back," I suggested, feeling the weight of the cavern pressing down upon us. "Hopefully, there's a simple explanation, so we don't need to go hunt for the other two."

"Are you sure you're alright, Avery? You look a little pale."

Avery offered a weak smile. "I'm fine, really, Roman, I promise. It's just tiring sometimes, I suppose."

"We will be able to rest soon. Real soon by the looks of it. We're going to have to go home to get Emma. We can take some time when we get there." My heart skipped a beat at the prospect of home.

"Nik," Roman scratched his head, "Lysaria mentioned something about her fated connection to Osric when she was in the mortal realm. Do you know anything more about that? It could be important."

"It might be true, but I honestly don't know. We will find out when we're back, I guess."

32: Avery

As we re-entered the Citadel, Lysaria stood there, beaming like sunlight breaking through storm clouds. She looked radiant and rejuvenated.

"Osric sends his regards," she announced, her voice filled with warmth. "He wishes you success, though; I see you were successful, so it doesn't matter anymore. Now, before we continue, let us discuss the matter of the Lunar Stone."

We all stared at her in confusion.

"Osric has agreed to give Nik the Lunar Stone," Lysaria revealed, her eyes shining with joy. "In exchange, when his time on our world expires, he will ascend to the Celestial Citadel and join me here." She reached into a small pouch at her waist and pulled out a beautiful stone shimmering in shades of silver and blue.

"But how can he get in?" I was curious since he failed the test and all.

"The Citadel rewards acts of redemption and punishes those of impure spirit. He really has changed, I am pleased to tell you. He will hopefully be more amenable as you finish your journey together."

Nik's eyes widened, a mix of awe and anxiety as Lysaria held the Lunar Stone out to him. Hesitantly, he reached for it, his hand trembling slightly.

"Thank you, Lysaria," he whispered, his voice filled with emotion as he accepted the stone.

"Osric believes this is the best course of action to defeat Belial once and for all. We were stronger together because of our mate bond, just as you and Avery tied. Your connection will bolster your chances of success. His soul is much changed, but I can see the light struggling with the dark," she continued. "But now we must discuss how to help Emma absorb the Shadow Stone."

Gabriel scratched his chin thoughtfully, then spoke up. "We need to ensure that Emma can control the power of the Shadow Stone without being consumed by it, right?"

"Perhaps we could find a way to create a barrier between the stone and her mind, something that allows her to tap into its energy without being overwhelmed," Roman suggested.

"That could be something," Nik agreed. "But what kind of barrier would be strong enough to contain such power?"

"Maybe there's a magical artifact or spell we can use? Something to help her harness the Shadow Stone's power safely." I had no idea if there was such a thing, but since Elloria had conveniently gone missing, we had to try to figure something out.

"Let's research ancient texts until Elloria is back," Lysaria recommended. "Though time is of the essence, we must be thorough in our search. I can only guide the Seraphina. Dark Faeries are not my forte. Let's go to the library."

As we discussed our plans, Nik clutched the Lunar Stone; his gaze fixed on it as if he were attempting to unlock its secrets. Suddenly, the stone began to glow softly, a gentle silver light enveloping his hand. His eyes widened in surprise as the stone seemed to melt into his skin, leaving behind an intricate pattern of silver veins trailing up his arm.

"Are you alright, Nik?" I asked with a smile, reminiscing on my own experience.

"I... I think so," he replied, flexing his fingers experimentally. "It feels...strange, but not painful."

"Your acceptance of the Lunar Stone was successful; congratulations, Lycan," Lysaria said, her eyes filled with relief. "Now, we must focus on helping Emma do the same with the Shadow Stone."

As our group huddled together, pouring over ancient texts in search of answers, the door to the chamber creaked open, revealing Elloria. Her footsteps echoed off the floor as she rushed towards us.

"Enough with the books. I have consulted the spirits and discovered a way to help Emma control her powers."

"Please enlighten us," Lysaria bowed, giving her attention to her friend.

"First, we need to understand the nature of Emma's abilities," she began, her hands weaving intricate patterns in the air as if painting invisible runes. "The Shadow Stone is an ancient artifact that bestows immense power upon its wielder. In Emma's case, it grants her the ability to manipulate shadows - to bend them to her will and even step into their realm for brief periods."

"Shadows? Like...literal darkness?" Roman asked skeptically, raising an eyebrow.

"Indeed. Through the Shadow Stone, Emma can harness the very essence of darkness, using it as both a weapon and a shield. Much like Avery has her dream realm, we have the shadow realm, yet they operate differently and cannot be used for prolonged periods of time. She must learn to maintain a delicate balance between her own spirit and the stone's power."

"Balance? How can she achieve that?"

"Emma must form a bond with the Shadow Stone. She must accept and embrace the darkness within herself and learn to channel it. Only then can she wield the stone's power without succumbing to its corrupting influence. If she absorbs it as Nik did, she will not complete the reunification."

"Is there a specific technique she needs to practice or perhaps a ritual to perform?" Gabriel searched for practical solutions.

"Rituals can help, but ultimately, it is a deeply personal journey," Elloria said, her tone gentle. "Each of us has darkness within us - fears, doubts, regrets. Emma must confront hers and find a way to harmonize them with the power of the Shadow Stone."

"Sounds like a tall order," Nik rubbed his arm, gazing down at its pattern.

"Indeed, but I have faith in Emma's strength," she replied, a small smile playing on her lips. "And she has all of you by her side."

With my heart feeling a little lighter, we decided to leave and head home.

"Thank you both for everything," I hugged Lysaria and Elloria in turn, "you've been most wonderful. If you see Alara... or my Aunt Sapphire, can you tell them I love them?"

Lysaria nodded, "of course I can. Stay strong, Avery, no matter the doubts that seep into your mind, you can do this."

The guys each said their goodbyes before we turned towards each other in a huddle.

"Alright," Gabriel began. "We need to make sure we have everything we need before we leave. Roman, you take care of gathering supplies; I'll try to plan the quickest route home. The land might be unfamiliar, but I remembered most of what we journeyed."

"Got it," Roman disappeared into a nearby chamber filled with various provisions.

"Be sure to grab some extra water bottles," Nik called after him.

"I've been thinking," I interjected, "how are we going to help her control the Shadow Stone's powers against Belial? Training is one thing, but war is another. We can't just throw her into battle without a plan."

Lysaria, who had been quietly observing our preparations, stepped forward. "I've spoken with Elloria about this matter, and she believes that Emma will need to undergo rigorous training to harness the stone's energies properly. She suggested finding an isolated location where Emma can practice without endangering anyone."

"An excellent idea," Gabriel agreed. "We should search for such a place while we're en route. The sooner she can begin her training, the better."

"Also, let's not forget about rest," I added, our earlier conversation still fresh in my mind. "We need to make sure we're all taking care of ourselves mentally and emotionally, too."

"Agreed," Nik smacked my ass. "I'm missing my time with you."

"Speaking of togetherness," Roman's voice echoed from the chamber as he returned with his arms laden with various supplies, "I got us matching travel cloaks!"

"Matching cloaks?" I asked, raising an eyebrow as amusement bubbled within me.

"Absolutely!" Roman grinned, revealing four identical deep blue cloaks. "We'll be the most stylish adventurers out there."

"Roman, you're incorrigible," Gabriel teased, accepting one of the cloaks with a shake of his head.

"Hey, we might as well look good while saving the world, right?" Roman winked, draping another cloak around my shoulders.

"Right," I agreed, unable to suppress a smile. Roman always had a way of raising my spirits. "At least they'll keep us warm."

"Okay, let's go home," Gabriel clapped his hands.

Together, we stepped out of the crumbling archway and into the unknown, our determination burning brightly amidst the encroaching darkness.

The sun sank low, casting a warm golden glow over the gardens surrounding the Celestial Citadel. Birds sang their farewells to the day as we gathered our supplies and prepared for our departure.

"Wait," Gabriel said suddenly. "How are we even going to approach Emma with all this information? We can't just shove the stone at her and be all, 'Here's a magical stone; absorb it, and you're going to come with us to defeat a demon lord.'"

"Right. Maybe we can.... take her to dinner or something."

I leaned against a nearby tree trunk, my fingers unconsciously twisting the hem of my new cloak. "How will we know if she's making progress?" I asked, my voice tinged with worry.

"Elloria mentioned that Emma must learn to channel her energy through the Shadow Stone," Roman replied, his brow furrowed in thought. "Perhaps we can devise some exercises for her to practice while we're traveling."

"Like meditation?" I suggested.

"Exactly," Roman nodded. "Meditation, breathing exercises, anything that helps her focus on controlling her power rather than letting it control her. Basically, what we did with Gabe until he learned to control himself; as far as telling her, I vote we just tell her the truth. Wouldn't you want to know the truth if it were you, and also that you were part of this kickass team of adventure warriors?"

"Of course. The name of the game is teamwork." I burst out laughing as Roman struck a pose.

"Speaking of which," Nik winked at me, "are you sure these matching cloaks are absolutely necessary?"

"Hey, I stand by my decision!" Roman protested, feigning offense. "A little morale boost never hurt anyone."

33: Roman

As we left behind the mysteries of the Citadel, our bags heavy, but our hearts were full. I spotted a figure leaning against the ancient stone wall. His posture seemed weary, but there was an unmistakable aura of strength surrounding him.

"Osric," I murmured. Recognition flickered in his eyes, and he straightened up, offering me a nod in greeting.

"Roman," he replied, his tone cautious but friendly. "I've been waiting for you guys."

"Waiting for us?" I raised. "Why? I thought you'd have left after you saw Lysaria."

"Because it's time for me to go," Osric said solemnly, his gaze flicking to Nik before returning to mine. "I've given my Lunar Stone to him so the torch of the last Lycan can be carried on. Without it, I will die soon."

"Die? But Lysaria said you would finish with us?"

"There is no need anymore, pup. I have given you the source of my advanced strength. In a few days you'll have eclipsed me if you train and work to understand it. You don't need me anymore."

Nik scratched his head, "so why not just come finish with us? What about Selene tying you to Avery? If you die, then she dies, and I think that's pretty shitty."

"Because Lysaria is here," Osric explained, his eyes growing distant as if he could see her face in the air before him. "She is my fated mate, and we have been apart for far too long. I cannot bear the loneliness any longer, and now that the burden of being the last Lycan has been passed onto you, I am free to join her. As far as Avery, she is now tied to you. The last Lycan."

"Osric... thank you." Nik choked up, "I know you were pretty much an asshole to us, but this means everything."

"Promise me you'll do better than I did, son," Osric implored, clasping the younger man's shoulder with surprising gentleness. "Protect our people, cherish your mate and your brothers, and never forget the legacy of our kind."

"I promise," he vowed, his voice thick with emotion. "I will honor the Lycans and do everything in my power to be someone they could have been proud of."

"Thank you," Osric stepped back, releasing Nik's shoulder as he looked over at Avery. "Take care of her, all of you. She's worth more than you know."

"Goodbye, Osric," I murmured, feeling an unexpected lump in my throat. He smiled at me before stepping through the archway, vanishing into the Celestial Citadel to reunite with his beloved Lysaria.

"May they find peace," Avery whispered, her hand coming to rest on Nik's arm as we watched the gates close behind him.

"Alright, everyone, let's get moving. We have a long journey back home," Gabe announced. He'd never liked the ancient God.

He took point, leading us through winding passages that we hadn't walked on the way here. I guess his map was better than just wandering aimlessly. I could have sworn it took us a week to get here, and we've only been walking a few hours, and the terrain has shifted. Or maybe the Gods took pity on us and pulled the terrains closer together. Whatever it was, I was glad. I want my own damn bed for once.

"Good, because we don't have much farther to go," Gabe said. "Just a bit more, and we'll be there."

The path before us was shrouded in a thick, eerie mist that swallowed all light. After passing by a frog with six eyes, I'd just about thrown up. Why was everything so extra here? Like two eyes wasn't enough. Nooo, everything had to have a million eyes and look like someone threw them in a meat grinder and sewed them back together.

"Look!" Avery cried out suddenly, pointing towards a faint glimmer up ahead. "Could that be our way out?"

"Only one way to find out," Gabriel took her hand as they walked forward.

As we neared the source of the light, the mist began to dissipate, revealing a swirling vortex that looked like a cosmic whirlpool.

"Is that...?" Avery stammered, her eyes widening with awe.

"Our realm," I finished for her, my voice hushed. "We'll have to pass through it to get back."

"Sounds about right. The map maker said there was a portal here, so good job, love." They exchanged glances, and Avery stood on her tiptoes to kiss his cheek.

Gathering our courage, we stepped into the vortex, our bodies wracked with tremors as the energy surged around us. The light swallowed us as a wave of nausea hit me.

"Are we home?" Avery asked breathlessly once we emerged from the vortex.

"Only one way to find out," I muttered, scanning the landscape for any sign of familiarity. There! The training field. Finally!

The pack house finally came into view, like a lighthouse in the distance, guiding our weary bodies home. A sense of relief and exhaustion settled deep within my bones. We stumbled forward, physically and emotionally supporting each other as we made our way to the entrance.

"Home sweet home," I sighed, leaning against the doorframe as the others filed in.

"I am so happy we're back... I wonder where everyone is," Gabriel murmured, his normally stoic face etched with weariness.

"Hey, at least we didn't have to fight any more of those strange beasts," I joked, trying to bring some levity to our situation. "I mean, who knew that multi-eyed creatures could be so... cuddly?"

"That one almost but my arm off, might I remind you," Gabriel chided, though the hint of a smile played at the corners of his mouth.

"Come on, Gabe. Lighten up a bit. We made it back alive, didn't we?" I grinned.

"At least we're home," Nik shrugged.

"For now," Avery sighed before turning to go upstairs. "I just want you to know I'm grateful for each of you."

"Aw, don't make me blush," I felt the heat rise and spread over my face.

"Too late, lover boy," Gabriel teased, his smile finally breaking through.

"Say, do you think we can put 'fighting otherworldly creatures' on our resume? I mean, it's not every day you get to navigate through different realms and dimensions with your mate."

"Yes, Roman, you can add it to your resume," Nik laughed. "Though I think we've had enough excitement for a while."

"Agreed," Avery said, letting out a contented sigh as she sat on the stairs. "Let's just focus on recovering and starting Emma on a training program."

"Sounds like a plan," I trudged up the stairs behind Avery. If anyone was going to shower with her, it was going to be me.

The pack house reconstruction had finished while we were gone, but there were no beds in here. At least they put in some couches, so we have that to be grateful for, I guess. My gaze lingered on Avery for a moment and the purple bags under her eyes. She had carried so much responsibility throughout our journey; it was time for her to take a well-deserved break.

"Come, let's shower." She smiled as I picked her up and carried her to the massive ensuite bathroom.

My fingers traced lazy circles around the small of her back as she rested her head on my chest. I kissed the top of her head before moving so the water cascaded down her body. Of course, there was no soap because why would anyone think we'd need soap in a bathroom? I washed her hair as best I could before stepping out and looking for a towel.

"Looking for this?" Nik stood, holding a tea towel.

"Better than air drying, I guess," I grumbled. First thing tomorrow, we are going to deck this place out. I get we've been gone a while, but really? No one thought of this?

By the time we'd painstakingly dried ourselves, Avery was close to passing out. Tucking her onto the couch, I kissed her forehead and turned off the light. *Sleep well, baby.*

The first light of dawn crept through the window, shining in my eyes like an asshole with a flashlight. Gabriel and Nik were still asleep, their chests rising and falling with each breath. Avery sighed, looking over the side of the couch at all of us sprawled on the floor.

"Morning," she whispered groggily, stretching her limbs and rubbing at her eyes.

"Good morning, babe," a smile stretched over my face at the sight of her sleep-softened face.

"Did you sleep well?" Our eyes locked, and for a moment, I was lost in the depths of her gaze.

"Better than I have in a long time," I admitted, "but damn do I want a bed and some toothpaste. My breath could blast open a bomb shelter."

"Oh, Roman, you're so dramatic."

I pulled up to kiss her, and she scrunched her nose.

"Dramatic, huh?" we burst out laughing.

"Guys, wake up," I said to Gabriel and Nik, who stirred but didn't quite wake. "We need to talk about what's next."

"Five more minutes," Gabriel mumbled, burying his face deeper into his arm. Nik only grunted in response.

"Fine," I relented, knowing full well that we all needed a few extra moments or days, if I'm being honest. "But no longer."

"Deal," Gabriel replied, his voice muffled.

"Think we got enough time for a quickie?"

"No, Roman, though that sounds lovely, we really do need to get going. This place is so beautiful but so empty. And we need to find Emma." She sighed as she ran her fingers through her hair.

Adulting sucks.

"Alright, alright," Gabriel grumbled, sitting up and rubbing at his eyes. "Let's get this show on the road."

"Fine," Nik yawned. "What's the plan?"

"First things first," I began, my mind racing with ideas. "We need furniture."

"Agreed," Avery chimed in. "And we should work on strengthening our defenses here at the house if they haven't already done that. It was pretty easy to get in here, which makes me a bit nervous. We can't afford to let our guard down. And we need to find Emma and tell her... about all of this..."

"Sounds like a plan," Gabriel rubbed his hands together. "Let's split up and tackle these tasks. We'll regroup later to discuss our findings."

34: Nikolai

The crisp morning air nipped at my skin as I stepped out of the new prison and into the rising sun. The prison was fantastic; all upgraded equipment, the latest in supernatural tech, basically impenetrable cells. Everything had been rebuilt in our absence, a testament to how well we ran our pack. We operated based on mutual respect, and our people responded in kind.

We'd been out attending business for the better of three hours, and I was getting antsy. Everything looked great, and now that the adrenaline had worn off, I wanted a nap. Or to bury my dick inside Avery, or to nap with my dick inside Avery.

"Hey, Nik," Roman approached with Avery and Gabriel in tow.

"Morning, guys," I replied with a smile, my breath condensed.

"Can we go see the new baby cows that just came in? I don't want to deal with the Shadow Stone stuff right now." Avery sounded excited as she bounced up and down. Her love for the animals was infectious – she had a way of making even mundane tasks enjoyable.

"You mean calves?" I laughed, and we set off towards the paddock where our cattle grazed.

"Well, yeah, but baby cows sound cuter." She grabbed my hand with a giggle.

Upon reaching the paddock, we spread out to check on the health of each animal, murmuring words of encouragement and affection. The mooing of the cows, mixed with the bleating of sheep, brought a sense of normalcy. We were run differently to most packs. We always strived for self-sufficiency, but most of all, we wanted everyone to find a place where they found peace. Some of our more traumatized members found solace among the animals, so we ensured they were trained and able to care for them. It was a symbiotic system.

"Looks like everyone's doing well," Roman reported, rubbing the head of an amicable cow.

"Good," I responded. "We'll need to keep a close eye on them, especially since they're new here. I'll let Farah know. Let's move on to patrolling the borders."

As we navigated the dense forest, I wondered about Emma. I wanted us to move a bit faster in regard to her training, but Avery suggested we get her to move into the house first and get her comfortable being around us. She'd only briefly met us ages ago when we saved her. I guess it made sense, but the longer we waited, the longer it was until we saw Onyx and Aurora again.

"Have any of you seen Emma today?" I asked as we passed by the stream that marked the edge of our territory.

"No," Avery replied. "But I'm sure she's around here some-where."

"Let's keep an eye out for her while we patrol," I suggested. "We can ask around if anyone's seen her."

As we continued our patrol, we encountered various mem-bers of our pack tending to their own duties. We inquired about Emma each time, only to be met with puzzled expressions and shrugs. Worry gnawed at my gut. What if she left and no one noticed?

"Guys, I'm starved; I'm going to go make lunch. The bou-tique said they'd have our new items delivered by noon, and it's probably well passed, considering how hungry I am."

"Sure, baby girl, see you in a bit, okay?"

She nodded and took off towards the house.

"Hey, Nik! I didn't know you were back." a familiar voice from the trees called. He swung down from a branch, landing gracefully on the ground before us. "What brings you this way?"

"Hey, Ivan. Actually, we're looking for Emma," I explained. "Have you seen her around?"

"Emma? Yeah, I saw her earlier," he replied, scratching his chin thoughtfully. "She was heading towards the old oak tree near the western border."

"Thanks, man," I said gratefully. "We'll check there."

"Good luck, and nice to have you back," he called out as we hurried towards the western border.

A gentle breeze blew through the leaves of the old oak tree, its gnarled branches reaching into the sky. Emma was seated with her back against the trunk, a book in her lap, and an expression of serene contentment on her face. She looked up as we approached, surprise flickering across her features.

"Hi, I didn't know you guys were back," she greeted, closing her book. "What brings you all here?"

"Hey, Emma. We've been looking for you. We wanted to invite you to join us for lunch at the pack house."

"Really?" Emma's eyes widened, curiosity piqued. "I'd love to."

"Great," Roman said with a warm smile. "Avery should be close to finished by now if now is a good time."

"That would be lovely. I'm sorry, can you reintroduce yourselves? It's been a while," her cheeks were red as she asked.

"Of course, how rude. I'm Nik, that's Roman, and there's Gabe. Nice to officially meet you."

The walk to the house was filled with easy conversation, Emma asking questions about our pack and how it functioned. It seemed she had been fairly reclusive during her time here. Pride swelled within me as I spoke of our close-knit community, our shared duties, and the support we offered one another. I'd have to check in on Lola, the one in charge of new members. It was odd she didn't help Emma adjust.

We filed inside, and Avery had already set the table, an array of mouth-watering dishes laid out before us. We took our seats, the fragrant scent of roasted vegetables and grilled meats wafting through the air as we filled our plates and began to eat.

"Emma," Roman asked between bites, "what's your favorite food?"

"Really? What's your favorite food?" Gabe frowned.

"What? I didn't know what else to ask!"

"Um..." She pondered for a moment, tapping her fork against her lips. "I'd have to say lasagna. I love layering all the ingredients together and baking it until it's nice and bubbly."

"Ooh, I love lasagna too," Avery said. "Maybe we can make it together sometime."

"Sounds like fun," Emma agreed, her smile bright.

"See? It wasn't a bad question!"

We burst out laughing. "It was a good question, Roman. Don't worry, I appreciate the icebreaker."

As we continued eating, the conversation shifted towards hobbies. Roman regaled us with his corny jokes while Gabriel spoke fondly of his nerd stuff. Emma just listened and watched.

"So, where have you guys been?" Emma asked. "I mean... I haven't seen you guys around much, and no one is telling me anything because I haven't officially become a pack member... And then I saw Avery's face warning me to stay here, without much context so I've been a little on edge. Keeping to myself."

"Actually, yes," I answered, "we've been out searching for guidance and found it. Though, it's nothing that needs to be discussed right now."

"Okay, I understand." Before changing the subject, she said, " I love how you all look at each other... it's like... you're more. I hope I find someone who looks at me like that one day."

"We are," Avery smiled. "They're everything."

Emma asked a few more surface-level questions, and I realized I was quite fond of her. She was a really good person with a kind heart. I hoped that she would be as easy to train as she was to talk to.

As the last morsel of food disappeared from our plates, I glanced at Avery, who seemed to be thoroughly enjoying herself. It was nice seeing her interacting with a friend—one who didn't want anything from her. The camaraderie between us all felt genuine and effortless, and it was time to extend an invitation that could change her life for the better.

"Emma," I began, my voice warm and sincere. "We've really enjoyed having you here with us today. As you've seen, our pack is like a family, and we would love for you to be a part of it. Would you consider living with us at the pack house? We know you haven't felt at home here yet, and we want to change that."

"Not as, like, a partner or anything, but as someone we want to spend more time with."

"That still sounds like we want to date her, Gabe." Avery laughed before turning to Emma. "As beautiful as you are, we're all full on mates. That being said, we feel a kinship with you and would like you to be closer to us so we can form a friendship if that's something you'd be interested in doing."

Her eyes widened in surprise, and she hesitated before responding, clearly weighing her options. "It's a generous offer, but I don't want to impose."

"Please, don't worry about that," Avery reassured her, reaching out to touch her arm gently. "We have plenty of room and we'd be thrilled to have you here. Besides, it would be nice to have another woman in the house. We can do your pack ceremony tonight so you feel more welcome."

Roman chimed in. "The ceremony comes with many benefits. We support and protect each other, and you'll never be alone. There are responsibilities, of course – contributing to the well-being of the pack and respecting our customs and traditions. But the bonds you will form here are priceless."

Gabriel nodded in agreement. "We all take care of one another, and there's always someone available to help if you need it. What do you think?"

I practically could see the wheels turning in her head as she considered our words. Finally, she offered a small, tentative smile. "I'd love to."

"Welcome to the pack, Emma!" Avery exclaimed with joy, enveloping her in a warm hug.

We turned our attention to the practicalities of our new living situation, staring at the house. "We'll need to get some furniture for your room," I mused, glancing around the pack house. "At least the boutique delivered the rest of the order."

"Maybe Avery can go with you."

"Sounds perfect, Nik."

Emma smiled as we made plans for the day, "Ummm, I'd have to grab a few things. They set me up with a guest cabin, but I have some clothing and stuff I'd like to bring."

"Of course. We can grab it on the way!"

A few hours later, the women returned in a whirlwind of laughter, some of our burly men toting boxes of furniture.

"Have a good time?" I winked.

"We did, but it's a lot of building, so... chop chop."

"Alright, let's do this," I said, clapping my hands together.

As we unpacked and assembled the furniture, Emma watched us with a mixture of curiosity and admiration, occasionally lending a hand when needed. The ease between us was palpable; the air filled with laughter and teasing as we worked together.

"Thank you, all of you," Emma said once we finished, her eyes shining with gratitude. "I can't tell you how much this means to me."

"Of course, Emma," Avery replied, pulling her into a hug. "You're part of our family now."

With the furniture set up and the pack house feeling more like home than ever, our stomachs growled, reminding us of the time. Avery glanced at the clock on the kitchen wall and clapped her hands.

"Looks like it's a few hours past dinner time, everyone! Let's make something to eat."

We rummaged through the pantry and refrigerator, gathering fresh vegetables from our garden and cuts of meat from the cellar. Thank God the butcher was on the ball.

"Roman, you're on salad duty. Gabriel, can you handle the potatoes?" Avery directed. She was so cute when she was in control.

"Of course," they both replied, moving to their respective stations.

"Emma, would you like to help me prepare the meat?" I asked, offering her an opportunity to contribute.

"Sure, Nik. I'd be happy to."

As dinner came to a close and the last of the dishes were cleared away, Avery shot me a sultry glance from across the table. I could sense her desire for intimacy, and my heart raced in anticipation.

"Hey, guys," she said, addressing Roman, Gabriel, and me. "Wanna meet me upstairs?"

"God, yes," I replied, feeling a surge of excitement course through me. The others nodded in agreement, their eyes conveying their shared eagerness.

"I'll clean whatever's left," Emma smiled, "go enjoy your evening."

35: Nikolai

As Emma went about her thing, Roman locked the front door before joining us upstairs.

"Excited, are we?" Avery stared at my hard cock.

"Can't blame me; it's been like, weeks," I already felt pre-cum wetting my boxers, and we hadn't done anything yet. She was just so sexy without even trying.

"Shirt off," Gabe said, sitting on the couch, just watching.

She curtsied with a smirk and pulled it off before Roman picked her up and threw her on the bed.

My fingers twirled around her nipples, and they stiffened in response. I leaned in and sucked on her neck, my tongue exploring the soft flesh of her throat. Roman slid his hands into her panties and began teasing her. She moaned as he began to move his fingers in circles around her clit.

She scooted closer so that she was sandwiched between us both, her back against my chest. Pushing two fingers inside her pussy, I pinched her nipples hard. Her body quivered as I increased the pressure and pace. She released a low moan of pleasure as we worked her over. So long without release, and she was already ready to cum.

"Yes, oh my Goddess, yes baby, more, please."

Roman smiled, shooting me a wink as he pinched her clit, pushing her over the edge.

We lay there for a moment, savoring this moment of pleasure before Gabe stood, replacing me at her back. He lifted her and sat her on his cock while we sat and watched.

His pace was slow and deep as he rocked her hips back and forth, allowing her to take control. Her head fell back as she pulled on her nipples, sliding her free hand down her stomach before circling her clit.

She gazed at Roman with hunger in her eyes before bending forward and taking him in her mouth, sucking hard. Gabe shifted, so he knelt behind her and grabbed her hips.

"I love you," she whispered before pushing Roman down her throat and holding him there while he came.

"Good girl," he said as he wiped a drop of cum off her lip.

She smiled up at him before jerking her head for me to take his place.

"Hold on, I'm close," Gabe grunted as he thrust hard and fast, only pausing as he came.

He reached down and pulled her up, kissing her neck before whispering his love for her and moving back to the couch, allowing me a moment with her alone.

I lay down and pulled her on top of me, my face lined up with her pussy and my cock pushing against her lips.

"Ohhh, this is a new one, babe," she lowered herself on my face, moaning around my cock as I ate her.

She was soaked; her juice mixed with Gabe's cum dripped down my chin as I kicked and sucked. Her blow job was sloppy, unable to stop writing and gurgling around my cock.

Her pussy clenched as she sat and rode my face, taking everything I had to give as she came.

"Holy fuck," she moaned, her hips slowing as she rode the wave before bending over and taking me back in her mouth.

The view was perfect. Her round ass hovered above me, and her pussy slowly dripped into my waiting mouth. She hardly had to suck, I was so turned on. Pushing my hips upward, I came in her mouth, and she swallowed before slowly rolling off me.

"That was so hot. Like... so hot," Roman said from his spot next to Gabe.

I'd pretty much forgotten they were there, but hey, if they got off again, all the better.

As Gabe so aptly put it, we were the sharers of the angel.

"You're perfect, baby girl," I kissed her temple, and we all piled into bed. Sweaty, slick with cum but content.

"Please... don't stop," she gasped, her fingers gripping the sheets tightly.

My eyes opened to Avery riding Roman as the sun streamed into the room. Damn, my insatiable little minx.

"Your wish is our command, my love."

He drove his hips into her as his hands grabbed her breasts, pinching her nipples as her head fell back.

I stayed quiet, watching as she came around him. Her lips parted, and her hand rested on her chest as it heaved. So perfect.

She kissed him deeply before resting her forehead on his. It was all they needed to do. No words, no sweet nothings, just a simple gesture of love and adoration.

If I wasn't as hard as a rock, I'd probably think it's cute, but as it were, I wanted next.

"Been up a while?" she teased as she looked between Gabe and me.

"Huh, Gabe's up too?"

"You think the bed rocking didn't wake me? Naw, I was just enjoying our girl riding our brother."

She smiled and moved to the other side of the bed before opening her legs and spreading her pussy. Her fingers began to work, but Gabe was on her in a flash before she could finish.

"Don't you dare cum," his voice was low.

"My, my, I thought being demanding was for Nik, but look at you," she smirked as he pulled her into him and started fucking her.

Roman and I joined in. Clearly, he was a stallion because he was ready to go, just like that.

As we pleasured Avery, we were attuned to her reactions, adjusting our movements according to her needs and desires. When her breathing became ragged and her body trembled, we knew she was close to the edge.

"Are you ready, Avery?" Gabriel asked when she was thoroughly soaked.

"Y-yes... please!" she cried out.

In unison, we entered her. Roman slid inside her ass while Gabe fucked her pussy, and I held her hair while she tongued my cock. I watched her mouth engulf me before turning back to watch Roman fucking her tight ass. She seemed to have taken a liking to anal sex, and it drove me wild—little vixen.

All three of us thrust our cocks into her with abandon – searching for the perfect rhythm, the ultimate sensation, and the most intense connection. As Roman thrust, she cried out against my shaft, sending vibrations shooting through my cock. The sensations were intense, and my cock twitched. I pulled on her ponytail, watching in delight as her eyes squeezed shut and her throat bobbed around me.

"Such a good, good girl. I'm going to cum, and you're going to swallow every drop."

A gurgle was my response as she allowed me to cut off her airflow and spill my load down her throat.

Roman and Gabriel finished soon after, and once again, we were sweaty and smelled like sex.

"We should shower and then go chat to Emma about everything," Avery said, breaking the comfortable silence.

In the back of my mind, I knew that the Shadow Stone would eventually demand our attention. But, honestly, I was enjoying this. We'd missed so much while we'd been away, and I missed connecting with her like this.

"Right."

One by one, we had a shower and put on clean clothes before going downstairs to an empty kitchen.

Shit, did we scare her away? I wouldn't be surprised by the way Avery was howling.

"Did anyone hear from Emma after we left her last night?" I asked as we made a simple breakfast.

"Actually, she sent me a message this morning," Roman replied, pulling out his phone. "She said she's going out for a bit to read."

"Wow, on texting and checking in level already," Avery said with a pout.

"Babe, she needed one of our numbers in case. You know I'd never do anything to put you in a state of jealousy, but it is kinda cute."

"Ugh, you're the worst." She smiled.

"Okay, great. Let's make breakfast for her when she gets back. Then we can get on with it and tell her what we were doing and start her on training."

"Yes," Roman said, eyeing the new furniture that now filled our pack house. "I think we all did an excellent job yesterday. This place really feels like home now."

"Agreed," Avery gave him a kiss. "I'm so glad we're home."

"The only thing missing is a giant naked portrait of our angel right there," he said, pointing to the hallway.

"Ha...ha."

"Bedroom, then?" Gabe offered

"Alright, lovebirds," I teased, wondering how we could make that happen. "Let's get some food into these growling stomachs of ours."

"Are you ever not hungry?" Gabriel quipped, bumping his shoulder against mine playfully.

"Can't help it," I shrugged. "All this running around as Alpha is hard work, you know."

36: Avery

With the sun shining and the birds chirping, I decided to find Emma, and I had an inkling of where she might be. She hadn't come home for breakfast, but I don't blame her. We are pretty... intense in the bedroom, and I have no idea how well the walls are for soundproofing. It was the kind of afternoon that begged for leisurely strolls and quiet contemplation. As I walked along the worn path, my boots crunched softly on fallen leaves. I spotted Emma sitting under the massive oak tree at the heart of the grove.

"Emma?" I called out gently, not wanting to startle her. She looked up from her sketchbook, a faint smile gracing her lips. "Hey, Avery. Isn't it just beautiful out here today?"

I sat beside her and noticed the intricate drawings covering the pages of her sketchbook—delicate flowers, twisting vines, and small woodland creatures. "It certainly is. I might steal your spot if I ever need to get away from the guys. It's peaceful here."

As we sat there, enjoying the warmth of the sun on our faces, we chatted idly about our day. She shared stories of her latest artistic inspirations while I recounted tales of some of the crazy creatures I'd seen. Our laughter rang through the grove, as easy and carefree as the rustling leaves above us.

"By the way, have you noticed how the weather has been lately?" Emma asked, tilting her head back to gaze at the sky. "It's been so mild and sunny, almost like summer's trying to hold on just a little bit longer. It should be much colder by now, but I don't mind. This place has like a micro-ecosystem."

"Indeed," I chuckled, following her gaze upwards. "It's as if nature itself is reluctant to let go of these peaceful days. But eventually fall will come, and then winter."

"Hopefully not for a while," she agreed before glancing at me with a playful grin. "Speaking of adapting, I love having some friends around. Roman is a hoot."

"Ha!" I laughed, shaking my head in mock exasperation. "It's been quite the adventure, I'll tell you that much. But they're amazing guys."

"Sounds like a handful," Emma teased, closing her sketchbook and standing up. She brushed the stray blades of grass from her clothes and extended a hand to help me up. "Shall we head back to the house? I'm sure there are many more stories to be told over lunch. I skipped breakfast. Got too engrossed in my latest drawing."

"Sure," I accepted her hand and rose to my feet.

The house was alive with rock music and boiling pots. The guys stood in the cozy kitchen; the scent of freshly baked bread made my stomach growl. The three of them glanced up when we entered, their faces lighting up with welcoming smiles.

"Ah, Avery, Emma! Perfect timing," Roman exclaimed, gesturing to the simple lunch spread out on the wooden table. "We were just about to sit down."

"Everything smells delicious," Emma said appreciatively, eyeing the bread and muffins.

"Thank you," Gabriel replied, his cheeks flushing slightly at the compliment. "I'm glad you think so."

"Come on, let's dig in," Nik urged, motioning for us to take a seat. "I'm so hungry, I could eat a horse."

"Didn't you eat breakfast?"

"Yeah, but then I spent the morning training the army. Wanted to test and see if they kept it up, and sure enough, they were all fit as a fiddle. Except Gary. Dude needs a diet."

I was content as we sat down and began filling our plates. Gathered together like this and sharing a meal was such a simple pleasure yet profoundly grounding.

"Emma," I said, waiting for a lull in the conversation before turning my attention to her. "There's something I've been meaning to tell you." My heart raced, knowing that this revelation would forever alter the course of her life.

Her gaze met mine, curiosity piqued. "What is it, Avery?"

Taking a deep breath, I plunged straight in. "You are the last Dark Faerie in our realm, at least," I watched as her eyes widened in surprise. "Unfortunately, I don't have time to word this any more gently... time is... short."

"A Dark Faerie?" she whispered, disbelief etched across her face. "But how?"

"Your lineage has been hidden from you, but the truth is within your very blood," I explained. "And there's more - you have been entrusted with a Shadow Stone, an ancient artifact that will unlock your shadow powers."

"Shadow powers?" Emma's voice trembled, "you guys are kidding. What are you even talking about."

Shaking my head, I plowed on. May as well get it all out and let her sit in shock for a while. Then we can answer all her questions at once. "Once you accept and absorb the Shadow Stone, you'll be able to access your full potential. It won't be an easy journey, but you're not alone. We're here to help you every step of the way."

Silence fell over the table before she burst out laughing.

"Damn, you're good. Either you're joking, or you're just crazy."

"Emma," I said softly, reaching out to place a reassuring hand on her arm. "You were born for this, and I know you have the strength and courage to embrace your destiny."

"Destiny? DESTINY? I'm an orphan who was stalked by a lunatic and happened to find my way here. There is no *destiny*. Only a series of choices and consequences for those choices. You're insane."

I allowed her a moment and just observed as she looked around the table at each of the guys. None of them cracked a smile. None laughed along with her.

"What? No, this can't be real."

"It is." Gabe said, "It's nothing to be concerned about; it's a blessing. From your ancestors. Their way of protecting you and your gifts. The stone holds the key to your heritage."

A tear rolled down her cheek. "I still think you're insane, but I'll hear you out."

We hesitated, unsure of where to start. Thankfully, Roman began at the beginning, making sure not to leave anything out. Gabe chipped in now and then when he derailed, but overall, he did a good job of explaining the last few months.

She looked up at me, her eyes shimmering with a mixture of fear and resolve. "Okay," she whispered. "I'll do it. I'm still in shock. So you'll have to bear with me."

"Basically, how I felt when I found out I was the last Seraph ina... and Nik... the last Lycan," I said.

After a few moments of silence, I knew it was time to offer Emma the path forward. "There is a forest outside the pack boundaries where we can train you. It's a place hidden from the rest of the world, where you can learn to harness your powers without fear of being discovered."

Emma looked at me with wide eyes, both excited and nervous. "You mean... I'll be able to control these shadow powers?" she asked hesitantly.

"Sure you will," I replied. "With proper training, you'll learn to manipulate shadows, channel darkness, and probably more. It's a powerful gift, but one that comes with its own set of risks."

"Risks?" Emma's voice quivered ever so slightly as she sought clarification.

"Darkness attracts darkness," I explained, choosing my words carefully. "The more you use your powers, the more attention you may draw from other supernatural beings – some of whom might not have the best intentions. But don't worry, we'll teach you how to protect yourself and stay hidden when necessary." My thoughts lingered on the countless dangers that awaited her. "You also run the risk, as Nik did, of being consumed by it. He is still learning to control his balance, and so must you."

"Okay. I'll do it. When can we start?"

"Tonight, if you're up for it. We'll begin after sunset, under the cover of darkness. It's the best time for you to connect with your new abilities."

"Thank you, Avery," she murmured. "For everything."

"Of course," I assured her, giving her hand a comforting squeeze. "You're one of us now, and we'll always be here for you."

As the hours passed, anticipation hummed through the air like a current, electric and alive. It was a mixture of excitement and trepidation, as we all knew that Emma's training would either make or break us.

Night finally fell, shrouding the world in darkness. As Emma and I ventured into the grove, the moon cast its silvery glow upon the earth.

"Are you ready?" I asked.

Emma took a deep breath, drawing strength from within. "Yes. Let's do this."

In the shadows, surrounded by the ancient trees, Emma stood ready. Ready to embrace her destiny and unlock the power hidden deep within her soul.

I watched as she twiddled her thumbs in the center of the clearing, her eyes wide and alert. She took a deep breath, searching for something deep within herself. The moonlight filtered through the canopy, casting shadows on her face.

"Alright, let's begin with some basics," I instructed, my voice steady. "Your shadow powers come from your connection to the darkness. You'll be able to manipulate shadows and use them to your advantage."

She nodded, a determined look in her eyes.

"First, focus on the shadows around you," I guided her. "Feel their energy and try to connect with it."

She closed her eyes and took a deep breath. Slowly, she extended her hands toward the ground. The shadows seemed to respond to her, reaching out and intertwining with her fingers like tendrils of smoke. Her face lit up with wonder. She wore a look of shock as they wrapped around her arm, humming with energy.

"Amazing, Emma! Now, let's try to make the shadows move." I demonstrated by lifting my own hand and moving it back and forth. She mimicked my movement, and the shadows obeyed her command, swirling around her, dancing and alive.

"Wow," she whispered, staring at her arms with an expression of pure amazement. "I never thought I'd be able to do this. Or that I'd be doing this at all."

"You're doing great," I encouraged her. "Now, let's try something more advanced. Focus on creating a shadow shield. This will protect you from harm."

"Okay," she said, taking a deep breath. She manipulated the shadows into a solid barrier around her with intense concentration. It shimmered with dark energy.

"Emma, that's incredible!" I praised, watching her progress with awe. "You truly have a gift for this. You're learning so quickly! It took me forever to figure some stuff out, but you've got a knack for this. I can't wait to see what you can do with the stone."

As she continued to practice, her confidence and mastery grew. The shadows seemed to bend to her will effortlessly, as if they had been waiting for her all along.

"Can I tell you something?" Emma asked hesitantly, her eyes meeting mine.

"Of course," I replied, curious about what was on her mind.

"Growing up, I always felt different," she admitted quietly. "I never quite fit in with others. There was this feeling deep inside me... like there was something special about me, just waiting to be discovered. I used to dream of a dark angel clothed in black going on adventures and protecting the planet. Whenever I was bullied, I thought of her; it brought me peace."

"Emma," I said softly, wanting her to understand how important she was. "That feeling you had? It wasn't wrong. You are special – not just because you're the last Dark Faerie, but because of who you are. And now, with these powers, you have the opportunity to make a real difference in our world."

As she absorbed my words, I could see the weight of her identity slowly settling upon her shoulders. But instead of fear or doubt, there was a spark of determination in her eyes. She was ready to embrace her destiny. She had found the forgotten piece inside of her and was grabbing onto it.

With the moon watching over us from above, we intensified our training. I devised a rigorous schedule for her, ensuring she would be prepared to wield her powers with precision and control.

"Alright, Emma," I began. "We'll start with two-hour sessions every evening, gradually increasing the duration as your stamina improves. We'll focus on honing your skills in manipulating shadows, moving through them, and even using them as a weapon."

"Got it," Emma nodded.

"Remember, it's crucial to maintain balance within yourself," I continued, watching her closely. "Too much power can overwhelm you, so we'll also work on exercises to help you stay centered, like meditation."

"Right." She replied, wiping the sweat off her brow.

"Awesome, let's get back to work. So much to do, so little time." I said, smiling as she resumed her battle stance.

37: Gabriel

The air grew heavy as a sudden chill ran down my spine. Nik was restless as he scanned the horizon, his muscles tense beneath his skin. It was clear he sensed something we didn't.

"Gabriel," Nik whispered, his voice strained with urgency. "They're close. Sion and Belial's forces... I can feel them."

"Are you sure?" I asked; the thought shattered my hope for this nightmare to just disappear.

"Positive," he replied, his jaw clenched. "We don't have much time. A week, maybe. Two at the most. Don't you feel the shift?"

I could see the flicker of uncertainty in Emma's eyes as she looked between us. Avery stood beside her, her hands clenched tightly against her side. We had been reading ancient texts to understand more about the bonds of magic between the three of them. Almost all had come up with nothing, except that they needed to be able to use their powers as one... and Emma needed to accept and absorb the Shadow Stone, which she had yet to do.

"Alright," I said, taking a deep breath. "Whatever time we have left, we use to train."

I went to work and devised new strategies and techniques to strengthen their abilities; I had taken the role of trainer extraordinaire since my thirst for reading was unquenchable... and Nik was too distracted figuring out what new powers he had with his Lunar Stone. With every passing day, the air grew heavier with impending danger, but we had no choice but to push forward.

"Emma," I called out as she sparred with Avery. "Focus on your movements. Each strike must be precise, calculated."

"Got it," she responded, her dark hair flying behind her as she spun, landing a solid hit on Avery's side. She winced but quickly recovered, retaliating with a swift punch that sent Emma stumbling back.

"Good. Now, Nik," I turned towards the Lycan, who was practicing his agility. "You need to be faster, more agile. Use your senses to anticipate your enemy's strikes."

"Really, man? Why don't you train? You're out here yelling at us when we're the ones doing all the work," he grunted, leaping over a series of obstacles I had set up, his body twisting mid-air. The sound of his claws scraping against the ground grated against my ears.

"Again!" I ignored his whining. The time for whining had passed. We only had time to perfect their connection to each other.

As the days wore on, I watched Emma, Avery, and Nik grow more and more confident in their abilities. Every bruise, every ache, and every drop of sweat drew them closer to unification. They practiced relentlessly, honing their skills and learning to work as a cohesive unit.

"Gabriel," Avery said one evening after an intense sparring session. "Do you think we're ready?"

I hesitated for a moment, my eyes meeting hers. "We have to be. We don't have another choice."

Her shoulders slumped as she walked back to the house. Morale was low, and I wasn't sure how to boost it because I felt it too. Death. It clung to the air the nearer darkness drew.

The following morning, I found Emma sitting on a moss-covered rock, her eyes fixed on the Shadow Stone clutched between her delicate fingers. The sky was clouded with an eerie darkness, casting an ominous shadow over our training grounds.

"Emma," I said gently as I approached her. "We need to talk."

"About what?" she asked, her gaze never leaving the stone.

"About that," pointing at the stone, I smiled. "You need to absorb it as Avery and Nik absorbed theirs. It becomes a part of you. You're ready for it, and if there was ever a time, this is it. Do you feel it? The harmony inside of you?"

"I do," she said, her grip on the stone tightening. "For once in my life, I feel like I have a purpose, a meaning."

"I'll be here to help you, Emma. I won't let you do this alone." I guided her through a series of breathing exercises and mental techniques to help her focus. As she concentrated, the stone began to pulse with dark energy, its shadows reaching out to entwine with Emma's essence.

"Feel the connection between yourself and the stone," I watched as her face contorted with effort. "Embrace its power and allow it to become an extension of your being."

As she continued to focus, the Shadow Stone came alive in her hands. The dark within the stone danced and swirled, responding to her every thought and emotion. It was a mesmerizing sight, but I knew we were only scratching the surface of its potential. As we watched, it suddenly melted into the palm of her hand, disappearing as dark veins spread through her body before she returned to normal. Just behind her ear, I saw a dark star imprint itself like a tattoo.

"Emma, the three of you were chosen long ago to wield these powers. Just because it's new to you right now doesn't mean your blood, your bones, don't remember."

She nodded. "I understand. Honestly, I don't feel much different, and maybe that's a good thing. I was expecting some kind of weird evil to take hold of my soul, but I feel peaceful so far. If anything, I feel better than I have in days. Stronger, perhaps."

The sun dipped below the horizon, casting an eerie glow over the training grounds as we regrouped. Roman and I stood at the front as the Trinity formed a line.

"Alright. We've covered individual techniques; now it's time to practice working together. Remember, our enemies won't be fighting one-on-one, either. You three need to figure out how to work as a unit."

Avery cracked her knuckles and grinned at Roman while Nik flexed his muscular arms, ready to shift at a moment's notice. Emma looked thoughtful; her brow furrowed.

"Emma," I said softly, drawing her attention. "You need to dig deep to figure out how to use your powers. Avery has had months. Nik knows what to do, but you need to focus. Focus on amplifying your strengths and countering enemy attacks."

"Got it," she replied, nodding. She closed her eyes, took a deep breath, and then opened them again, her hand pulsing with a shadowy glow.

"Ready?" They assumed their battle stances, their faces locked in concentration.

"Begin."

As I watched them spar, I was struck by how fluid their movements were, each one seamlessly transitioning from offense to defense, their actions perfectly complementing one another. The air crackled with energy as Avery unleashed her light, wings unfurling, her strikes swift and deadly. Nik's Lycan was a blur of fur and muscle, darting in and out with precision. And Emma, who it appeared, was a natural, wove shadows around her companions, bolstering their abilities while hindering their imaginary foes.

"Excellent!" I shouted, unable to contain my enthusiasm. "Keep it up!"

As they continued to refine their tactics, I felt hope rise for the first time in a while. We could do this. They could do this.

"Alright, break," I called eventually, sweat glistening on their brows. "Now that you've got a handle on working together, it's time to put your skills to the test."

"Meaning?" Avery asked, panting slightly as she wiped the sweat from her forehead.

"Meaning..." I grinned wolfishly, "We're going on a demon hunt. I've seen changes in the woods just outside the border. Roman went to check and confirmed my suspicions. There's a small outpost. We are going to take them out."

We set off under the cloak of darkness, moving stealthily through the woods. The tension was palpable; we all knew how high the stakes were—the first test.

"Showtime," I muttered, adrenaline surging through my veins.

We readied as we prepared to face our enemy head-on. This would be our first real challenge as a team, and I hope that our training has prepared them for it.

The moon hung low in the sky, casting a strange glow on our surroundings as we trekked through the forest. Shadows danced around us, creating a haunting atmosphere, but for once, it didn't feel eerie. Emma was in control.

The demon's lair was a grotesque sight. Its walls were slick with a sticky substance, and the air reeked of decay. We moved in cautiously. Footsteps light and precise.

"Stay focused," I whispered. "We can do this."

Nik let out a low growl, his Lycan instincts on full alert. He motioned for us to stop, then pointed at something lurking in the shadows. A pair of glowing red eyes stared back at us. Showtime.

"Here we go," Roman muttered, shifting effortlessly. His muscles rippled beneath his fur, and he bared his teeth menacingly and lunged forward.

38: Gabriel

The battle that ensued was intense and brutal. We fought with everything we had, relying on the skills and techniques we'd honed during our training sessions. Emma used her Dark Faerie powers to immobilize the demon while Avery, Roman, and Nik attacked it relentlessly.

"Keep pushing!" I shouted as a giant demon tried to regain its footing. I tried to flank behind it but got stuck between lesser demons and a wall.

Just as victory seemed within our grasp, it unleashed a powerful counterattack, knocking us all back with a deafening roar. Avery cried out in pain, clutching her arm. As she screamed, the demon paused, allowing me a chance to escape and rush to her.

"Are you okay?"

"Yeah," she breathed, wincing. "Just a scratch. Keep fighting."

"Stand behind everyone," I tried not to sound panicked, but my heart raced. "Heal yourself before you come back."

"Right," Avery nodded.

The demon suffered deep wounds as I circled it, finding a spot where its skin hung off its body. Grabbing a hold of it, I ripped and slashed until it started swaying back and forth. Nik and Emma worked to finish it off. She created a barrier around him as he leaped up and beheaded it with one powerful swipe of his claws. Dust kicked off the ground, and it fell with a thud.

"You guys were incredible," Emma beamed, her face flushed with adrenaline.

"Couldn't have done it without you," Roman said, shifting back into his human form and clapping her on the shoulder.

"Let's get out of this place," Avery shuddered, glancing at the remains of the demon. "I don't like it here."

"Agreed," I said, leading the way out of the lair. "Let's eat and rest. We did well today."

We left the darkness behind us, deep in thought. Despite our setbacks and imperfections, we had grown closer. Our bond was finally complete; the Trinity was whole. Light, dark, and the balance that binds them together.

"Guys," Emma's voice broke the silence. "I've been thinking about the Shadow Stone. I believe there's more power within it that I haven't tapped into yet. I feel stronger, but I also... sense stuff."

"Interesting. What stuff do you sense? Like visions?"

Emma nodded.

"That's amazing, Emma! That will come in handy whenever Belial decides to show up."

She beamed, "I'm glad I'm a part of the group, Avery. Even if just a small part."

"You're not small, Emma, you're anything but."

"Alright, we're almost home. Since we're on our own for the most part, you're just going to have to see what happens and when it happens and go from there."

"Okay, Gabe."

Once we made it back, we decided to have a bonfire to celebrate our victory. Roman busted out the s'mores, and Nik poured hefty drinks. Soon, we were all relaxed and having a good time.

"Man, we should have showered first; we stink." Roman sniffed his armpits and gagged, "Gabe, you're a brutal trainer, man. If this is how bad I smell, I can't wait to see how bad Avery smells."

"Gross!" She giggled as she chugged her drink, Nik at the ready to pour her another one. Eh fuck it, let them have fun. Those demons were close for a reason.

"I miss the twins," Avery said as she sighed and sat down next to me. "I also miss you. Can we go and talk while Roman and Nik entertain Emma?"

"Sure, my love. Hey guys, we will be back in a bit," I yelled.

No sooner had we left their visible line of sight did she thrust herself upon me. "Just in case tomorrow doesn't show." She whispered before her lips consumed mine. I was shocked for a moment but soon let go of all my inhibitions. Her kiss was passionate and hungry, and I could feel the heat radiating through her body. Her hands were all over me, pulling me closer as her lips passionately moved against mine.

We broke apart, both gasping for breath. "I've been wanting to do that for so long," she said, her voice low and husky. "It feels like we never have time for each other anymore."

She was right. We'd been having more group sex lately, which was great, but I craved time alone with her. "Me too," I admitted before leaning in to kiss her again. This time, our kiss was slower, more tender, and full of unspoken promises and desires.

Taking her hand, I led her to a nearby tree. Placing one hand against the trunk of the tree, I wrapped the other around her waist as I pulled her closer to me. My fingertips explored every exposed inch of her body. Her hands explored me in return, leaving trails of fire on my skin wherever she touched. Soon, our clothes were discarded, and we stood there with nothing between us but the air itself.

My fingers slipped inside her warmth as I thrust them into her throbbing depths. She moaned loudly, pushing hard against my hand as she rocked her clit against my palm. Hitting the right spot, she reached orgasmic bliss in my arms. Her pussy clenched, and her juice ran down my hand until I popped my fingers out and licked it off. Delicious. She wanted to continue, but I just wanted this moment to be about her. Avery always gave freely of herself, but this was about loving her. No expectations, no giving back.

"It's getting really late," Avery whispered, pulling her pants back up. "We should get some sleep."

By the time we got back, someone had already put the fire out, and the night was still. The house was quiet as we made our way to the shower, quickly cleaning ourselves and dropping into bed next to a snoring Roman. Nik had just about fallen off the bed, one leg on the floor, arms spread wide.

I shoved them aside and placed Avery in the middle, cuddling up against her and wrapping her in my arms. My thoughts drifted to the twins, the beautiful babies my angel had brought into the world, and all I could think about was seeing her swollen with child again and again as we expanded our family with her. The only thing that caused me to shake that thought was the fact that there was a giant, looming dark cloud of evil that we had to battle… and I didn't know whether we would all make it home.

"I love you, my beautiful warrior princess. You are everything to me and more." I whispered into her hair as she sighed and wiggled her butt against me.

39: Gabriel

The air was thick with tension as we approached the pack-house from the training grounds. The scent of burning wood filled my nostrils while the distant screams and chaos reached my ears. Avery gripped my hand tightly as we surveyed the scene before us – the once-welcoming town hall was now engulfed in flames and swarming with demons. The carpentry was on fire. Shit. It had been a week since we fought the demons in that cave, a very silent week. And now this.

"Gabriel, this doesn't look good," Nik said.

"We need to protect the women and children."

"What do you want us to do, Gabe?" Avery looked panicked as she surveyed the destruction.

"Fight," I said, planting a reassuring kiss on her lips before turning my attention back to the battlefield.

"Follow me!" I shouted to the strays, charging forward into the fray. The sound of ripping flesh followed as our army descended into the horde of demons, unafraid.

"Gabriel!" Roman yelled. He was fighting two at once while he was half-shifted. His claws were slicing at them, and soon enough, they lay dead at his feet. "We've got more coming!"

"Keep pushing, we're almost there!"

As we neared the entrance to our underground bunker, I caught sight of Belial, his face twisted into a grin amidst the carnage. Our eyes locked for a brief moment, his hatred palpable even from a distance. He would pay for what he'd done.

"Roman, Nik! You two handle the rest of these demons, clear the path. I'm going to gather the women and children."

"Be safe, brother," Nik urged, his eyes full of concern.

"Take care of our girl," my gaze never left Belial as I moved quickly towards the terrified women and children scurrying around, desperately trying to get out of the way of advancing demons.

"Always," Roman affirmed, nodding solemnly as he and Nik continued to battle.

My heart pounded, but I couldn't let fear control me – lives were at stake. Surveying the chaos unfolding around us, I quickly assessed our situation. Our pack members were scattered and disoriented amidst the battle, making them easy targets. Within minutes, Emma had cut a sizeable dent in the demons, allowing a straight shot to the pack members huddled together. Her shadows were holding them at bay as they made a break for the center of her shield.

"Everyone, listen up!" I bellowed, cutting through the screams and chaos, before switching to mind link, reaching everyone at once. "Run as fast as you can to the bunker! Quickly, go!"

As they ran, Emma strained against the increasing number of attackers pushing against her barrier. Avery rushed and stood beside her, creating another shield of light. If we weren't in the middle of a deathmatch, I'd say it was pretty damn beautiful, the way the colors swirled together.

"Gabriel, what do we do?" one of our younger warrior members asked.

"Fight back with everything you've got," I instructed. "Protect each other and trust your instincts. You'll make it through this."

Nodding resolutely, he joined the others in forming a defensive line against the invader. Hope ignited within me as the pack members began to work together, coordinating their attacks and shielding one another from harm. Despite the odds stacked against us, we wouldn't go down without a fight.

"Let's show these monsters they picked the wrong pack to mess with!" I roared. The pack took up the rallying cry, our voices merging into a fierce battle anthem that echoed across the battlefield.

"Belial will pay for what he's done!" Roman vowed, his eyes blazing with fury as he joined me. As Emma's shield broke, Nik was ushering the women and children into the bunker. She looked exhausted as she stumbled back. But there she stood, my Seraphina. She glowed as her barrier pulsated with light. Looking back at us, she nodded. She was okay, and her energy was stable as she bought us more time.

"Everyone, follow me to the underground bunkers!" I shouted as we picked up small children on the way—their parents were nowhere to be seen.

"But Avery-"

"Avery will be fine, Roman; trust in her. Get your ass moving and get these kids to safety. Now."

"Emma, make sure no one gets left behind."

Without any further delay, we ran, our footsteps pounding against the earth in unison as we sprinted through the pandemonium unfolding around us. The air crackled with tension, thick with the bitter tang of smoke and the acrid scent of fear.

"Watch out!" Roman bellowed as a demon lunged at us from the shadows, its twisted form barely visible in the darkness. Nik sprang into action, his claws slid through the creature with lethal precision as he swiftly dispatched it back to the infernal depths.

"Keep moving!"

"Almost there, just a little further!" Avery encouraged, suddenly appearing beside me. "It broke. I took down as many as I could as it shattered. It bought us a few moments."

I nodded. With a final burst of speed, we reached the bunker entrance, working together to push people inside.

"Inside, quickly," I ordered, my gaze sweeping over the frightened faces of our pack as they scrambled to follow my command. "We'll hold them off as long as we can."

As the last of our pack disappeared beneath the ground, I couldn't help but feel a fleeting sense of relief. They had made it – for now.

"Let's do this," Roman muttered as he slammed the bunker door shut.

The five of us stood and faced an army and a demon lord.

Do or die, it's our time to shine.

40: Nikolai

The air was thick with the stench of sulfur as we approached the front lines. I could feel the heat of the battle lick at my skin, urging me to join the destruction. My chest tightened with anticipation, and my heart raced in tune with the adrenaline coursing through my veins. I glanced over at Avery, so beautiful as her wings spread wide and her palms glowed. Beside her, Emma wrung her hands nervously, but she held her chin high, ready for the fight.

"Are you ready?" I asked them.

"As we'll ever be," Avery grabbed Emma's hand and squeezed before releasing it.

We moved closer to Belial's position, and Roman and Gabriel shifted, their bodies morphing with a sickening crunch of bone and sinew. Their fur bristled, muscles rippling with power as they snarled at the demons surrounding us. The sight gave me goosebumps, and excitement coursed through me; my brothers were powerful as fuck.

"Emma, you're up," I said, nodding toward the sea of demons that lay between us and our target. She closed her eyes briefly, her hands weaving intricate patterns in the air. As if in response, shadows began to swirl around us, forming a barrier that repelled the demons as we advanced. She began to tire, so Avery stepped forward.

"Nice work," Avery whispered appreciatively. Palms facing outward, she unleashed a powerful gust of wind that cleared a path straight through the demon horde. They flew left and right their bodies hit the ground, bones gutting out of their skin. Emma brought up the rear, holding her barrier to prevent any stragglers from hitting us from behind.

"Keep moving!" I shouted, ripping apart any demons that made it through Avery's vortex. "We're almost there!"

Roman and Gabriel tore through the demons with brutal efficiency, leaving a trail of destruction in their wake. Their ferocity was both awe-inspiring and terrifying, but it was exactly what we needed to reach Belial—unrestrained havoc.

As we finally broke through the last line of defenders, Belial loomed ahead, his grotesque form pulsating with dark energy. This was it – the moment we had been training for. Exhausted but not without hope, we formed a triangle with Emma at the helm. She looked so small as she stood there, looking up at him in defiance.

Roman and Gabriel flanked us, tearing any creature that dared approach to shreds. It was just us and Belial.

"Watch out!" Avery shouted. A demon lunged at Roman from the side, but before it could reach him, Avery conjured a whip of light that sliced through the air and decapitated it with chilling precision. He howled in response.

I focused on my own strengths, pulling down deep. My roar just about deafened me, but it was enough to distract him from hitting the women with whatever goop he was throwing at them. The angrier I got, the bigger I became, my body stretching and pulling at itself until I towered above the battleground, hitting half of Belial's height. Running forward, I felt Emma's shadows stretch around my arms, forming shadow swords. Each strike seemed to chip away at the dark shield surrounding him, but I knew we needed something more. All this was doing was serving to deplete us before we were even close to killing him.

"Emma, Avery, get ready," I said, gritting my teeth as I felt my strength waning. "We need to combine our powers to bring him to his knees."

"Understood," they replied.

As Roman and Gabriel continued to tear through the demonic horde, Emma, Avery, and I moved closer to Belial. We joined, our abilities flowing like streams converging into a raging river.

"Ready?" I asked, feeling the power within us building to a crescendo.

"Ready," they both answered, their eyes locked on our target.

"NOW!" Avery and Emma's energies swirled around me. Light created a shield and darkness gave me weapons. As the two mixed and muddied, ancient runes burned onto my skin, lighting the battlefield in an explosion of color. The air crackled with energy as we poured everything we had into this final assault. The ground trembled as I ran forward, swords raised.

Belial stepped back as I swung at him, laughing when he clipped me in the shoulder before he screamed. The runes burned him. Good. Let him feel pain.

We pushed forward as a unit, one, but three. The light held firm as the shadows swirled and danced before reforming into my swords to slash at him again and again. As his blood spewed from his wounds, it ate away at the ground.

"Don't let his blood hit you. It'll eat right through you," I yelled as I cut off his arm.

Just as we were on the verge of victory, something hit me with a bolt of lightning. I barely had time to register the pain. Avery gasped as she frantically looked around.

"There! Sion!"

"Roman, Gabriel, go kill that bastard," I called out, catching a glimpse of Sion at the edge of the battlefield, his hands weaving intricate patterns as he sent a volley of magical blasts into our ranks.

"Got it, Nik!" They dashed and weaved as they tore after him.

"Emma, can you create a diversion?" I choked out as Avery's light pushed and probed at my wound, healing it as fast as she could.

"Leave it to me," she replied, darkness swirling around her like a tempest of shadows. With a flick of her wrist, Emma summoned a horde of writhing spirit serpents that slithered towards Sion, their fanged maws snapping hungrily.

The sudden change of focus startled Sion, forcing him to shift his attention from us to defending himself against the ravenous spirits. It wasn't enough to drive him off entirely, but it bought us the precious time we needed.

"Let's move!" I urged my mate, feeling a surge of determination. We had to press our advantage while Sion began to run for his life at the sight of two massive werewolves descending upon him, shadows swirling around their forms in a protective casing.

"He's gone," Avery yelled, her voice steady despite the chaos that surrounded us. "Roman and Gabe drove him off; let's finish this."

My body was strong; it felt near invincible as the runes glowed brightly, illuminating the battleground.

"Emma, we need to break through his defenses," I grit my teeth as I slashed at him again. He seemed to be regenerating before our very eyes. Where his hand was once missing, a new one was in its place. Bastard. Sion bought him just enough time to heal.

"Got it, Nik," Emma panted, her hands moving in fluid, intricate patterns, weaving a spell that would hopefully weaken Belial's defenses. Magic swirled around her as she concentrated. Soon, Avery joined her, the two chanting in ancient tongues, conjuring a spell together.

"Focus your energy. Combine it with mine," Avery urged, her own energy connecting with mine and Emma's, creating a brilliant rainbow of white, grey, and black. The surge of combined power between us pulsated with raw intensity.

"This is it!" I yelled, feeling a height of power I had never felt before crackling through my body. The resulting blast sent shockwaves rippling through the battlefield, cracking Belial's defenses and causing him to stagger back in surprise.

"Urgghh, what is this?" Belial snarled, his voice a guttural growl as he struggled to maintain his footing.

"The end," I retorted. This was our chance; we couldn't let it slip away.

"Roman, Gabriel – go for his legs!" Avery commanded. They darted in to bite and slash at his lower limbs, forcing him to divide his attention between them and us.

"Emma, we need another opening." With all of us focussing on Belial, the demons were starting to box us in. "Can you summon more of those shadow things?"

"Of course," she replied, a wicked grin on her face as she once again conjured the writhing masses. They slithered forward, their fangs sinking into Belial's flesh, eliciting roars of pain from the demon lord. Her hands shook as bolts of darkness struck into the horde that was moving in.

"Let's finish this," Avery whispered fiercely, each of us pouring the last of our strength into one final, devastating blow. Our powers intertwined, a harmonious dance of light and dark, as we attacked as one.

There was no clapping, no chorus of angels as the demon lord fell with a thud, his body split open as his blood soaked the ground.

As he fell, so too did his army, their screams of defeat echoing through the night like the cries of tormented souls. Exhausted and battered, we stood victorious, each of us knowing that we had only succeeded through our unwavering trust in one another.

"Oh, my Goddess, we did it. Holy shit, man, we did it!"

"Yes... it appears we did." Avery said, sweat shining on her brow as she looked upon the slowly dissipating body. Her worn face shone brightly as she hugged Emma.

We'd hardly had time to celebrate when Roman started shouting. "Look, Sion!" He pointed at the fleeing figure in the distance.

"Everyone, regroup! Let's go after him!" I commanded, my heart thundering in my chest as the adrenaline from our victory coursed through me. *Two birds, one stone. Two birds, one stone.* I repeated the mantra as we tore after him.

The ground beneath our feet felt uneven and treacherous, littered with the remnants of the defeated demons. The stench of their demise clung to the air.

"Gabriel, can you use your speed to catch up to him?" Avery asked, her breaths coming in shallow gasps as she tried to keep pace with the rest of us.

"I'll try." He tore off, leaving the rest of us desperately trying to catch up.

"Emma, if he gets away, can you track him?" I questioned, glancing at the Dark Faerie. Her eyes were narrowed in concentration, her hands glowing faintly with power.

"Perhaps, but it won't be easy. I don't track as well as you do, Nik," Emma admitted, her frustration evident in her tone.

"I can only track with my nose. We will think of something."

As we neared the edge of the forest, Sion slipped into its depths like a shadow disappearing into the night. We were too late. The dense trees and underbrush would make it next to impossible to follow him now.

"Damn it," Roman muttered, kicking at a fallen branch in anger. "Why can't anything ever go smoothly?"

"Because life isn't a fairy tale, Roman," Avery said softly, her voice tinged with fatigue. "But we did what we were meant to do. We defeated Belial."

"True, but now we have another problem. Sion is still out there, and who knows what he'll do next." Honestly, this was a buzzkill. The thought of him plotting another attack weighed heavily on my mind.

"Let's head back," Emma suggested, her shoulder slumped. "We need to regroup and heal before we can even think of doing anything else. We've won great today, but the war isn't over yet."

As we turned away from the depths of the forest, I felt a strange mixture of hope and regret churning within me. We had triumphed against a formidable foe, but Sion remained beyond our reach. We had achieved so much, yet it still felt like we were always behind.

41: Roman

The moon hung heavy in the sky, a lone nightingale bearing witness to the aftermath of the fierce battle that had raged mere hours before. I surveyed the battlefield, my heart still pounding, the taste of victory bittersweet on my tongue. The scent of blood and sweat clung to my skin as my mate and brothers stood beside me. We did what we were meant to do.

"Are you right?" I saw Avery tremble as she stopped to rest.

"I'll be fine," she replied, her voice soft and weary. "We did it, Roman. We won."

Gabriel's face bore a gash that would surely scar, even as it rapidly healed, but his eyes shone with pride. "We fought well together. We are stronger than ever."

"Yep, still didn't get Sion, though," Nik was bitter. We all felt the same, but he always took the lion's share of bitterness for some reason. He sighed before continuing. "But let us not forget those who fell protecting our pack. They died protecting our home, our family."

We unlatched the bunker, and bleary-eyed people made their way out. Women and children who no longer had their husbands or fathers. Sisters without brothers, mothers without sons. They had fought bravely as the demons first descended on our people, and they will never be forgotten. We saved many when we chose to take on Belial alone, but the pain that we got here when it was too late to save them all, would stay with us forever.

"Tonight," I announced, "we honor our victory and the sacrifices of our fallen brothers and sisters. Their bravery will never be forgotten."

A mix of sobs and cheers erupted from the pack as they filed out of the bunker, tired voices raised in both triumph and defeat. The victory was bittersweet, but it was a victory nonetheless, and we had to hold onto that.

We went down to see that everyone had made it out, but a few were still sitting around. Jasmine had already administered first-aid to most who were injured, many minor, but one looked pretty bad. Nik carried him out and laid him on the ground.

"Roman, grab some bandages from my bag," she instructed, gently probing the injured wolf's side. I did as she asked, finding the items quickly and handing them over.

"Thank you," she muttered, working carefully to wrap the wounded warrior's torso. "This one will recover, they got him with silver, but there was another..." She trailed off, glancing at the lifeless wolf with sorrowful eyes. The weight of the loss hung heavy in the air.

"May your spirit soar, brave one," I whispered, bowing my head in respect.

"A few others never made it back."

When every last warrior had been accounted for, we gathered the pack together and announced plans for a grand celebration of life to honor their courage and sacrifice.

By dusk the next day, preparations were well underway, and the atmosphere in our territory began to shift from somber to joyous anticipation.

We had built an immense pyre constructed from logs and branches. It was situated in a large clearing near the heart of our land, a place where countless generations of our kind had gathered to celebrate victories, mourn losses, and solidify bonds. As the sun dipped below the horizon, the fire was ignited, and soon, an enormous blaze roared to life, casting flickering shadows on the trees that encircled us.

"May our fire cleanse our wounds and celebrate our triumphs," I declared, my voice booming over the crackling flames. "Tonight, we honor each and every one of you who fought bravely to protect each other. We honor those who go home with heavy hearts. You are the pillars on which this pack is built."

As the bonfire blazed, a sense of unity washed over us all. The flames seemed to reach out, touching our very souls and binding us together in a way words couldn't.

"Let the festivities begin!" Nik raised his glass and then downed it in one gulp.

As the pack reveled in the festivities, I couldn't help but steal glances at Avery, her eyes shimmering like stars in the firelight. She stood beside me, her laughter and joy infectious to everyone around her. Wherever she went, people crowded, wanting to bask in her presence.

"Can we have your attention, please?" Gabriel asked loudly, his deep voice cutting through the chatter and laughter that filled the air.

The noise gradually died down as everyone turned their gazes towards us, their curiosity piqued. Nik, Gabriel, and I exchanged knowing looks before turning our focus on the woman who had captured our hearts.

"Avery. This ordeal has shown us how much you mean to us, how much you've become an essential part of our very souls." Tears pricked at my eyes.

"Your strength, courage, and love have guided us through the darkest of times," Gabriel added, his eyes never leaving her face. "We can't imagine facing another day without you by our sides."

Nik chimed in. "Baby girl, we know this is not conventional, but the bond we share transcends tradition. We love you more than words can express, and we're willing to face whatever challenges may come if it means we can be together forever."

"Will you marry us, Avery? All three of us?" my heart raced, and I broke out in a sweat.

Her eyes glistened with unshed tears as she looked between the three of us. Her smile was radiant and full of love. "Yes," she whispered before yelling. "Yes, oh my Goddess, yes, I will marry all of you."

We pulled her into a group embrace, our relief and joy palpable as we held one another tightly. The pack erupted into cheers and applause, their excitement loud and catching.

"Everyone!" I shouted, raising my voice above the din. "Meet your new Alpha!"

She looked up at me, stunned.

"What, you didn't think we'd make you a Luna? Though Luna's are equal to Alpha's, we felt it more fitting to have us all with the same title given what we've been through."

"Oh, Roman, you are something else," she threw her arms around me and kissed me passionately.

"Let this celebration mark not only our victory in battle but also the beginning of our future together," Gabriel declared, his joy evident in his wide grin.

"Here, here!" Nik proclaimed, raising his hand to the sky as if toasting the heavens themselves.

"Here, here!" the others echoed, their voices strong and unified.

As the pack's cheers reverberated through the air, I couldn't help but notice the few individuals who seemed less enthusiastic about the impending union. A hushed murmur echoed between a small group of elder wolves, their eyes narrowed and brows furrowed as they exchanged glances.

"Roman," Avery whispered in my ear. "Do you think everyone is okay with this?"

I met her gaze, seeing the fire flickering behind her eyes that ignited whenever she was passionate about something. I pulled her closer, reassuring her. "Our love has brought us this far. There will always be some who are resistant to change, but we'll face it together."

"Love conquers all," Gabriel grabbed her hand and gave it a gentle squeeze.

The celebration continued around us, oblivious to the grumpy old wolves gossiping in the corner. Tables laden with food lined the perimeter of the clearing – freshly caught game, fruits and vegetables harvested from our fields, and jugs of sweet honey mead. Laughter and conversation filled the air, punctuated by the occasional howl of triumph.

Nik, who surprisingly was becoming the life of the party, led a group of younger wolves in an impromptu dance around the fire, their movements wild and uninhibited. The beat of drums accompanied their steps, the rhythm pulsating through the ground beneath our feet.

"Come on," Avery said, pulling me towards the dancers with a mischievous grin. "Let's join them."

Her laughter rang like silver bells as we danced, her hand entwined with mine. As we swirled through the excited throng, our eyes locked, and for a moment, it was as if the entire world had ceased to exist.

"Roman," she murmured, her breath warm against my cheek. "Tonight is perfect. Defeating Belial... our engagement... it's all so surreal."

"Almost perfect," I replied, brushing a stray lock of hair from her face. "There's just one thing missing."

"What's that?" She asked.

"Our babies," I said as her face creased in a soft smile, tears welling in her eyes. "It's almost time to go bring them home."

The fire burned lower as the night wore on, and the music softened to a gentle, lilting melody. We stood near the edge of the clearing, arms wrapped around each other, swaying to the delicate rhythm.

"Everything feels so right," Avery sighed, resting her head against my chest.

"Because it is," I murmured, pressing a tender kiss to the top of her head.

The celebration gradually wound down; the once roaring bonfire was now reduced to embers as pack members began to disperse, stumbling around after a few too many. The night sky, punctuated with stars, served as a reminder that a new day was dawning, bringing with it the promise of a fresh start.

I stood by Avery's side, my arm protectively wrapped around her waist. She leaned into me, her soft smile lighting up my world. Nik and Gabriel exchanged warm handshakes and pats on the back with the remaining pack members before they joined us.

"Thank you," a soft voice from behind startled me, and Emma smiled. "For everything."

"We're family," I replied. "We'll always be here for each other. Besides, we should be thanking you. You didn't have to take all of this so easily, but you did, and it's with your strength that we were able to defeat him."

Avery nodded in agreement, and we watched as Emma disappeared into the night, her silhouette swallowed by the darkness.

"Even after the battle and all the tension tonight," I thought to myself, "our pack has shown incredible resilience."

"Let's head back," Gabriel suggested, fatigue evident in his voice as we turned and walked back.

As the first light of dawn began to paint the horizon, everyone returned to their homes.

"Home at last," Gabriel sighed as we entered our home, the familiar scent of pine and earth welcoming us.

"Tomorrow is a new beginning," Avery sighed. "For all of us."

42: Emma

The sun was setting as I stood before my new home, a large cabin nestled among the towering trees in the woods just outside the village. It had been a week since the whole Belial thing, and listening to Avery with her men was... enough. They put in a rush job for this cabin in the spot I picked. The sweet scent of cherry blossoms welcomed me home as a light breeze rustled the leaves above me. It felt like a sanctuary, a much-needed reprieve.

I stepped onto the wooden porch, the boards creaking softly beneath my feet, and turned the brass doorknob, stepping inside. Warmth enveloped me in an instant, the golden glow from the fireplace casting flickering shadows on the walls. The cabin was spacious yet cozy, with high ceilings adorned with wooden beams and plush furniture that invited one to sink into their comforting embrace.

"Welcome home, Emma," I whispered to myself as I closed the door behind me, feeling a sense of peace wash over me. This was my safe haven, my own little corner of the world where I could escape the chaos that had been my life for so long.

The open-concept living area boasted a generous kitchen with sleek appliances and polished countertops gleaming under the soft lighting. A sturdy wooden dining table sat at the center, surrounded by cushioned and inviting chairs. I ran my fingers along the smooth surface, marveling at the craftsmanship as I imagined sharing meals with friends and family within these walls.

A floor-to-ceiling bookshelf lined one living room wall, filled with countless novels and volumes that begged to be read. My fingertips grazed the spines of the books as I took in their titles and genres. From romance to history, fantasy to science fiction, it seemed as though every subject imaginable was represented here.

I explored each nook and cranny and felt a sense of gratitude for everything that had led me to this moment. I'd fought alongside Avery, Roman, Gabriel, and Nik to protect our pack, and in the process, I'd discovered strengths within myself that I never knew existed.

Upstairs, there was a spacious bedroom with a four-poster bed draped in luxurious linens and an ensuite bathroom that featured a deep soaking tub and a glass-enclosed shower. The thought of relaxing in a hot bath after a long day was enough to make me sigh with longing.

My heart swelled with pride as I took in every detail of my new home, knowing that I had earned this sanctuary through my courage and determination. This cabin was more than just a place to rest my head; it symbolized the life I was building for myself – a life of independence, strength, and resilience.

The warmth of the fire crackled and danced upon my skin as I nestled into the plush sofa. Soft shadows cast by flickering flames played along the wooden walls, giving the room a cozy, almost magical atmosphere.

A sudden knock on the door shattered the tranquility, and I tensed, unprepared for the intrusion. Warily, I rose from the couch and approached the door, my heart pounding.

"Who's there?" I called out.

"Amrin," came the deep reply. "I need to speak with you, Emma."

My fingers brushed against the doorknob, hesitating for a moment before turning it. As the door swung open, I found myself face-to-face with Amrin, his tall, muscular frame filling the doorway. His dark hair fell across his forehead in an unruly manner, framing piercing blue eyes that seemed to see straight through me. Scars ran up and down his face.

"Emma," he began, his gaze never leaving mine, "you are my mate."

I blinked at him, taken aback by the intensity of his words. Shock rippled through me, followed by a wave of disbelief. "Y our... mate?" I stammered, feeling the weight of his declaration settle upon me like a heavy cloak. What the absolute hell. Why don't I have a moment of rest? Didn't someone else say I was their mate, too? What was his name? Luke or something? What happened to that guy? Did this one kill him?

"Yes," he replied, his voice unwavering. "You are my other half, the one I am destined to be with."

The very idea sent shivers down my spine, as intimidating as it was alluring. My mind raced with questions, doubts, and uncertainties, but one thing stood out above all else: the raw sincerity in his eyes. He truly believed what he was saying, and that alone was enough to make me take a step back, my heartbeat thundering in my chest.

"Um," I breathed, "I... I don't..."

"Please," he interrupted, his tone softening. "Let me explain. We can talk about this, Emma. Just give me a chance."

I hesitated, torn between the instinct to slam the door and the curiosity that gnawed at me like a persistent itch. The gravity of his words hung heavy in the air, and despite my reservations, a part of me couldn't help but wonder what it would mean to be someone's mate. With a deep breath, I stepped aside, allowing him to enter my home. This was probably stupid, but who really cares at this point? I killed a demon lord, I could handle a super sexy wolf.

"Alright," I relented, meeting those intense blue eyes once more. "We'll talk."

He settled onto the rustic wooden chair near the fireplace, his muscular frame making it look almost fragile.

"Emma, I know this is a lot to take in, but let me explain what it means to be mates," he said, his deep voice soothing my frayed nerves. "Mates are usually two werewolves who are destined to be together and share a deep, unbreakable bond. This bond isn't just physical; it's emotional and spiritual, too. You're not a werewolf, but I am, so I still feel the bond, even if you don't."

I couldn't help but laugh at the earnest way he was explaining this to me. "Amrin, I've been living with the pack for a while now, remember? I've seen how the wolves and their mates interact. I know about the bond."

He raised an eyebrow, a hint of a smile playing on his lips. "Ah, I see. You're not as sheltered as I thought. But knowing about and experiencing the bond are two different things, Emma."

My laughter died down, replaced by a flicker of uncertainty. He was right; I had observed the bond between other pairs, but I had no idea what it truly felt like.

"Alright," I said slowly, meeting his gaze. "I'm willing to try and understand this... connection between us. But I need time, man. Time to get to know you better. Like how the hell you even knew I was here... and how you knew I was your mate."

"Of course," he agreed, his eyes softening. "I want that, too. I want us to learn about each other to build trust and friendship. Our bond may be fated, but it's important that we grow together as well."

Over the next few days, my initial reluctance gave way to tentative curiosity. Amrin's presence in my life was like a whisper in the wind, gentle but impossible to ignore. We took long walks through the lush forest surrounding my cabin, exploring the vibrant world that had become my sanctuary. He explained all about being Avery's mate... his part in bringing about Belial, his death, and ultimately, Selene giving him another chance through me.

Honestly, this would all sound absolutely insane, except for the fact I was a nobody, became the last in the line of Dark Faeries, absorbed a STONE in my SKIN, and beat Belial. My life was one insane event after another. What's adding a mate gonna do?

As we walked side by side, he shared stories about his own life—his family, his friends, and his experiences as a werewolf. I found myself opening up to him in return, telling him about my dreams and my fears, things I had never dared to share with anyone else.

With each passing day, the bond between us grew stronger, pulling us together like an invisible thread. His emotions resonated within me, a strange yet comforting reminder of our connection. And though fear still lingered in the back of my mind, I couldn't deny the growing attraction I felt for this man who had unexpectedly entered my life.

"Emma," Amrin said one evening as we sat on the porch of my cabin, the setting sun casting a warm glow over the forest, "I know you're still hesitant, but I want you to know that I'll be patient. I'll give you all the time you need."

His words washed over me like a balm, soothing the last of my doubts. At that moment, I realized that I was willing to take a chance on him, on the bond we shared, and on whatever future lay ahead of us. Together.

After that, we fell into a comfortable routine. We would start our mornings with a walk through the woods, then we would have breakfast, laze around for a while and find something fun to do.

"Did you know that I'm quite the hunter?" Amrin interrupted my thoughts as he pointed out tracks left by a deer. "I can track down prey like no other."

"Really?" I raised an eyebrow, genuinely intrigued. "Well, I suppose that's a useful skill to have as a werewolf."

"Indeed," he agreed, a proud smile spreading across his face. "But it's not just about the hunt for me; it's also about understanding the balance of nature and respecting the life we take. There's something almost spiritual about it."

As we continued our walks, I discovered that Amrin had a deep love for history, often regaling me with tales from the past—stories of significant battles, legendary leaders, and ancient civilizations. We spent hours discussing these histories, sharing our thoughts and opinions on the events that shaped the world around us.

On one particularly sunny afternoon, we sat beneath the shade of a large oak tree, taking a break from our usual stroll. I pulled out my sketchbook and began to draw the lush scenery before me.

"Is that what you do for fun?" he asked as he peered over my shoulder, his breath warm against my neck. "Draw?"

"Among other things, like reading," I replied, feeling a blush creep up my cheeks at his proximity. "But yes, I love to capture the beauty of the world around me. It helps me appreciate the little things."

"Can I see more of your work?" he asked hesitantly, as if afraid he might be intruding.

"Of course," I said, flipping through the pages of my sketchbook for him. His eyes widened in admiration as he took in the detailed drawings of landscapes, people, and animals.

"You're incredibly talented, Emma," he breathed, his blue eyes meeting mine with a gaze full of wonder.

"Thank you."

As we continued to spend time together, sharing meals and opening up about our interests, it became increasingly clear that we were more than just two people bound together by fate—a genuine connection formed between us, which went beyond our bond's physical and spiritual aspects. Days flew by, and I grew more comfortable in his presence, slowly allowing my fears to recede into the background.

One evening, as we sat by the fire, I noticed tension building over the last few weeks.

"Emma," Amrin said softly, reaching out to tuck a stray strand of hair behind my ear. "I have to admit, I'm really enjoying spending all this time with you."

"Me too," I murmured, feeling the heat rise in my cheeks as our gazes locked.

"Want to play a game?" he asked, a mischievous glint in his eyes. "Strip poker?"

"Are you sure you want to lose, Amrin?" I teased, my heart pounding at the thought of where this game might lead.

"Bold words, beautiful," he challenged, grabbing a deck of cards from the nearby shelf. "Let's see if you can back them up."

The game progressed, and our drinks continued to flow; the atmosphere grew increasingly charged. With each lost hand, we shed another article of clothing until there was nothing left but our mutual desire laid bare before one another.

"Amrin," I whispered, feeling my pulse race as he pulled me close, his muscular arms wrapping around me. Our lips met in a fiery, passionate kiss as if we were trying to consume one another.

That night, we made love for the first time, and I marveled at the intensity of our connection. It was as if our bodies were speaking a language that only we could understand. Every touch and caress sent shivers down my spine.

This was everything I had been missing.

43: Gabriel

The carpentry house, where we had spent countless hours working together, now lay in shambles – its wooden beams splintered and crushed like the bones of a fallen warrior. The scent of charred wood permeated the air, mingling with the stench of blood and death that didn't quite seem to leave. We'd been so busy building Emma's house that we'd just... let this slide until now.

"Gabe, where do we even start?"

I looked into Avery's eyes, a sea of emotions swirling within their depths – grief, fear, anger, and love.

"Piece by piece, my love, piece by piece," I replied, focusing on the task at hand. "We'll start by clearing the debris and salvaging what we can. The foundations are still strong; we just need to rebuild."

Roman, who had been silent until now, added with a hint of his usual wit, "Well, at least we won't run out of firewood for a while."

Despite the circumstances, a small smile tugged at the corner of my mouth. Leave it to Roman to lift our spirits.

"Alright," I said, clapping my hands together and drawing the attention of the others. "Let's get to work. We'll divide the tasks among ourselves and ensure everyone is focused on the reconstruction."

We began the arduous task of rebuilding. the wind continued to howl around us, but now it seemed less like a cry of despair and more like a rallying call. At that moment, I thought of the countless generations who had come before us, their spirits woven into the very fabric of our land. And as I looked upon my mate and fellow wolves working together in harmony, I knew that we would honor their legacy by creating a bright future for all who called this place home.

I stood on a hill overlooking the bustling activity below a few days later. The air was filled with the sounds of hammers hitting nails and the low hum of voices as everyone worked together to rebuild their lives.

"Gabe," Avery approached me, her gaze serious. "I think we need to address something."

I turned to her, my brow furrowing. "What's on your mind?"

"Emotional healing," she said. "While it's great that we're rebuilding the physical aspects of our lives, we can't forget about the emotional scars left behind. We've all experienced trauma, and if we don't deal with it, it'll fester and cause problems down the line."

"Right," I agreed, nodding thoughtfully. "That's why we started the group therapy sessions and one-on-one counseling, right? To help everyone cope with what they've been through."

"Yes, but we need to make sure everyone understands how important this is. Emotional healing isn't just a luxury; it's essential. I've noticed not many have signed up..."

"Alright. Let's gather everyone together. I'll address them all and emphasize the importance of attending these sessions and seeking support when they need it."

As the evening began to settle in, we gathered everyone around a large bonfire.

"Listen, I know we've been working tirelessly to rebuild what we lost, and I'm proud of our progress. But we can't forget that to truly heal, we must also address the emotional pain we've endured. Many of you have lost family members or experienced trauma. It's not a sign of weakness to seek help – it's a sign of strength. That's why we've organized group therapy sessions and one-on-one counseling. I urge each and every one of you to attend these sessions and support one another during this time."

As I finished speaking, they exchanged glances, some nodding in agreement while others wiped away tears. The road to recovery would be long and complex, but we were united in our determination to heal both physically and emotionally.

I turned to Avery who reached up to give me a kiss, "Thank you."

"Anything for you, my love."

Amidst the chaos of rebuilding, Avery approached me with a glimmer in her eyes and an infectious smile. "We need to start planning the wedding," she clapped her hands.

"Okay," I agreed, casting a glance toward Roman and Nik, who were working nearby. Their tired faces lit up at the mention of the wedding, and they eagerly joined us, and we set off back home for the day.

"Let's start with the venue," Avery suggested, flipping through a pile of brochures that she had printed. We huddled around her, our eyes scanning the lush gardens and elegant ballrooms depicted on glossy pages. As much as our land held a special place in our hearts, we decided on an enchanting forest clearing just outside our territory – a place where nature would be our witness, and our love could flourish.

"Menu next?" Roman asked, rubbing his hands together in anticipation. Our conversations about food quickly became animated, each of us contributing ideas based on our preferences. Soon, a hearty feast was planned, with dishes that represented each of our unique tastes.

"Music..." Nik mused, tapping his foot rhythmically as he contemplated the soundtrack to our celebration. He suggested songs that ranged from traditional folk tunes to modern hits, creating a playlist that would have everyone dancing and laughing late into the night.

As we continued to plan, our attention began to wane. The pressure of the rebuilding efforts weighed on us, even as we tried to focus on the joyous event ahead. Eventually, Roman sighed and leaned back, "I think we could use some help."

"Right," I chimed in, running a hand through my hair. "Avery, why don't you go ask Emma for assistance? She has a knack for organizing events, and I'm sure she'd be thrilled to be part of the planning process."

"Good idea," Avery said. "I'll talk to her right away. I haven't seen her in a while; catching up will be good."

"First..." Nik grabbed her and swung her over the shoulders. "Have you been a good girl?"

She giggled, "No, Daddy."

"You boys gonna come watch me punish our girl?" Without waiting for a response, he ran up the stairs.

Roman sighed, "I wish, but I can't."

I just nodded and followed them up the stairs. Watching was almost as much fun as participating; I got to see all her angles, the way her face lit up, and how incredible she looked choking on a dick. By the time I got to our room, he already had her naked on the bed.

As I watched from the side of the bed, Nik's lips consumed Avery's pussy with relentless fervor, his long tongue dancing between her folds and delving deep into her wet heat. The sight of him pleasuring her made my cock twitch in anticipation. His head bobbed rhythmically as he worked his magic on her; his hands gripped her smooth thighs tightly and pulled her closer to him. Every now and then, I caught a glimpse of Avery's face contorting in pleasure - sometimes soft moans sometimes gasps - which only added to the raw intensity of the moment. I could almost taste her arousal in the air; it was thick and intoxicating.

And then, he finally pulled away with a satisfied smack of his lips. He looked up at me with a grin that spoke volumes about what he intended to do next. Without giving me another glance, he reached onto the nightstand and pulled out a tube of lube. He coated two fingers before sliding them into Avery's tight ass, and she groaned. She bucked her hips against him as he slowly finger-fucked her. It was clear she liked it – she always did – but this time was different: there was an edge of desperation in her cries that told me she wanted more.

She arched her back, biting her lip and gasping as he finger-fucked her deeply, stretching her anal ring with each thrust of his knuckles. My cock throbbed in my pants as I watched him pull out her pleasure.

"Ready for me, baby?" he whispered against her ear, his voice low and rough. "You want my big cock in that tight asshole of yours?"

She whimpered in response, her breath coming in short gasps. "Please, Nik..." She turned towards him, grabbing his hard length through his pants. "Gabe... I need you both."

Nik slowly pulled off his pants, revealing his thick cock that glistened with pre-cum at the tip. He lubed it up and lay underneath her, letting her sit in reverse cowgirl while he guided his head towards her asshole. She gasped as she felt the blunt head of his cock press against her entrance. Closing her eyes, she braced herself for the inevitable invasion. He pushed gently, and she let out a long, low moan as he slid inside her tight ass. She arched her back again before laying on top of him, exposing her pussy and her cock filled ass to me.

He slowly started to move in and out of her ass; each thrust met with a grunt of pleasure from both of them. The slap of their skin, the smack of their hips coming together, the creak of the bed frame - every sound filled the room and made me harder.

Avery's eyes met mine for a brief moment, filled with lust and need, and then she closed them again as she focused on the sensations overtaking her body. Her pussy was dripping wet; I could smell her arousal from where I sat.

Her tits bounced beautifully with each movement, her nipples hard and begging for attention. I wanted nothing more than to suck on one of those perfect peaks while buried deep in her pussy, but I waited. I wanted to watch her face as she came around his cock, before I watched her cum around mine.

As Nik started slamming deeper into Avery's ass, her moans and gasps became more frequent, her body arching and shuddering under his powerful thrusts. She looked like she was in heaven, her face contorted in pleasure, her eyes rolled back in her head as she gasped for air. The scent of sex filled the air around us as I watched my best friend fuck our woman like the animal he truly was - raw lust taking over every rational thought.

Her ass was made for him; it clamped down on his cock with every forceful stroke, her pussy leaking onto the bed beneath her as she took it all in. She exploded, her legs trembling as he held them in the air, and her head rolled back in ecstasy. There it is, the look I'd been waiting for.

With primal ferocity, I jumped on the bed and thrust my cock into her.

"Fuck yeah," she moaned, clutching onto me as she reveled in the sensation of being filled by two men at once. She was so tight around my cock, it almost made me cum. I started to move with Nik as we stretched her, fucking her slowly at first and then faster.

She was tight and hot, and as I looked down at her beautiful face contorted in pleasure, I lost myself in the moment. Her lips parted as she moaned, her tongue darting out to lick them. She bit her lower lip before letting out a long, low groan as we fucked her.

As she writhed beneath me, I leaned down and captured one of her nipples between my teeth, tugging gently. The taste of her skin, mixed with desire, filled my mouth, sending a shiver down my spine. She arched into the sensation, moaning loudly as Nik grunted, both of us pounding into her with unbridled lust. Her body shook under our force as she tried to take us both in deeper. Her gasps and grunts echoed off the walls around us while we took turns whispering dirty things in her ear that made her shiver and squirm.

She was so fucking beautiful like this: eyes closed, lips parted in a silent moan, body trembling with pleasure as we took her to new heights.

Before I could utter another word, she tensed around us, triggering us both to cum inside her as she clenched and un-clenched, riding the wave of her orgasm. I kissed her deeply before rolling off so she could breathe.

"Holy fuck."

"Holy fuck is right," Nik said as he got up to grab a towel. "That's what you get for being a bad girl."

"Damn, guys. I gotta be bad more often," she said with a wink. "Now go, I got shit to do. Tomorrow, we're going to get the twins."

44: Nikolai

I took a deep breath and exhaled slowly, savoring the crisp morning air. Avery, Roman, and Gabriel were beside me; each lost in their own thoughts—our journey to see our twins had finally begun.

"Can you believe it's been almost a year since we last saw them?" Avery asked, breaking the silence. Her voice was tinged with a mixture of longing and excitement. "It feels like we left them just yesterday... so much has happened and robbed us of our time."

"Time flies when you're busy saving the world," Gabriel said softly, a small smile playing on his lips. His reserved nature often made him seem distant, but I knew he missed them just as much as the rest of us.

"One year is too long," Roman interjected, his typically goofy demeanor momentarily replaced by seriousness. "I can't wait to see how much they've grown."

"Me neither. Let's get going."

As we entered the forest, I couldn't help but feel a sense of exhilaration. The prospect of reuniting with our children far outweighed the physical challenges of the four-hour drive ahead of us. Avery finally let me buy some ATVs. I fully loaded them with headsets, and the best helmets money can buy. She never wanted to ride on my back for whatever reason, so this was the best compromise I could make.

"Who do you think they'll take after more?" Avery teased as she clipped her helmet on.

"Only one way to find out," Roman replied, his usual playfulness returning as he poked Avery gently.

"Hurry up, please. I miss the kids. The construction took forever, and now it's done, and now we can finally get our babies and have a relaxing, boring, familial life. Let's go." I was impatient as I revved my engine.

"Sometimes I wonder if they'll even recognize us," Avery murmured, her gaze distant as she pondered the impending reunion with our twins.

"Of course they will," Roman reassured her, placing a comforting hand on her shoulder. "Richard and Helen must have been showing them pictures and telling stories about us."

"Besides," Gabriel added softly, "we're their parents. There's an innate connection between a parent and child that can't be severed by distance or time."

We drove for a couple of hours until we hit a particularly gravelly area and heard Avery stifle a moan. *Oh shit, she's getting off. God, this woman. Kind of works out, though, our last hurrah before the babies come home.*

"Guys..." Avery began hesitantly, her cheeks flushed with color as she looked at me. "I think we should... take a break."

"An excellent idea," I replied, my tone steady despite the anticipation coursing through my veins. We searched for the perfect spot, eventually discovering a secluded grove nestled amongst the trees. Turning off the ATVs, we walked until we found just the spot.

"Here," I said, my voice low and commanding as I gestured for Avery to join me on the soft bed of moss that lay before us. Roman and Gabriel exchanged glances, their expressions a mix of excitement and apprehension.

"You good to share?" Gabriel asked, his eyes locked onto mine.

"Absolutely," I replied.

"Me too," whispered Avery, her lips brushing against my ear as she wrapped her arms around both Roman and Gabriel.

Roman put his hand down her pants and started fingering her while Gabe went to work on her mouth and nipples.

"Please... Nik..." Avery moaned, her voice thick with longing.

"Is this what you want?" I asked, my fingers tracing intricate patterns on her skin, causing her to shiver with delight.

"Yes... all of us... together..." she gasped, her eyes bright with desire.

We surrendered ourselves to the moment; the world outside seemed to fade away, leaving only the sounds of moans and sloppy sex. It didn't take long until we all came undone and were back on the ATVs, ready to go.

"Ugh, we're so close," Roman groaned, his voice static through the headset. "I can't wait to see those little rascals again."

"Me too," Avery replied quietly, her voice tinged with fatigue. "We've been away for far too long."

"Let's keep going; we're almost there," Gabriel urged.

We drove the last couple of hours in comfortable silence.

"Look, there it is!" Roman exclaimed, pointing down the hill towards Avery's parents' house. His goofy grin was contagious, and we were all smiling before long.

"Let's park here and walk the rest of the way. Don't want the engines waking the babies if they're asleep." Gabe said.

"That's really smart," I replied, shutting off my engine and hanging up my helmet.

"Remember when we first set out? When we left them behind?" Avery said as we walked, "We've come such a long way since then."

"We have, and we will be better parents because of it."

"Stronger and wiser," Roman chimed in, striking a mock strongman-like pose that had us all laughing.

"Especially you," Gabriel teased. "You haven't lost a single bit of your charm."

"Hey, it's all part of my thing," Roman retorted playfully, causing more laughter to ripple through the group.

As we walked down the hill, Avery smiled as she saw the smoke rising from the chimney, "They're home!"

"You mean you didn't call ahead of time?"

"No, Gabe, I did not. I didn't think that far ahead."

"Almost there," I reached out to squeeze Avery's hand.

"Almost there," she echoed, her smile lighting up her face.

The mood was light-hearted as we descended the hill towards the house, our steps quickening with each passing moment. The reunion with our twins was now moments away, and we couldn't wait to embrace them again.

45: Avery

As we stepped onto my parents' doorstep, the door swung wide open, revealing their warm smiles and sparkling eyes.

"Welcome home, sweetheart!" my mother exclaimed, her voice full of love and excitement. Her arms wrapped around me in a tight embrace, and I breathed in the familiar scent of lavender and vanilla that always clung to her.

"Hey there, kiddo," my father said gruffly, his eyes softening when they met mine. He pulled me into a bear hug, and I couldn't help but laugh as he lifted me off the ground. Roman, Nik, and Gabriel chuckled at our antics, and soon enough, they were also enveloped in hugs.

"Roman, Nik, Gabriel," my dad said, nodding warmly at each of my mates in turn. "It's good to have you all back."

"Thank you for taking care of our children," Roman replied, his voice filled with gratitude.

"Of course," my mom beamed, her gaze flicking between all of us. "Now, come in! It's time to catch up and get comfortable. You must be exhausted after your journey."

The moment we crossed the threshold, I felt a surge of warmth wash over me – not just from the heat emanating from the fireplace, but from the sense of being home, surrounded by the people I loved most in this world.

As we stepped into the familiar living room, I felt at peace. The scent of my childhood home, a mix of lavender and pine, enveloped me like a warm blanket.

"Make yourselves at home," my dad insisted, gesturing to the plush couches that were adorned with soft blankets.

"Your children have missed you so much," my dad said, his voice thick with emotion. "They've grown so much in the past year."

My heart ached at the thought of all the moments I had missed while we were away. I knew that my parents had taken good care of Onyx and Aurora, but nothing could replace the time lost.

"Let's go see them," I suggested, eager to reconnect with my little ones. My men nodded in agreement, and together, we made our way down the hall to the room where our twins slept.

"Thank you," I choked out, tears streaming down my cheeks, stopping as I walked by my mom. "For everything."

"Of course, dear," my mom replied, rubbing my back soothingly. "Family takes care of family."

As we entered the softly lit bedroom, my breath caught in my throat at the sight before me. Onyx and Aurora lay peacefully in their cribs, their tiny chests rising and falling with each breath.

Their delicate features were a perfect blend of all of us despite the fact that these guys weren't their biological fathers.

"Dada!" Aurora gurgled when she saw me, her little arms reaching out for me as she tried to get up and wobbled unsteadily on her feet.

"Hey there, princess, it's Mama, but we got time to get that right," I said softly, scooping her up into my arms and pressing a gentle kiss to her forehead. Onyx soon followed suit, watching with wide eyes.

"Look at you two," I cried. "You're both already walking! Well, kind of." Aurora promptly fell on top of Onyx, who screamed and tried to push her away.

My parents stood in the doorway, beaming with pride, watching as we spent precious moments bonding with our children. We hugged and kissed enough to last a lifetime before bringing them to the living room and continuing to chat with my parents about our journey.

"Tell us everything," my mom asked.

As we recounted the harrowing tale of our struggle against the dark force, I felt grateful for every person in this room.

"Here's to many more adventures – together, as a family," Roman toasted later that evening, raising his glass in celebration.

"Cheers!" we all chimed in, clinking our glasses and savoring the warmth and connection between us.

"Though," Gabriel added with a smirk, "I wouldn't mind fewer life-threatening situations."

We all laughed, enjoying each other's company as we played games and enjoyed a delicious meal together. Later, I took a moment to spend some time alone with my children, soaking in the love that filled the room.

The night drew to a close, and we settled down in the living room, our hearts full and content. Finally, my family was complete.

"Thank you, Mom," I murmured into her shoulder. "I've missed you too."

"Oh, dear, don't thank me. We thank you. This time with the twins has been more than we'd ever hoped. To have you back is everything, and I couldn't be more proud of my girl."

We spent the next afternoon in the sun-dappled living room, soaking up the warmth of family and love. Aurora and Onyx crawled about on a soft rug, their chubby little hands grasping at toys as they babbled with delight. My parents sat smiling, watching the twins with pride and adoration.

"Look at you two," my dad said, lifting Aurora into his arms and tossing her gently into the air. She squealed with glee, her blue eyes sparkling like sapphires in the sunlight. "You're growing up so fast."

"Time flies," Roman remarked, a tender smile gracing his lips as he watched our daughter giggle in my father's embrace.

"Indeed," Nik agreed, scooping up Onyx and tickling him under his chin. The delighted laughter that erupted from our son filled the room like music.

"Your mother and I were just talking earlier," my dad began, looking over at us with a proud smile. "It's amazing, isn't it? How quickly life can change. One moment, you're a young woman, running from an asshole, and the next, you have two beautiful children who bring so much joy to your life."

"Tell us," My mom chimed in, her eyes full of curiosity. "How did you defeat Belial, exactly? We've heard bits and pieces but want to know the whole story."

"Ah, yes," Gabriel said, shifting in his seat as he prepared to recount the tale. "It was an incredible battle that tested all our strengths and weaknesses."

"He was cunning," I added, recalling the fierce fight that had nearly cost us everything. "He knew our every move, anticipated our every action. But we refused to let him win. We drew upon the love we share, the bonds that tie us together, and found a strength we didn't know we had."

As Gabriel continued to regale our parents with the harrowing details of our victory, I watched my family—my mates, my children, my parents—and marveled at how far we had come. We had faced insurmountable odds and emerged victorious, our love for one another unwavering.

"Love truly is the most powerful force," my mom said after Gabriel finished recounting our story, her voice full of wonder. "It's what brought you all together, carried you through the darkest of times, and brought forth these beautiful little miracles." She gestured toward Aurora and Onyx, who were now curled up in their father's lap.

As the afternoon sun began to dip lower in the sky, casting warm golden rays through the living room windows, I noticed Aurora and Onyx growing restless. They squirmed on Nik's and Roman's laps, their little hands reaching out to grasp at the air. It was as if they were eager to explore and interact with the world around them.

"Look at them," Gabriel said softly, his eyes lighting up with pride. "They're so close to taking their first real steps."

"Well, they've been trying for a while. They kind of get up, walk a step, and fall down," My mom said.

"Yeah, but I mean, actually walking," Gabe chuckled.

Nik and Roman gently set them on the floor, their hands hovering nearby to catch them if needed. Aurora wobbled on her chubby legs for a moment before tentatively lifting one foot and placing it in front of the other. A gasp escaped my lips as tears welled up in my eyes – of all the milestones I'd missed, I was here for this.

"Come on, Little One," I encouraged her, kneeling down and holding out my arms, my voice thick with emotion. "You can do it." As she took another step towards me, Onyx followed suit, his face scrunched up with determination.

"Good job, kiddos!" Roman cheered, clapping his hands together. The rest of the family joined in, applauding and saying words of encouragement.

"Slow and steady," Nik advised, watching Onyx intently. "One step at a time."

They continued to wobble and stumble their way across the living room floor. My parents excused themselves to prepare a delicious meal for us all to enjoy. We gathered around the dining table, the twins in high chairs.

"Can you pass the potatoes, please?" my mom asked, smiling warmly at Roman as he obliged.

"Umm, these green beans are amazing!" Gabriel exclaimed, taking another bite. "Your recipe?"

"Family secret," my dad replied with a wink.

I excused myself from the table, feeling a sudden urge to spend some quiet moments with Aurora and Onyx. I scooped them up in my arms and carried them to their bedroom, sitting down on the plush rug with them nestled in my lap.

"Look at you two, growing up so fast," I whispered, brushing my fingers through their soft hair. "I promise to be here for every step of the way, every milestone, every laugh and tear."

I held them close to me as my heart ached. So much time was lost, yet dwelling wouldn't change it. I had to try move forward.

"Mommy missed you so much," I whispered.

"Hey, Avery?" Gabriel's voice came from the doorway. "Can we join you?"

"Of course," I replied, smiling through my tears. My mates filed into the room, each taking a seat on the floor next to us.

"Your mom told me about this game she used to play with you when you were little," Roman said, his eyes twinkling with excitement. "The one where you make animals with your hands?"

"Shadow puppets?" I laughed, wiping away a stray tear. "Yes, I loved that game."

"Let's try it out," Nik chimed in, and Gabriel nodded in agreement. We dimmed the lights, and soon enough, the room was filled with the flickering shapes of birds, rabbits, and other creatures dancing on the walls. Aurora and Onyx giggled in delight, their eyes wide with wonder.

"Isn't this something else? Being all together like this?" Gabriel mused as he expertly crafted the silhouette of a horse.

"It's something we deserve. We've been through so much, but times like these make it all worth it. Our family, our love... it's everything."

Nik reached over and squeezed my shoulder, his eyes meeting mine with a depth of understanding that only we shared. "I'm grateful too, Avery. For all of us, and for this journey we're on together."

"Me too," Roman added. "We'll face whatever comes our way as long as we're together."

"Always," I whispered, my fingers tightening around Aurora and Onyx. The love that filled the room wrapped around us like a warm embrace, a promise of the future we would build together. And in that moment, my heart overflowed with the deepest gratitude for this priceless gift of family and love.

Epilogue

As I stood in the midst of the twins' third birthday party, my hand instinctively cradled my swollen belly. A sense of tranquility washed over me as if the laughter and joy that filled the room had the power to dissolve any lingering fears or anxieties. The last Seraphina, carrying new life within her, surrounded by the people she loved most – there was a surreal beauty to it all.

"Happy birthday, little ones," I whispered, sending a silent prayer for their happiness and well-being.

"Careful there, Avery," Roman teased. "You don't want to pee on the kitchen floor like you did the battlefield way back when."

I burst out laughing. "True. But today is all about these two, so no peeing for me."

"Indeed, it is, love," Gabriel agreed, wrapping his arm around my waist protectively. His touch brought a wave of reassurance, and I leaned into him, appreciating the strength he provided.

"Come on, little ones! Let's see how high we can make this tower!" Nik exclaimed, his voice full of enthusiasm. He expertly balanced colorful building blocks with the twins, who squealed in delight with each successful addition.

"Higher, Papa!" Onyx demanded, clapping his hands excitedly.

"Careful now," Gabriel warned playfully, "we wouldn't want this masterpiece to come crashing down."

As I observed the scene, I couldn't help but marvel at how effortlessly my mates doted on our children, their love for them evident in every action. Seeing them so invested in their roles as fathers warmed my heart.

"Hey, what if we add this?" Roman asked, holding up a toy airplane with a mischievous grin. "Think it'll fly?"

"Only one way to find out!" Gabriel replied, sharing Roman's excitement.

"Wait, let me help!" Aurora yelled.

"Alright, everyone stand back!" Nik announced dramatically, guiding the twins to a safe distance. "Pilot Roman, prepare for takeoff!"

"Ready?" Roman asked, looking at our twins with anticipation. They nodded vigorously, their eyes wide and attentive.

"Three, two, one... Blast off!" Roman launched the toy airplane into the air, much to the delight of the kids.

"Again! Again!" they cried, bouncing up and down.

The scent of birthday cake wafted through the air as my parents set it down, adorned with six candles, three each. The plane forgotten, they rushed to blow them out before taking a slice and smearing it all over each other.

"Here, let me help you with that," Gabriel said softly, approaching me with a plate of cake. My mom had the foresight to buy two.

"Thank you," I murmured, gratefully accepting the sweet treat. It felt like such a small thing, but it meant the world to me at that moment.

"Are we going to play Pin the Tail on the Donkey?" one of the twins asked, tugging on Roman's sleeve.

"Sure thing, buddy," Roman chuckled, ruffling their hair affectionately. "Let's get it set up."

"Everything alright, Avery?" Nik asked gently, his concern palpable as he touched my shoulder reassuringly.

"Everything is perfect," I replied, offering him a genuine smile. And as I watched my family bask in the happiness of the moment, I knew that it truly was.

"Come with me," he whispered, his breath hot against my ear, sending shivers down my spine. He gently took my hand and led me away from the festivities towards a secluded corner of the garden.

"Is everything okay?" I asked, curiosity and concern mingling in my voice.

"Everything's fine," he assured me, his eyes filled with warmth and desire. "I just wanted to give you a little something special." My heart raced as he gently lowered me onto a soft patch of grass hidden from view by tall shrubs.

"Right here?" I questioned, glancing around nervously, but excitement coursed through me.

"Trust me," he murmured, kissing my lips tenderly before sliding down my body. I felt vulnerable as Nik lifted my dress and pulled aside my panties. I could hardly see him for my belly, but oh, I could feel him.

He expertly teased my clit with his tongue, eliciting gasps and moans that I struggled to stifle for fear of being heard. The pleasure he brought me was a welcome distraction from my growing belly and the weight of my pregnancy. His fingers gripped my thighs as he devoured me, bringing me closer and closer to the edge.

"Please, don't stop," I pleaded, my fingers tangling in his hair. Moments later, I was swept up in a wave of ecstasy, my body trembling with the intensity of my release.

Nik grinned up at me, his eyes sparkling with satisfaction. "You deserve to feel good, too," he said softly, helping me back up and fixing my clothes so we could return to the party.

"Thank you," I whispered to Nik, resting my head on his shoulder. He squeezed my hand in response.

"Anything for you, Avery. And I do mean *anything.*"

With my family all together, doting mates who would clearly do anything for me, and the blessing of another child, I thanked Selene for blessing me with the life I'd always dreamed of.

Acknowledgements

To everyone who was so patient while I got this done. You're amazing. I appreciate you.

Also By

Historical Fiction:

The Milkmaid: https://books2read.com/u/3yQJOe

The Betrayal: https://books2read.com/u/4NeqNx

Sweet Romance:

Twisted Candy Canes: https://books2read.com/u/bQeQqD

Fantasy Shifters:

Bonded to the Alpha Trio: https://books2read.com/u/mKVe95

Poetry:

Tempest. Vol 1: https://a.co/d/dUbYLA9

Tornado. Vol 2: https://a.co/d/gN5TcBp

Anthology:

Surviving The Unthinkable: https://a.co/d/cC5Ii45

Ream:

https://reamstories.com/stephanieswann

About the Author

A lways being told she is a daydreamer, Stephanie uses her gifts for escaping into a fantasy world to bring those worlds to life. Unable to write solely in one genre, she has found herself enjoying writing a wide array of books. From historical fiction to fantasy, Stephanie loves it all. Hoping to instill a love of books in her children, Stephanie spends her days reading, writing and going on adventures with her family, allowing imagination to lead the way and creativity to write the stories. Her favorite adventures are the ones where her son leads them through magical portals to new lands in discovery of the mystery that lies there.

Contact Stephanie

You can contact Stephanie at: stephanieswann.author@gmail. com if you'd like to know more about her upcoming works!

Instagram: authorstephanieswann
https://www.instagram.com/authorstephanieswann/
Facebook: Stephanie Swann
https://www.facebook.com/StephanieSwannAuthor/
Tiktok: stephanieswannauthor
https://www.tiktok.com/@stephanieswannauthor
Other Links:
https://linktr.ee/stephanieswannauthor

Printed in Great Britain
by Amazon

31134239R00195